WHERE SECRETS
LIVE

WHERE SECRETS LIVE

S. C. RICHARDS

WORLDWIDE

TORONTO • NEW YORK • LONDON
AMSTERDAM • PARIS • SYDNEY • HAMBURG
STOCKHOLM • ATHENS • TOKYO • MILAN
MADRID • WARSAW • BUDAPEST • AUCKLAND

WORLDWIDE™

Recycling programs
for this product may
not exist in your area.

ISBN-13: 978-1-335-01223-4

Where Secrets Live

First published in 2022 by Crooked Lane Books,
an imprint of The Quick Brown Fox & Company LLC.
This edition published in 2024.

Copyright © 2022 by Susan C. Richards

For questions and comments about the quality of this book,
please contact us at CustomerService@Harlequin.com.

TM is a trademark of Harlequin Enterprises ULC.

Harlequin Enterprises ULC
22 Adelaide St. West, 41st Floor
Toronto, Ontario M5H 4E3, Canada
www.ReaderService.com

Printed in U.S.A.

To Rod and Tim
For their endless supply of love and support,
and always for the laughter.
I love you tons.

"The human heart dares not stay away too long from that which hurt it most. There is a return journey to anguish that few of us are released from making."
                                                                —Lillian Smith

ONE

SOMETIMES YOU JUST KNOW, long before you're ready to accept it, that things aren't going to end well. You just know. I wanted to pretend that nothing was wrong. But even pretending didn't change what I already knew.

Twenty minutes ago, my cousin, Fred, showed up at my apartment and shook me awake with, "Lizzie, get your ass out of bed. We need to get out to Meredith's. Something's wrong."

And that's how it started.

Before I could even ask, he was gone, heading down the stairs. His final words before the front door slammed shut were "I'm parked out front."

Now, sitting in his maroon Jag as he wove in and out of traffic, heading toward the freeway from my apartment in St. Paul, I finally asked, "What's going on?"

A quick glance at me over the top of his Gucci sunglasses and then his eyes were back on the road. "Did you get any messages from Meredith last night?"

"I don't know." I fished my phone out of my purse. There was one call from my sister, I pulled it up and put it on speaker. "Ellie, call me back. It's important." Meredith was the only one who called me Ellie. There was a long pause, then, "I need to tell you what's been going on. I've gotten myself in the middle of something and…you need to know. Whatever happens, please don't hate me. Please."

Every part of Meredith's life was ordered—grounded— which made the message particularly disturbing. She was the one stable person in my life, the one I went to when everything was falling apart. So, if she thought she was in the middle of some catastrophe, then she *was* in the middle of some catastrophe, but I couldn't even guess what that might be.

Too much alcohol from the night before, my head throbbed in rhythm with the tires on the pavement. "I don't get it. What's going on?"

"I don't know. I got one too. Must have been after she called you." Fred's phone was hooked up to Bluetooth. He gave the command to retrieve his voicemail.

Her voice was strained, maybe she'd been crying. "Fred, I need you. Call me back. I can't reach Ellie. I need you guys. I'm… I need you guys." There was another long pause. She started to speak, then her voice became quiet. "I've got to go." Before she clicked off, almost as if she was moving the phone away from her face, it sounded like she said, "What are you…" so softly I almost missed it.

"Did you call her back?"

"I didn't get the message until this morning, but I must have called her ten times since then. Couldn't get her. Couldn't get you."

"What did she say at the end?"

He played it again. This time it was clear. Someone was there with her, but who?

My chest felt tight. A quiet terror settled in the pit of my stomach. Sometimes you just know.

The thirty-minute drive from my apartment to Meredith's house, east of Lake Elmo, Minnesota, felt like twice that, even though we probably made it in half the time.

I hit Meredith's number on my phone, willing her to answer. When she didn't pick up, I hit it again. And again. And again.

Fred finally put his hand on top of mine. "That's not going to change anything."

"Should I call the cops?"

"I don't know." He nodded his head toward the rural mailbox with the name "McCallister" printed on it. "We're here now. I guess we should find out first if"—he cleared his throat—"she's even home."

A graveled driveway led from the county highway to Meredith's stretch of land. Fred guided the car through the overgrowth until her three bedroom, one-story, brick house rolled into view.

Her Saab sat protected under the carport. Fred's Jag came to an abrupt stop behind it. He was the first one to the porch, twisting the doorknob, then pounding on the door when it wouldn't open. He banged his fist against the green painted wood, yelling for Meredith while I fumbled to find her house key on my key ring. I handed it to him and he stuck it in the lock.

An unearthly stillness wafted toward us and made my skin prickle, Fred reached for my arm. I pushed him away and ran down the long dark hallway, screaming Meredith's name.

She was facedown on the living room floor, her cell phone inches from her right hand, a cranberry-colored stain soaking the carpet around her. Sometimes you just know.

Fred was two steps behind me. "Oh God!"

When I knelt beside her, he tried to pull me back. "Don't."

"Let go! I have to see if she's all right. I have to help her."

"Lizzie, don't. You can't help her now."

I looked up at him and we stared at each other. Seconds ticked by. No. He was wrong.

I crumpled on top of her body and put my lips against the side of her face. "Be okay, Meredith. Please. Be okay." Her skin was cold, a sticky wetness caked against my arms.

Fred put a hand briefly on my shoulder, then moved away. From a great distance it seemed, I could hear him moving around the room, talking, giving directions. But I felt as if I were drowning. I couldn't breathe.

He came back and grasped my shoulders, pulling me up. It was a dream—no a nightmare—and someone had come to rescue me. He was going to save me. He was going to save my sister. It would be all right.

"We have to go outside," Fred said.

Okay. I would go outside and then I would wake up.

He took my hand and started to draw me away from her.

I looked into his eyes, and I knew it wasn't a dream. He was fighting back tears, and there was so little color in his face.

"No. I have to take care of her…"

"Lizzie, please don't make this harder than it already is. You need to come with me." He took my arm and pulled me toward the glass door that opened onto the patio.

We stepped outside onto the flagstones and waited. Waited for the police to arrive. For the ambulance to come. For the world to stop spinning.

Fred walked over to the low stone wall that separated the patio from the backyard. He sat down and started to cry, his face buried in his hands, his shoulders heaving. That was more than I could do. If I let go now, everything inside me would unravel. I paced the flagstones, tried to breathe—and waited.

I started at a movement at the edge of the woods that bordered Meredith's property. As I turned, someone took off running into the trees.

"Hey!"

Fred looked up. "What?"

"Did you see someone over there?"

He glanced toward the woods, but the figure was gone. "No."

Now I wondered if I'd imagined it.

Sirens blared into the front yard just then. Car doors slammed, someone yelled instructions. Fred stood up, wiped his eyes with the back of his hand. "Are you coming?"

I shook my head and he went around the side of the house.

Muffled voices filtered through the glass door. I turned and walked down to the lake, thinking of the last time I'd been here, Memorial Day weekend. We'd all come out to the lake for a barbecue, the whole family—a typical American celebration, only without the typical American family. We tried so hard to look the part, but we couldn't even get that right.

We were the McCallisters. Deep roots. Old money. It had taken generations to perfect our dysfunction, but we'd done it well. Fred, Meredith, and I had been the last of the leaves on the family tree.

And now Meredith was gone, and I didn't know what I'd do without her. Not that I'd seen much of her lately. It had been two and a half months since I'd been out here. Two and a half months of sidestepping every invitation.

Memorial Day weekend it had been obvious that some-

thing was very wrong—something about her was seriously
off. I didn't have a clue what it was, but it scared me. It
frightened me to see her like that, but the thought of being
pulled in, terrified me even more, because if I found out
what was wrong—I just knew I would somehow be involved in something I wasn't prepared to handle. Whatever it might be.

So, instead of trying to help her, to find out what was
going on in my sister's life, I simply ran away. I didn't *want*
to know. Once you know a thing, you can never unknow
it, and whatever her angst had been, I didn't think I had it
in me to deal with it.

Strange men and drunken blackouts had become my an-
esthesia over the summer. And now I was just plain tired.

The guilt settled over me like a black shroud, and I
couldn't hold back the tears any longer—but I honestly
couldn't tell if I was crying for Meredith or for me.

TWO

"LIZ?"

Tom.

The voice came from behind me and from fifteen years out of my past, but I would recognize it anywhere. Maybe because I was already focused on Meredith.

Tom had been my sister's first serious boyfriend. He and Meredith, both five years older than me, had dated in high school, broken up, and reconnected in college. They were one of those adorable couples—the kind you see and you hope with everything in you that they're the ones who make it. That they can beat the odds and stay together. Unless you're a jealous little sister. The crush I'd had on him had been intense. And now here I was, sitting at the end of Meredith's dock, with my feet in the cool water, trying to be anywhere other than where I was at that moment. And he was speaking to me.

I turned. Those steel-blue eyes met mine. "What are you doing here, Tom? I didn't know you and Meredith still saw each other."

His look softened. "I'm an agent for the Bureau of Criminal Apprehension. I'm here to find out…what happened."

I don't know which seemed more out of place—Tom Martens being a detective or the oblique reference to my sister's death.

I rose slowly. "Then I guess you want to talk to me."

"I'm so sorry, Liz." He moved in to hug me.

He wasn't quite six feet, maybe about four inches taller than I am. Years ago, when he and Meredith were dating, he'd seemed so much taller. But then, I'd been seeing him with my petite sister. Next to her five feet two inches, everyone seemed tall.

After a few seconds, I pulled away from him. I didn't want the tears to start again.

Tom shook his head. "Who would want to hurt Meredith? She was so…"

"Perfect?" I said, surprised by the sudden resurrection of that old adolescent jealousy.

He smiled. "Yeah. Just about."

Yes, she was. Perfect and beautiful and kind. This time I couldn't hold back the tears. Meredith was the best person I'd ever known. She was the best part of me. And now she was gone.

Tom held me while I cried, my head buried in his shoulder. He smelled of Calvin Klein's Eternity and cinnamon rolls, and I wanted to stay there in his arms forever. I wanted to feel safe.

I finally pulled away from him again. "Are you gonna be okay?" he asked.

I dried my eyes. "I guess. For a while anyway."

He nodded toward the picnic table in the middle of the grassy lawn, and I followed him over and sat down.

He sat next to me, so close that our knees were touching. "It's good to see you again, Liz. It's a damn shame it had to be like this."

I took a breath. "Look, if you've got anything you want

to ask me, do it now. I don't know how long it's going to be before the waterworks start again."

He managed a crooked smile. "Sorry. I forgot. The Mc-Callisters have super powers and don't cry in public like the rest of us."

I sort of smiled back. My life. The reference, we both knew, was to my stepmother, Ruth, who believed well-bred people didn't parade their emotions in public. What she had yet to realize was that money did not equate breeding. We had money; breeding was a matter of opinion.

Tom rubbed his hand along his thigh. With the sun on his face, I could see the sporadic strands of gray in his wavy brown hair, the creases at the corners of his eyes. Undeniable reminders of the fifteen years that had slid away.

"So, did you and Meredith still see each other?" That wasn't the kind of news my sister would have kept to herself.

He shifted his weight on the hard, wooden bench. "Meredith called me out of the blue last spring and wanted to get together for coffee. I hadn't seen her since college. We met a few times, but that was it."

"Not a date?"

He smiled. "Not a date. I don't know why she called. It was good to see her, but…"

"But what?"

"I think maybe she wanted something from me, but it wasn't clear what she was looking for."

"And that was it?"

He nodded, then a subtle shift of his eyes told me nostalgia-time was over, and he was now in cop mode. "Did she mention someone she might be having trouble with lately? Boyfriends? Neighbors? Someone from work?"

The question was disturbing. "You think someone she knew did this?"

"There was no forced entry on any of the doors or windows."

Meredith knew. The phone calls—she knew something was going to happen. But Meredith wasn't stupid. If she'd known it would turn out like this, she would have left. She would have called the police. Still…she knew *something* was going to happen. I tried to process that.

Tom repeated his question, "Did she mention anyone she was having trouble with?"

I searched my memory of the past few months. "No. But I don't think she'd tell me if she was. I don't know who she'd talk to if she was having trouble like that. Maybe Fred. Maybe no one. You know Meredith; she never really talked about her problems."

"Oh yeah, right. McCallisters. Super powers. I forgot." There was the slightest hint of a smile in his eyes. "Was she expecting you out here today?"

"No. She called both Fred and me last night, but neither one of us picked up at the time. She left voicemails for both of us."

"I'll need to hear those."

I went to voicemail, put my phone on speaker, laid it on the picnic table, and walked away. I couldn't listen to it again. I couldn't hear her voice. I didn't want to be reminded that the one time in my life—the *one damn time* she'd asked for my help—I hadn't been there for her. And now she was dead.

I walked out to the edge of the dock again, looking out over the water. The lake was small, a dozen acres or so, with maybe eight cottages on it. Just big enough for swimming, fishing for panfish, and canoeing. Across the water, a girl stood watching us, her face half hidden by a baseball cap. I'm sure by now everyone on the lake was well aware that there were squad cars and a commotion at the McCallister house. The girl and I stared at each other.

A few minutes later, Tom moved in behind me. I turned to see my phone in an evidence bag in his hand.

I nodded toward the baggie, "Do I get that back?"

"Eventually. But first it goes to the lab geeks." An outboard motor revved up across the lake, and he moved in closer. "When did you get her message?"

"This morning, when Fred came to get me."

"What was going on last night that was so important you couldn't take your sister's call?"

For some reason, I felt like he already knew the answer to that. "I was busy."

He waited.

I looked him in the eye. "Getting drunk. Getting laid. Although, I have no idea in what order."

He raised an eyebrow but made no comment. "So, you have an alibi?"

"I guess." Although at the moment, I'd be hard-pressed to come up with a name.

"And Fred? Do you know where he was last night?"

I shrugged. "You'd have to ask him."

"I did. Just seeing if you could corroborate for him."

"So that's how we're playing this, Tom? Fred's a suspect? I'm a suspect?"

"To tell you the truth, Liz, right now everyone in the Twin Cities metro area and surrounding counties is a suspect."

"Okay. I don't know where Fred was last night. And I'm not too sure about where I was."

Again, the look with no comment.

Fifty feet from the main house was a small white bungalow. Tom jutted his chin toward the structure. "What's that?"

"The guest cottage."

"Anyone live there?"

"I'm not sure. I haven't been out here all summer."

He seemed to be getting the hang of this; he didn't even bother with the unspoken judgment, just nodded.

"Different people stay there." I looked him in the eye, trying to convince him that I wasn't totally removed from the details of my sister's life. "Whoever Meredith thought needed help and a place to stay. I know someone was living there at the end of May, but I never met him."

Uniformed officers were already heading toward the small boathouse behind the guest cottage.

"How did…how did it happen?" I asked.

He looked at me. "How did she die?"

I nodded.

His eyes met mine. "She was shot at close range."

I didn't want to ask the next question. "Was it quick?"

He gazed out across the lake, then back at me. "We won't know for sure until we get the coroner's report, but yeah, I think so."

"Lizzie?" I turned to see Fred standing there. "How much longer are you going to be? There are reporters out front. Someone should tell Ruth what happened before she hears it on the news."

Oh God. Ruth. I didn't want to do this.

I turned toward Tom. "I need to go see my stepmother."

He thought about it. "I want to talk to your family. I can take you."

"I think I need to do this alone. Please." My voice started to crack.

He watched my face. "Okay," he finally said. "I'll be in touch with you later."

"Do you want me to go with you?" Fred asked. I knew it was a half-hearted offer. He didn't want to go any more than I did.

"No. I guess this one's mine, but I'll need your car."

"I can give you a lift home," Tom said to Fred.

Reluctantly, my cousin pulled his keys out of his pocket. "Please, *don't scratch it.*"

I took the keys and started to turn away.

Tom put out a hand to stop me and nodded toward the front of my blouse. "You might want to get cleaned up first."

I looked down at my shirt and arms, covered with my sister's blood.

THREE

I AIMED THE car back toward St. Paul, thinking of Ruth, trying to figure out what I could possibly say to soften the news. The traffic was unusually sparse for a Saturday summer afternoon, and I could have made good time. Instead, I drove slowly, forestalling the inevitable.

Meredith and I never spoke much about our family in public. It always seemed too complicated to explain. It was just easier not to try.

My mother died when I was five. What few memories I have are of her sitting at her makeup table, getting ready to go to out. She was beautiful—blonde and petite like my sister—loved beautiful clothes, and pouted when she didn't get her way. She was killed in a car accident as she and my father were driving home from a party. He was driving, and although no one ever told me directly, I think he was quite drunk at the time. They both probably were. Neither of them was wearing a seat belt. My father was thrown clear of the car, but my mother—beautiful face and all—went right through the windshield.

I have vague, gray memories of visiting my father in the hospital and my mother's funeral, not that I understood at the time what was even happening—I had no frame of reference for death. It should have been traumatic for a five-year-old, but I don't remember missing my mother. I don't think we'd ever bonded. I had Meredith, and I guess that was enough.

A year after my mother died, my father married Ruth. In the tradition of Eleanor Roosevelt, Ruth had been a McCallister even before my father married her—a distant cousin, fourth or fifth. When I was younger, her lineage didn't much interest me. Now it merely seemed like ancient history.

Ruth was a middle-aged spinster when my father married her, having spent her adult life caring for an invalid mother. She and my father had nothing in common, and I could never figure out what attracted the two of them to each other.

As if our dynamic weren't complicated enough, less than a year after the marriage, my father disappeared in a boating accident on Lake Superior. His sailboat was found capsized on the rocks off one of the Apostle Islands. His body was never recovered.

For the first time that I could remember, I understood the loss, and unlike with my mother, I missed him. Whenever I talked about my birth parents, which was rare, it was always Katherine and Joseph, never Mom and Dad.

A year after that, Ruth married David Alder. So, in essence, Meredith and I were raised by two stepparents.

The trees on Summit Avenue cast dappled shadows on the windshield as I made my way down the block and turned into the circular drive that led to the three-story brick manse. It had been weeks since we'd had any rain. The neighborhood smelled like scorched grass and old money.

The house was dark and cool, and I stood just inside the front door, remembering what it felt like to live there. It seemed like such a long time ago. I don't think we were ever happy there—any of us. I'm not sure we were unhappy either. We merely existed. Four people, living under one roof, going in different directions, never quite connecting. In a twenty-two-room house, it was easy to get lost.

Music filtered through from the sun porch—Gershwin, I think. I started toward the living room, then looked down at my arms, covered in blood, and headed for the main staircase and my old bedroom.

My room was on the left, two doors down from the top of the staircase. I walked in and closed the door behind me. Nothing had changed much over the years; everything was crisp and white: a large four-poster bed, complete with canopy, sitting in the middle of the too large room. It wasn't at all the bedroom a child would have chosen, with bright colors and posters on the walls, but more the image of what a young lady's room should be. Ruth's image.

Ruth had put her stamp on every inch of the house, turning it into the home she thought it should be. She'd brought order to our lives, and as much as I'd rebelled against it, maybe that was a good thing.

I pulled a pink blouse and a pair of jeans out of the closet, took clean underwear out of the dresser drawer, and headed to the Jack and Jill bathroom my sister and I had shared growing up.

A certain numbness had settled in, and I watched the blood run down my arms and swirl around the shower drain. I stood beneath the pulsating water longer than necessary. When I finally realized that I couldn't put this off forever, I stepped out of the shower, dried off, got dressed, and went back downstairs.

This time, I followed the sound of the music through the living room to the French doors.

She sat in a high-backed rattan chair, near the window overlooking the garden, her eyes closed, her face peaceful. Masses of thick gray hair were piled loosely on top of her head. Her hair had once been as brown as mine and was the only thing about her that seemed to have changed over the years. Ruth had aged well. Her face was smooth, and she was still lean and fit. Nothing interfered with her daily walks, not even the inhumanly cold Minnesota winters.

She must have sensed me standing there. She opened her eyes and looked toward the door, smiling when she saw me.

"Elizabeth," she said with pleasure in her voice. "What a nice surprise, darling. I was hoping you'd call today, but this is even better. Come sit with me." She patted the chair next to hers.

I slipped into a matching chair. "Is David around?"

"He's been with the youth group all morning, making plans for the Labor Day camping trip. He should be home any minute."

David had been a volunteer with a local youth group ever since I left for college. He'd worked with hundreds of kids over the years—tutoring, supervising camping trips, taking an interest in their lives. I'd never been as close to David as Meredith had been. She'd been more of a homebody and spent more time with David than I could afford.

Maybe all the volunteer work with David is where my sister developed her drive to save the world, befriending every underdog that crossed her path. David and his do-gooder activities didn't interest me on any level. I had my own friends, and that was the sum of my existence.

My stepfather was a quiet, dapper man who'd inherited a butt load of money and then went on to make it bigger in the stock market. Where my father and Ruth shared nothing in common, both of my stepparents seemed much more in sync with all their volunteer and philanthropic activities. David was on the board of a number of charitable foundations and president of the church council. Ruth was always busy with some type of committee work.

"Elizabeth?"

I realized she'd been talking to me. "What?"

"Is something wrong, darling? You don't look well."

"Meredith is dead." It came out differently from the way I'd planned. I wanted to build up to it—prepare her. But how do you prepare someone for something like that? The moment I said it, I knew it was wrong.

I don't know what kind of reaction I'd expected, but not the one I got. She stiffened as if I'd slapped her. Her eyes filled with tears, and she covered her face with her hands as small, tortured sobs came from somewhere deep inside.

Her body rocked back and forth, as if searching for some rhythmic comfort. "No. No please—it can't be."

I stood and walked across the room, looking out the window at the front lawn. I could barely deal with my own grief. I wasn't prepared to handle someone else's.

"How?' she asked, her voice strained. "What happened?" When I faced her, tears were streaming down her face, revealing her seventy-odd years in a mask of pain.

"She was shot. In her house. This morning—last night—I'm not sure." I turned back to look out the window. I didn't want to be here. Someone needed me—Ruth needed me—and I wanted to be gone, far away. Alone with my own pain.

"Shot? My girl. My precious girl." She shook her head and wrapped her arms around her abdomen as if she could protect herself from another blow.

Minutes passed. Finally, she produced a tissue from the

pocket of her pale gray skirt. She wiped her eyes and blew her nose, then straightened her back. "The police? What are they saying?"

"Nothing yet. They don't know anything."

"We'll have to make arrangements," she said.

"Yes," I said softly, "we will."

Ruth stood and crossed the small room. Her arms went around me in a stiff embrace. "You're the only one I have left now, Elizabeth."

It was the first time she'd hugged me since I was seven years old. When my father died.

FOUR

I NEVER DOUBTED that Ruth loved us—Meredith and me. We were the children she'd never had. In her own reserved way, she even doted on us. But what little mothering I got came from my sister and Martha, our housekeeper. She and her husband, John, had worked for the family since before I was born, and I dreaded telling them the news even more than I had my stepmother.

After a while of awkward kindness, Ruth went upstairs to lie down, and I walked to the kitchen, looking for the comfort I so desperately needed from the two people who had been more like parents than any of the others who'd held that position.

They were both sitting at the table, Martha writing out a shopping list, John playing solitaire, a deck of cards spread out in front of him.

This had always been my favorite room in the house. This was where the warmth was that kept my sister and me anchored in a life that seemed too tenuous to grasp hold of.

They bore a striking resemblance to Ma and Pa Kettle. Martha, large and buxom with unruly hair. John, lean and wiry—a man of few words. But they had a normalcy about them that filtered into my heart and grounded me in a way nothing else had.

The afternoon sun flooded the room with light and made it feel safe and inviting.

"Elizabeth," Martha said without looking up, "are you going to stand there staring at us all day, or are you going to come in and have a cup of coffee?"

I slipped into the chair across from her. "How did you know it was me?"

"I saw you drive up."

When I was a child, I thought this woman possessed some mysterious psychic power. She always knew when I'd done something wrong or when I was lying. Now, I realized, she was just paying attention.

John winked at me and rose to get my coffee.

Then Martha looked up and saw my face. "Something's wrong."

John sat back down at the head of the table.

They both waited in silence as I studied the backs of my hands, then looked up at them.

"Meredith's dead." Those words weren't getting any easier to say.

Martha shrieked and clutched her chest, reaching instinctively for her husband's hand. "No, no, *no*!" She shook her head.

I'd never seen John cry before. A strangled agony erupted from deep in his throat, and he turned his head away from me, his shoulders convulsing under his shirt. I think that was the hardest for me to watch.

I wasn't sure I could do this again. I waited. I breathed.

The shock finally settled, and something else took over, some primal survival instinct where you know acceptance is the only thing that will keep you sane.

They cried and pulled themselves together and cried

some more, asking the same questions Ruth and I had covered. *How? When? Where?* But the *why* was where we stumbled. There would never be a reason we could understand.

We talked about everything that seemed important. Our sadness, the funeral, what a wonderful person my sister had been. An hour passed. I thought I'd played the obligatory role well—I'd taken care of the folks—and I was exhausted.

When I stood to leave, Martha came around the table and held me close.

"We'll get through this, baby," she whispered in my ear. "I don't know how, but we'll get through this—together."

John took his turn. He put strong arms around me and pulled me into his chest. An old familiar feeling of safety rose to the surface. I held on tightly, afraid of where I might land if I let go.

Finally, reluctantly, I took a step back. "I have to go now. Let me know if Ruth needs anything—if any of you need anything." I was unaccustomed to this new role. It was awkward and felt out of character for me. This was Meredith's gig. She was the one who always knew what to do, how to pick up the pieces, how to go on. Now there was only me, and I wasn't sure I had the strength to do it.

I passed through the front hall, hoping to make my escape. Ruth and David sat in the living room, facing each other on opposite, matching floral loveseats. My stepmother's face was ashen, but her eyes were dry. She would shed no more tears except in the privacy of her own room.

David's face was red and swollen from crying. When I stopped to say goodbye, he rose from his seat and came toward me, shaking his head.

"Elizabeth." He had to stop when the sobbing interrupted

his words. He wiped his eyes with a white linen handkerchief, then placed two pudgy hands on my shoulders.

"I still can't believe it," he finally said. "I'm so sorry. Are you all right?"

"Yes," I said stiffly. I couldn't take much more of other people's grief. I let him hug me, then pulled away. "I have to go now."

"Elizabeth," Ruth said, "I think you should stay here with us."

"No, Ruth. I have to go. The police will probably want to talk to me again, and there are some things I need to take care of." It wasn't exactly a lie—just a graceful way of making an exit. It was all about appearances, and Ruth had taught me well.

She nodded.

David followed me to the front door, trying to speak— to comfort me, I think. But he could barely get two words out between the sobs. I'm ashamed to say, I found it embarrassing and a little pathetic.

But then, he wasn't a McCallister—one of us. He didn't know how to hold it all inside until it started to eat away at you. Until there was no emotion left to feel.

FIVE

TOM MARTENS WAS sitting on my front steps when I pulled into a parking space in front of my building, an old, sprawling Victorian that had been cut up into five apartments. He stood as I made my way up the walk, sweat dripping down his face.

I maneuvered my way around him to unlock the door. "How long have you been here?"

"About twenty minutes." He was so close I could feel his breath on my neck. "It's so blasted hot out today."

"You could have waited in your car."

"Yeah. Well, then I'd have nothing to complain about."

He followed me inside. The window air conditioner was on, and the apartment was relatively cool.

I headed for the kitchen. "Do you want something to drink?"

"Diet Coke if you have it. Anything as long as it's cold."

He sat on a stool at the counter in the small kitchen, "How'd Ruth and David take the news?"

I handed him a can of soda and a glass of ice and sat down on the stool next to him. "David's a mess. Ruth is, well, Ruth."

"I'm sorry."

I wasn't sure if he was referring to my stepparents' grief or my family dynamic. I didn't ask.

For barely an instant, he rested his hand on my shoulder. Then it was gone, and he was back into cop mode. "Meredith said in her voicemail that she needed to explain what she'd done. What was that about?"

I looked down at my hands. "No clue." She'd also asked me not to hate her, which, to me, seemed more perplexing than whatever she felt she needed to explain. I couldn't imagine anything my sister could have done that would make me hate her.

"When was the last time you talked to her?"

"Yesterday. Or the day before. I'm not sure. Sometime this week. I think."

He raised his eyebrows. For the first time I felt his judgment. I wasn't sure if it was about not paying more attention to my sister's life, or maybe an unspoken commentary on what my life had become. I wanted his approval, and I didn't even understand why. For some reason it was important. I wanted to explain, but no words came. Maybe there were no words for what I'd done. Or what I hadn't done.

It had been obvious Memorial Day weekend that something was going on with Meredith. There was a sadness about her, an aura maybe, that she was headed someplace dark. I couldn't even guess where that was. And the truth is, I didn't want to know.

Meredith was my rock. If her life was unraveling, what would become of me?

So, I did what I always do. I ran away.

I think she wanted me to know what was going on—wanted to confide in me, but I deftly avoided the phone calls, made excuses for the lunch dates, made sure I had plans when she wanted me to spend the weekend at the lake. Whatever was going on with her scared the hell out

of me, and I felt that if she told me—if I was somehow responsible to help carry her burden—then I would crack. I
was certain of it.

Tom was talking again. "Meredith told me that she was
a social worker for the Eastside Victims of Sexual Assault."

"Uh-huh."

He scrunched up his forehead. "Do you know Scott Pederson?"

I shook my head. "Should I?" God, I wanted a drink. I
didn't want to do this.

"He's been living in Meredith's guesthouse for the past
six months." His eyes appraised me.

"I told you before, different people came and went out
there. Meredith thought it was her job to save everyone who
needed help. She mentioned a Scott, but I never knew his
last name."

"Scott Pederson is an accused sex offender, Liz. What
the hell was he doing living on her property so far from
town?"

"She must have thought she could—oh God, Tom, was
she raped?"

His look softened. "I don't know for sure. I don't think
so, but we'll have to wait for the autopsy report."

I hesitated. "What was he accused of?"

"Statutory rape. He was never prosecuted, but some
girl's father had reason to go to the authorities."

"But statutory rape, it's not like real rape, right? I mean,
it's consensual." I was grasping at straws here, and I knew
it.

"Technically, but it's a sign of a serious lapse in judgment."

I looked out the window. This was too much. Even on

a technicality, what were we doing, sitting here talking about rape and autopsies in the same breath as my sister? I couldn't grasp any of it. I moved into the living room and he followed me.

He was talking again. I forced myself to watch his lips and tried to connect the words. It was so hard.

"Meredith's birthday is coming up soon," he said.

I stared at him, trying to tie that thread to my sister's murder. "What?"

"She'd be thirty-four next month, right?"

I nodded.

"And then what?"

I was lost. "And then *what*?"

"The trust kicks in?"

My God. "Where are you going with this?" But I knew exactly where he was going with it.

Years ago, our grandparents had established a trust fund that would go into effect for each of us—Meredith, Fred, and me—on our thirty-fourth birthdays. I'd never paid attention to it—thirty-four seemed like a long way off—but now that I thought of it, the money had been sitting in trust, accruing interest, for decades. Meredith would be the first to inherit.

"Just thinking out loud," he said.

I raised an eyebrow. "No, you're not. You know damn well that the only people who would benefit from Meredith's inheritance would be Fred and me. Are we back to us as primary suspects?" Suddenly, so suddenly it caught me by surprise, I was angry. "You need to leave. Now."

He held up his hands. "I wouldn't be doing my job if I didn't look at all the possibilities. You know that, Liz. You also know that from the outside none of this looks very good for Fred."

"Fred? Are you kidding me? Fred loved Meredith. He's been like our brother."

"A deadbeat brother. You and Meredith always worked, the two of you earning paychecks like the rest of us. What has Fred *ever* done?"

The truth was, nothing. Meredith and I had both worked since college, although my career had encompassed seven years of job-hopping. And Fred? He aspired, with some success, to be your stereotypical playboy. Still, he was a good guy, and Tom was pissing me off.

"Okay, stop. I mean it. I don't want to talk about Fred. You're wasting your time when you should be looking for a fucking murderer."

"Don't be naive, Liz," he said, keeping his voice steady. "Just because you never cared, or *had* to care, about money doesn't mean that other people don't. Just think about it for a minute."

Tom was quiet for a while. "Okay," he finally said. "We won't talk about Fred right now. Do you know any of Meredith's friends?"

I didn't answer right away. I had to think. "I know her boss and some of the people she worked with. Why?"

"I told you before, there was no forced entry. Meredith was shot at very close range. Whoever killed her was allowed to get very close before he pulled the trigger."

My brain was on overload. I couldn't process any of this. I stood up and walked to the window. Sunlight glinted off the cars in the street below. I turned back and looked at him. "This doesn't make any sense. We're talking about

Meredith—remember? No one on this earth who knew her would want to hurt her." My voice was shaking.

"Apparently, someone wanted her dead."

I could almost hear her voice, so quiet on my phone: *"What are you..."* Who had she been talking to? Her murderer? And who hated her so much to commit such violence?

Tom was watching my face. "When was the last time you ate?"

The sudden change in direction caught me off guard. "What?"

"Food. When was the last time you had any?" He was starting to sound like Martha, but then I remembered that side of Tom, the caretaker—needing to fix whatever was broken.

"I don't remember," I said. And I really didn't care.

"Interrogation time is over. You need to eat."

"I'm not hungry."

"I saw a Pizza Hut on the next block over—we can order in. I'm buying."

Oh God, he *was* going to make me eat. "Okay, but I'm going to fix myself a drink. Do you want one?"

"Wine, if you have any."

I poured him a glass of chardonnay and fixed myself some vodka and orange juice—more vodka than orange juice. As the warmth of the alcohol hit me, I realized I was headed some place safe and familiar, a place where sadness couldn't touch me.

It was after eight by the time we finished dinner. Tom was right. I did need to eat, as I discovered once I started. And more than that, I needed to talk about my sister with someone who wasn't part of the family.

We reminisced about the old days when Tom and Meredith were in college and dating. About the night they didn't get home until four in the morning. Ruth was beside herself with worry. Fred was staying at our house that night, and when Tom brought Meredith home that morning, Fred, in one grand, misguided moment of chivalry, had cold-cocked Tom on the front lawn. The memory still made me laugh.

Tom cleared the table and took the dishes to the sink. It felt like a lifetime had passed since he'd been a part of our lives. So much had changed. Everything was different now.

I watched him move. Tom, the protector. Tom, who took care of the people in his life. Years ago, he'd taken care of my sister.

I needed him to take care of me now, to protect me... from the overwhelming loss that was pulling me into the abyss. From my guilt, knowing that Meredith had needed me and I hadn't even been able to show up in her life. But mostly from the night ahead and whatever it would bring.

From some place deep inside, those long-buried feelings began to stir. I walked up behind him, put my arms around his waist, kissing the back of his neck.

"Liz, don't," he said. But he didn't move.

My hand went under the front of his shirt, his muscles tightened as I rubbed my fingers over his chest. As wrong as this was, I couldn't stop. If I stopped now, he would leave, and then I'd be...alone.

My hand brushed the front of his jeans, and his response was evident.

He reached for my hand and turned to face me. "Elizabeth, don't..." His voice was stern.

I leaned in to kiss him. He grasped my shoulders, holding me back. "I think it's time for me to go."

Long after the front door closed behind him, I stood by

the sink in the darkening kitchen, tears sliding down my cheeks. I slipped to the floor and curled into a ball as the sadness took hold.

EVENTUALLY, I MADE my way upstairs and climbed into bed.

I dreamed about Meredith. It was part of a long-forgotten memory that wove its way in from my subconscious. I was eight years old, and some strange noise had awakened me. I lay in terror in the dark bedroom, waiting for whatever monsters I'd heard to come and eat me up. I finally summoned the courage to move and crawled out of bed, quietly making my way to the door of my sister's adjoining room. I knocked softly, waiting for her to reply, keeping a lookout over my shoulder for the ghouls that lay in wait for small defenseless children.

"Go to sleep, Ellie," came Meredith's muffled reply.

"Meredith, I need to come in."

"Not tonight. Go away."

I pushed the door open to see her sitting in a tight ball on the window seat, her small frame bathed in moonlight.

"I need to sleep with you." I closed the door on the unseen creatures lurking behind me and tiptoed to her bed.

"I don't want you in here tonight, Ellie," she said.

"But I heard *noises*, Meredith."

"*What* noises?"

"Awful monster noises."

She sighed. "All right."

We got into bed together, and I slept the rest of the night.

Meredith was up before I was the next morning, and I lay in bed, sleepy and content to have been saved from the terrors of the night before. I rolled over and froze. The sheets on Meredith's side of the bed were stained with blood.

The dream was almost as vivid as the experience had been. I stared at the ceiling in the bedroom of my apartment, wondering why that particular memory, of all the ones tucked away in my brain, I had chosen to recall.

I remember I ran, screaming for Ruth, certain that my sister was dying.

It was my introduction to anything remotely related to sexuality. Ruth was clearly uncomfortable as she tried to explain to me about girls and monthly periods. I came away more horrified than before, to think what awful fate had befallen my sister.

Martha came to my rescue. She sat me down in the kitchen, gave me milk and cinnamon toast, and calmly related the facts of life—or as many of them as an eight-year-old mind could handle. When she was finished, I was reassured that Meredith was *not* dying, that what she experienced happened to all girls eventually, and that it was a natural part of growing up.

The dream memory drove into my heart like a stake. Meredith had saved me from the monsters that night, and every night I had needed her to. She had always—*always*—been there for me. She was my protector. And now she was gone. There was nothing I could ever do to repay her. Nothing I could ever do to even the score except maybe find out what had happened to her. Find out what monster had come out of the night to take her from me.

"Whatever happens, please don't hate me." Her last words to me on a faceless cell phone.

How could I hate you, Meredith? You're all I ever had.

I got out of bed and headed for the bathroom. In fifteen minutes, I was in my car driving into the sunrise.

Half an hour later, I came to a stop in the driveway behind Meredith's Saab. The brown grass crackled underfoot as I made my way to the front door and slipped under the plastic yellow police tape that guarded the entrance to my sister's house.

I unlocked the front door and moved inside. The house was warm, and gray powder, compliments of the crime scene unit, covered most surfaces, a police outline marking the position of the body. The cranberry stain on the carpet jumped out like a bull's-eye and nearly drove me out the door.

I had to steel my courage and remember why I was there: this was about Meredith, not me. I breathed deeply for a moment until I was calm enough to look around. Tom was right—there were no signs of a struggle. Everything was in its place.

I walked down the hall toward the bedrooms. Meredith's was at the end of the house on the right. A large picture window framed a panoramic view of the lake.

"Just think of it, Ellie," she'd said when she showed me the house for the first time. *"I can wake up every morning and see the water. Dad would have loved this. Remember?"*

No, I didn't remember, but I couldn't tell her that. I'd nodded.

My heart aching, I opened the door, wanting to see her sitting on her bed. Painting her toenails, reading a novel, anything that meant she was alive, that I hadn't lost her.

The stillness of the room was the only thing that greeted me. The queen-sized bed with the blue comforter had been made. The curtains were open. Everything neat and tidy.

I walked to the nightstand and sat down on the bed. There wasn't much there: a bedside lamp, a digital alarm clock, and a mystery by James Patterson. I picked up the book and fanned the pages, and a bookmark fluttered free. She was only halfway through with it. Now she would never know how it ended.

I looked at the small slip of yellow paper she was using as a bookmark. It bore the name "Dana" and a phone number with a local area code. I stuffed it into the pocket of my jeans.

I walked around the room. Meredith's room. Unlike mine, everything would be in its own assigned place, including whatever it was I was looking for.

I pulled open a few drawers but found nothing but clothes, color sorted and neatly folded. Nothing of interest in the organized closet. There had to be something here that would speak to me about her life, something that the police would never find.

As a child, Meredith used to hide things in her room, private things that she didn't want Ruth or me to find. She had some great hiding places, but after years of practice, I was pretty good at finding them.

I started my search again, recalling the challenge involved in the hunt. I slipped my hand into the pillow shams, under the shelves of bookcases, through every article in her underwear drawer.

It was under her bed, inserted in a small opening slit on the underside of the box springs.

The book felt heavy in my hand as I drew it out into the light. It was her journal. But why here? Without the intrusion of a younger sister, why would she feel the need to hide it? Or maybe this was her insurance in case something ever happened to her—she *knew* that I would find it.

Just to make sure, I felt around in the opening under the box springs one more time. Something hit my hand and fell to the floor. I fumbled around and found a small plastic flash drive, which I stuffed into the pocket of my jeans, along with the phone number.

I sat down on the bed and thumbed through the small book, filled with her tight, cramped handwriting. I flipped back to Memorial Day, to get some sense of what was going on with her that day, what had happened that made her so withdrawn.

Family here today, she wrote. *I wanted to spend time alone with Ellie, but that wasn't possible. I need to tell her what's going on before this whole thing blows up. But maybe I would have said too much. I don't know yet what's going to happen, how this is going to end. I only know I have to do something now. Too many people have been hurt, too many lives destroyed. It's time.*

I was suddenly crying. "Shit. You could have told me, Meredith. You could have fucking told me. I would have helped you."

But even as I thought it, I knew it wasn't true. I stood up and paced the room. Meredith was gone. I couldn't go back and pretend that I would have been a different person, a better sister.

All I could do for her now was to keep searching, to find out what had been going on in her life that had caused her so much pain. I would do that for her. I would do that for me, and I would find the bastard who did this.

After a few minutes, I went back to the search.

Pushed back in the bottom drawer of the desk in the living room, I found a stack of letters beside her address book. The letters were old, and the police must have already decided there was nothing worthwhile in them. Still, I slipped them into my purse next to her journal. A photo album lay on the shelf in one of the bookcases. I tucked it under my arm.

I looked around, thinking of those desperate calls to Fred and me. Had she known what would happen? Had she known how dangerous it would turn out to be?

Ruth had never liked the idea of Meredith living alone so far from town. Her housewarming present to my sister had been one of my father's prized guns, a Ruger MKIII.

When we were younger, Ruth had made sure that we both knew how to handle a gun, part of our turning-out process to become well-rounded young ladies as Ruth had been— old-school, country-club material. We took riding lessons, shooting lessons, tennis, piano, and ballet. Ruth finally gave up when she realized that both of her stepdaughters had two left feet and tin ears. We failed miserably at dance and piano, but we could both outshoot any boy we knew.

I wondered now if my sister had known someone was coming and had armed herself that night.

There was a locked door in the built-in bookcase in the living room, where Meredith kept the pistol. I found the key in the desk, unlocked the storage door, and withdrew the metal box that held the gun. Even as I took it from its hiding place, I could feel the weight of the gun in the box. I unlocked the box and saw it sitting there.

Maybe Tom was right: Meredith had been shot by some- one she knew and trusted. Or at least trusted enough to assume they wouldn't kill her. She had been frightened, distraught, but she never bothered to get the gun.

I put the gun back and took one last look around, feel- ing the loss of all the memories we'd shared in this small, cozy house. I locked the door behind me and ducked under the police tape.

Tom was leaning up against my car, arms folded across his chest. "You're not supposed to be here. I could arrest you for tampering with a crime scene."

"I just needed something of Meredith's, something personal to get me through the next couple of days." I produced the photo album from under my arm.

"This is an active investigation, Liz. That's police evidence, along with everything else in the house."

"Are you going to confiscate it?"

He didn't move.

"How did you know I was here?"

"Lucky guess. Did you take anything else?"

I shook my head. "I just needed to be here one more time."

He watched me for a minute, trying to read my face. "Go home. I don't want you out here again, do you understand?"

I nodded. He moved away from the car and I got in, made a tight turn, and started down the driveway. He watched me until I disappeared into the thicket of trees.

If he thought I was done, he was very mistaken.

SIX

I DROVE HOME, locked the door behind me, and headed up the stairs, carrying the things I'd taken from Meredith's house.

I sat down on the unmade bed, propped some pillows behind my back, and opened the slim red photo album. The pictures were recent, going back over the past eighteen months, all of them dated and in chronological order. So very Meredith.

My heart ached, looking at my sister's delicate, smiling face, knowing I would never see it again. But there was also a sweet comfort to be able to look back and share some of her memories.

There were pictures of the three of us—Fred, Meredith, and me—at the amusement park Valleyfair last summer. Christmas snapshots from the office party. Quite a few of Fred, doing what Fred does best—drinking, eating, sleeping sprawled on the patio furniture.

The last pictures were of the family on Memorial Day weekend. Ruth seemed to be enjoying herself. David's pale skin was red and puffy from too much sun. Fred was, well, being Fred. I looked distracted, remembering how eager I'd been to be gone. And then there was Meredith, smiling dutifully for the camera, a look of sadness in her eyes.

I remembered the look.

One of the pictures Fred must have taken, showed us

all seated at the picnic table, our faces turned toward my cousin. In the window of the guesthouse behind us, a man's face pressed up against the pane, watching.

I pulled back the plastic and removed the picture. Another photograph was hidden underneath—the family portrait of an unfamiliar family—a mother, father, and two small girls, all dressed in red sweaters and black slacks. From the woman's hairstyle, the picture was probably fifteen years old. I looked closely but didn't recognize any of them, and wondered who they were and why this picture was snuggled in behind another.

I flipped to the back of the album and found blank pages, so she hadn't run out of room in the book and had to piggyback pictures. They could have been any family—the Christmas photo of a coworker, the family of a client, a neighbor at the lake. But why were they hidden in the book? Maybe I was reading too much into this simple act. I just didn't think so.

The studio's name, printed on the back of the photo, showed the business address in Bloomington, a suburb south of Minneapolis.

I put the picture and album on the nightstand and opened Meredith's journal to a random page.

February 15th: *So weird that Lee called today out of the blue. I haven't seen her or even thought about her in ages. But, so good to hear a voice from the past. She was adamant that we get together soon, I think it would be fun to catch up.*

March 3rd: *She called today. I know I should be happy. She wants to meet with me, but I don't know if I can do this. The memories are still so vivid. They haunt me, and I don't think I have it in me.*

March 10th: *I did the craziest thing today. I feel stupid, but with all that's going on, I had the strongest feeling that I needed to see Tom. After all these years, I wonder what he'll think. I called him today. I think he was surprised but he agreed to meet.*

March 12th: *I met Tom for coffee. I didn't realize how much I'd missed him. He hasn't changed much. He's still so damn handsome—and kind. We talked for the longest time. Lee showed up, and the three of us together felt like the old days. A part of my life I thought I'd lost.*

March 19th: *Tom and I had dinner at that little place we used to go to in Dinkytown when we were in college. Again, we ran into Lee. I'm loving all the memories these two are bringing back into my life.*

She sounded so happy. There was no hint of trouble ahead or impending murder. I skipped ahead several pages.

April 8th: *I saw the pictures today, and I know it was him. There was no doubt in my mind. And the hardest part of seeing his face again was how happy he looked. He has no idea what he's done. I despise him. How could he have done this to me? How could any of them have done this? I want him to suffer like I've suffered. I want them all to suffer.*

Chills went down my back. What the hell? I read a couple of earlier entries, then through to the end, but Meredith never talked about who "he" was or what he had done. It was like she either didn't want to remember it or didn't want to commit it to paper. Was this man somehow tied to the memories that still haunted her? I needed to find out who he was, but I didn't have a clue where to start.

An hour later, I was in the kitchen, telling myself I needed to eat—telling myself I was looking for food—but all I could think about was the vodka in the cabinet above the sink. I started to reach for it.

A voice behind me said, "Kind of early for that, don't you think?"

I jumped, then turned. Fred stood in the doorway, perspiration dripping down his cheeks.

"God, you scared me. How did you get in?"

"I have a key, remember? Same one I used yesterday morning. Same one I've had for the past five years."

"Oh yeah. I'm a little jumpy."

"I think we all are." He watched my face, then nodded his head toward the cabinet over the sink. "Is that really necessary?"

I pushed the hair back off my face. "Right now, it feels very necessary. It's been the longest twenty-four hours of my life."

"Drinking isn't going to change anything, Lizzie—you know that. It's not going to make this any easier."

"Really? Thanks for the info. I had no idea." I wasn't in the mood for a temperance lecture from anyone, especially not from Fred. He'd been my drinking partner way too many times for me to take him seriously.

Neither of us moved for long uncomfortable seconds.

I finally stepped away from the sink, and he relaxed his vigil. "What are you doing here?"

"I just picked my mother up at the airport and dropped her off with Ruth and David. I needed a break." He sat down at the counter and put his head in his hands. "It's going to be a very long week."

Rachel was my father's sister, who usually only flew in for Christmas and our annual attempt to be a family. Her arrival was another reminder that we had a new family function— to bury my sister. "So, you spent maybe an hour with her and you had to leave?"

He rubbed his forehead. "It felt longer."

"What are they doing now?"

He looked at me and all his Fred-ness slipped away. "Making funeral arrangements," he said quietly. "You really should be there."

I walked over to the window. He got up and moved in behind me.

"I want her back, Fred. I need her." I turned and buried my head in his shoulder and cried. His arms went around me, and I could feel his hot tears on my cheek.

My tears finally turned into nothing but a vast, deep emptiness that crept up my insides. Fred held me for a long time. Minutes passed. Finally, he stepped away. I reached for a tissue in the box on the windowsill and wiped my eyes.

"What the hell do we do now, Liz?"

"I don't know. I just know I can't sit around waiting for the police to do whatever the hell it is that they do."

"Meaning?"

"I have to do something. I have to find out who did this to her. I owe her that much."

He narrowed his eyes. "Wait. You're thinking of looking for her killer?"

"Yes. No. I don't know. I just know that something horrible was going on in her life, and I need to find out what."

He shook his head. "You can't get involved. That's crazy."

"I have to. I have to do this for her." Even I heard the desperation in my voice.

I tried to convince him. I told him Tom's theory about her being murdered by someone she knew and about the journal and the picture I'd found hidden behind the other picture, and I tried to explain some of the turmoil I'd seen in my sister's face, starting last spring.

"I saw it too," he said, "but she was Meredith. I figured whatever was going on she'd land on her feet." He was quiet for a long time. Finally, he said, "Okay. I'm in."

"What do you mean?"

"If you're doing this, then I'm in too."

"I didn't ask for your help."

"Dammit, Lizzie, could you think about someone else for once in your life? You're not the only one who's hurting here. You're not the only one who lost her."

The pain in his voice was intense. I took a breath. "Okay."

I turned toward the cupboard over the sink again. Fred reached out and took my arm. "That isn't going to change one damn thing. It's time to stop."

"This isn't any of your business."

"You're wrong," he said, his eyes filled with concern. "When you love someone, it's always your business. I need you now, Lizzie, and I need you sober. And Meredith does too. Promise me you'll try. Just for a while? Please."

He didn't have a clue what he was asking. He didn't

understand it was the only thing that kept the demons at bay. But he was right. I knew that much. It wasn't going to change one damn thing. "I'll try, but I'm not making any promises—just that I'll try."

"That's all I'm asking. And I'm here for you whenever you need me."

"And you?"

"And me what?"

"If I have to do this sober, what about you?"

He looked at his hands, then back at me. "I've been sober for nine months."

"What? Seriously?"

"Seriously. I had my own demons to drown, but it wasn't working as well as I'd hoped. Actually, it wasn't working at all. So I quit. Besides, I met someone, and it was getting in the way of our relationship."

Sobriety and commitment, sides of my cousin I'd never seen. "Why didn't you tell me?"

He shrugged. "In the beginning, when I was getting sober, I had no idea if I'd make it, and I didn't want to talk about it. I guess it was the same with the relationship. I needed to know first if it was real."

"And it's real?"

He smiled. "It's real."

"Who is he?"

"His name is Charlie. Charles. He's a surgeon at Fairview Hospital. I want you to meet him. He's great."

I smiled. "A doctor. Your mother will be so proud."

He groaned. "Ouch. That'll have to wait. We need to get through the funeral. And I need to prepare Charlie for what he's in for."

I wanted to be happy for Fred, but the truth is, I was

more than a tad jealous. My handsome gay cousin was in a serious relationship, which was more than I'd ever been able to achieve.

And sadly, as with Meredith, I hadn't been paying attention to his life. I hadn't been there to share his struggle or his joy. But he also hadn't invited me in. Which made me wonder, why were we all living these secret lives? Why didn't we trust each other enough to share who we really were deep down inside? And the bigger question was, what the hell was wrong with us—why couldn't we just be normal?

Fred was watching me again. I looked at him and smiled. "I can't wait to meet him."

Fred heated up some canned chili and put a box of soda crackers on the table. We ate and talked and planned. I went upstairs to retrieve the picture I'd found hidden in the photo album.

Back in the kitchen, I handed it to Fred, very aware that I might be giving too much meaning to a random act. "Do you know them?"

He examined the faces. "No. You think this is important?"

"I'm not sure."

"I'll check it out." He took a picture with his phone of the front and back of the photo and said he'd pay a visit to the photographer the next day.

It was a longshot, I knew. I fished the flash drive out of my pocket.

"What's that?"

"It was Meredith's. I don't know what's on it, but for some reason, she felt the need to hide it."

"Okay, I'll look at it later." He put it in the pocket of his polo shirt.

Monday morning, I'd visit Meredith's office. Since I knew most of her coworkers, it wouldn't be at all unusual for me to be there to gather her personal things. The plan was for me to get her appointment book and anything else I could find that might help us figure out what had been going on in her life lately.

Part of me felt relieved that we had a direction, but that little voice in my head kept asking, *Do you really want to know?*

AT SIX O'CLOCK, there was a knock at the door. I opened it to see Tom looking hot and tired and holding a bag from the Thai restaurant two blocks over.

"If I bring food," he said, "then you can't turn me away."

"Is that how it works?"

"Yup." He moved past me in the doorway and headed toward the kitchen.

When he'd walked out the night before, I'd thought he was angry. Now I was confused.

He put the bag on the table. "I'm dying. You mind if I grab something to drink?"

"Go ahead."

He made his way to the fridge and pulled out a beer. "You want one?" He looked over his shoulder.

I shook my head. "I'm surprised you're here. I thought you were mad at me."

He wrinkled his forehead. "Why would you think that?"

"Well, last night…and this morning…"

"I'm not mad. You shouldn't have been at Meredith's this morning, but I understand." He stopped.

"And last night?"

He looked at something over my shoulder, then back at me. "I'm not mad about last night, Liz. It's just that this isn't the time for either of us. You're too vulnerable right now, and it would be inappropriate for me when I'm investigating your sister's murder."

"Okay. I get it." I walked over to the cupboard and reached for the plates.

"Now *you're* mad."

"I told you, I get it."

He stepped out of my way in the small kitchen as I moved to put the dishes on the table.

"You know you didn't invent grief sex," he said behind me.

I turned to look at him. "What are you talking about?"

"Grief sex—when all you want to do is numb the pain. Like getting drunk. The only problem is, once the sex is over or you sober up, the pain is still there. You didn't make it go away." He was watching me with an intensity that made me uncomfortable.

"I don't want to talk about this anymore. Let's just eat."

We were both quiet as we loaded up our plates with vegetable curry and panang chicken.

"Why are you here?" I finally asked.

"I wanted to see how you're doing. I brought you this." He took the evidence baggie containing my phone out of his pocket and handed it to me. "And... I got the autopsy report back right before I left the office."

I wasn't prepared for that. "I'm not sure I want to hear this."

"Okay. We don't have to talk about it if you don't want to, but some of it might be reassuring."

"Like what?"

His eyes met mine. "She hadn't been raped. There were no signs of sexual assault."

I didn't realize I'd been holding my breath until it started to slowly escape my lungs.

"And," he said, "you wanted to know if she died instantly. The medical examiner is pretty sure that she did. The bullet went right into her heart."

Tears came to my eyes. Small comfort, both of those, but I was in no position to bargain with God; I'd take what I could get. Knowing my sister's final moments had come quickly was enough for right now.

He was watching me again, a look I couldn't read. "What?" I said.

"You never told me that Meredith had a child."

"She didn't."

"The autopsy clearly showed that she'd given birth at some time."

"No, that never happened. I would have known."

The autopsy report had to be wrong. They'd gotten her mixed up with someone else. She had never even been pregnant. Those were the things that were going through my head, but the look in Tom's eyes told me how mistaken I was. I stood up and started for the liquor cabinet, stopped, and sat down again.

"It surprised me too, so I called the M.E. He was sure that a pregnancy had occurred, one that resulted in an actual birth."

I looked at Tom. "Was it yours?"

"What? No." He shook his head. "You think…"

"You guys dated for over a year in high school and then for over a year in college. Certainly a possibility, right?"

He looked uncomfortable. He stood and walked to the window, with his back to me. I thought he was considering the possibility of an unknown child somewhere. Finally, he turned around. "We never had that kind of relationship."

"What kind of relationship?"

"We never slept together. Trust me, I was more than willing, but Meredith kept putting me off. I thought maybe with her Catholic upbringing that she was, you know..."

"A virgin?"

"Well, yeah."

"I don't understand."

He seemed at a loss. "It's hard to explain. In high school, we were both so young and inexperienced, we mostly just hung out together. Meredith never seemed to want more than that. And then in college, when we got back together again, well, we didn't move much beyond that either. As time went on, I realized that she just wanted to be friends. She was going through some identity crisis or something, and I was her sounding board."

That surprised me, and bothered me on a level I couldn't even comprehend. I'd always thought that Meredith and Tom had some deep, intimate relationship, that they were destined to be together forever like star-crossed lovers. When they broke up, I'd felt a certain jealous satisfaction, but there was also a twinge of sadness that they hadn't ended up together when they seemed so perfect for each other.

"What?" he asked.

I shook my head. "I was just thinking. I guess I had your relationship all wrong."

I COULDN'T REMEMBER the last time I'd woken up without a hangover. Too long. It felt pretty good, but I wasn't kidding myself. One night of sobriety might be all I had in me.

I called my boss at Silver Springs Publishing, a children's book publisher where I'd worked as an editor for the past eighteen months, which was a record for me. It was still early enough so I wouldn't have to talk to anyone, and I left a voicemail telling her what had happened and that I'd be out for the next two weeks. Then I threw on some clothes and stepped out my front door into the heat.

Meredith had been pregnant. When? And by whom? Tom was the longest relationship Meredith had ever had, even though now I knew it wasn't really a *relationship*. Or so he said.

I needed to talk to Fred, but he wasn't answering his cell.

I tried to think of who else she'd dated in high school and college and beyond. Meredith and Tom had dated through most of her freshman year at high school and somehow had reconnected again in college. There were a few other boys along the way, and later a few men, but not many. No one at all that I could think of in the last couple of years. She was a homebody. I was the one who'd turned Ruth's hair gray, as she often reminded me.

So, who? And why hadn't she ever told me?

The only time we'd ever been apart was Meredith's sophomore year in high school, when Ruth sent her to boarding school in Chicago. At the time, it just seemed like another Ruth thing, to turn us into the young ladies she thought we should be. But nine months away at school, would be the perfect way to hide an unwanted pregnancy.

Still, I was surprised that Meredith had never told me. All these years later, would she still feel the shame?

Fred and I had our assignments for the day. He was going to track down the photographer of the unknown family from Meredith's photo album. It was an old picture, and I had little hope that he'd find anything. And for all we knew, the family portrait could have been anyone.

I walked into Meredith's office building on Lexington Avenue, certain that by now everyone already knew from the news what had happened to my sister. Diana Valentine, the receptionist, looked up from her computer. She was probably in her late fifties, a little on the dumpy side, with spiked pink hair. Well, it was pink today.

Crumpled tissues covered her desk, and her eyes were swollen and red. So, they knew. Diana looked surprised to see me. It took her a beat to compose herself.

She pulled another tissue from the box, dabbed at her eyes, then came around the desk and engulfed me in a bear hug. "I'm so sorry, Liz. I'm so very sorry. Everyone here was shocked. How're you doing?"

"Hanging in there."

"Meredith was one of the kindest people I knew. I don't know what we'll do without her."

"Is Barb in yet?" Barb Forseman was Meredith's supervisor.

"She's with someone right now. Some man. He was here when I got here this morning. It shouldn't be long. Do you want to wait?"

"Do you mind if I wait in Meredith's office?"

"That's a good idea. No one will bother you there."

I passed through the waiting area and entered Meredith's office, closing the door behind me. I didn't know how much time I'd have.

The mid-sized office had windows looking out over the parking lot and onto Lexington Avenue. The faux wood desk, angled in the corner, faced the door in a feng shui sort of way. Plants and family pictures perched on top of the file cabinet and surrounding bookshelves.

The desk was locked, but I knew where Meredith hid the key. I'd seen her lock up often enough while I waited for her to go out to dinner. The large side drawers held client files. I scanned the names on the tabs of the manila folders, looking for any that might sound familiar. None of them did.

I slipped her appointment book out of the center drawer, so glad my sister was pretty much a technophobe and didn't keep her appointments on her computer, where I'd have to come up with a password. Starting back in May and moving forward, I read each page.

Appointments from the first two weeks in May, simply had the initials "JM." Could have been a client, but I didn't think so. She coded those by first name and last initial. One of the entries had a phone number with an area code I didn't recognize. I ripped the page out and shoved it in my pocket.

The last week in June, she had a two o'clock appointment with Lee Atwater at the Tullerman Building in downtown Minneapolis. I thumbed back through the spring and saw other appointments with Lee Atwater. I knew the name but couldn't remember from where.

Then it hit me, Meredith and Lee had known each other in high school; then they'd gone to the same college and even been sorority sisters. But as I recalled, Lee had hated Meredith with a passion. Lee had been dating Tom in high school—ninth grade, I think—when he dumped her for Meredith—the *first* time. Tom and Meredith were together for over a year.

Then, almost as an instant replay, Tom and Lee had been dating in college—they may have even been engaged—when he left Lee again for Meredith.

How and why after all these years had Lee and my sister hooked up together? And was this the Lee from her journal?

There was movement on the other side of the door, and I quickly closed all the drawers. My hand was on the appointment book, ready to shove it into my purse when the door opened. Barb Forseman stood there with Tom, who was looking at me over her shoulder. His jaw muscles tightened. He narrowed his eyes and shook his head. I removed my hand from the appointment book.

"What are you doing here, Liz?" His voice was not at all friendly.

"I wanted to see Barb and didn't want to sit in the waiting room, so I came in here."

I could tell he wasn't buying it, but it was good enough for Barb. She moved around the desk and hugged me. "I'm so sorry, Liz," she said. "I wanted to call you when I heard the news, but I figured you'd be with Ruth, and I didn't want to intrude. So, how're you doing?"

I liked Barb. I don't know why. She was a little too touchy-feely for me, but she was compassionate and sincere and had been a good mentor for my sister. She pulled away and I avoided her eyes. They were too deep and too blue and too damn kind. Instead, I focused on her curly black hair with the silver threads running through it.

"I'm doing okay. If you're not busy, I was wondering if I could talk to you."

"Sure. Why don't you come into my office?" She turned to Tom. "Do you need me for anything else, Agent Martens?"

"Not at the moment."

Barb started out the door, but Tom stepped in front of me. "What do you think you're doing? I told you to stay out of this."

"My sister is dead. Barb was a good friend of hers. I just want to talk to her."

"Liz, if I find out that there is more to this than you've said, I will throw your ass in jail. Do you understand?"

I met his gaze. "Yes," I said.

Reluctantly, he moved out of my way.

"Can I get you a cup of coffee?" Barb asked when we were seated in her office.

"No thanks, I'm fine."

She slid a box of Kleenex across the desk toward me, tears filling her eyes. "What can I do for you, Liz?"

I tried to detach myself from the emotion. I'd never make it through if I lost it now, so I cut to the chase. "Was Meredith in some kind of trouble?"

She looked away for a second, then back at me. "What kind of trouble are we talking about?"

"The fact that we have to clarify it tells me that she was. So, what was going on with her?"

She arched her neck and looked at the ceiling. "I wish I could tell you."

"Barb, this is my sister we're talking about…"

She held up her hand to cut me off. "It's not that I *won't* tell you. It's that I *can't* because I don't know anything."

"But you just said…"

"As I told Special Agent Martens, something was definitely going on, but for the life of me, I don't know what it was. For several months now, she'd been agitated and distracted. I thought maybe her caseload was too heavy, so I cut it back as much as I could. That didn't seem to help."

Barb ran a hand through her curls. "I encouraged her to take some time off. She took a few weeks in early May and went up to Bayfield, but she came back in even worse shape. I thought maybe something was going on with the family—that maybe you or Ruth might be sick, but when I tried to talk to her about it, she said everything was fine. She was losing weight and had those dark circles under her eyes. I suggested maybe she should see a therapist, and she said she already was."

Barb spread her hands out on the desk in front of her. "I wish I had more to offer you, but I don't know anything."

"But something was definitely wrong?"

"Definitely."

She watched my face for a long time while I tried to think. "And everything's okay with the family, aside from what you're dealing with now?"

"As far as I know."

"Then I haven't got a clue."

"What about clients? Coworkers? Any problems there?"

"Just what comes with the territory." She paused. "This may not be relevant, but there was this man who kept showing up around here."

"A new boyfriend?"

She shook her head. "I don't think so. He came to the office a few times—an older man, big guy. And I ran into them at Starbucks one morning, but Meredith didn't introduce us. I saw him maybe five or six times."

"Do you have a name?"

"No. I just know that it felt secretive. And that doesn't help you any more than anything else I've said, does it?"

"Not really." But I filed it away, hoping somehow, I could track down this mysterious man.

We talked for a few minutes more, but there was nothing else to say. Barb asked about the funeral, and I told her I'd let her know. She looked down at her desk, and I knew she was trying to hold back the tears for my benefit. "I'm going to miss her more than you can imagine." Her voice shook. "She was a wonderful social worker and a good friend."

As I stood to leave, she came around the desk and hugged me again. "I'm here for you. If you need anything—anything at all—call me."

I pulled away and there were tears in her eyes. "Thanks, Barb, but we'll be fine."

Her hand rested on my arm. "I mean I'm here for *you*, Liz. I don't want you to keep this all bottled up inside like your sister would have done. If you need an ear to listen or a shoulder to cry on, I'm here."

I had my hand on the doorknob when she said, "Maybe if Meredith had talked to someone, none of this would have happened. Maybe we wouldn't be talking about her funeral."

SEVEN

WELL, THAT WASN'T exactly what I needed to hear. I didn't want to believe that my sister had, even unwittingly, contributed to her own death.

The car was stuffy and I sat in the parking lot, waiting for the air conditioner to kick in.

The passenger door opened and Tom slid into the seat. "You know I was being a nice guy yesterday when I didn't arrest you at Meredith's house for tampering with a crime scene."

"Am I supposed to thank you?"

"You're supposed to keep your nose out of an official police investigation is what you're supposed to do."

"I haven't done anything."

"Yet." He watched my face. "So, did you find what you were looking for?"

I raised my eyebrows.

"I haven't got time for games, Liz. You went through her appointment book and her desk. What was it you were looking for?"

Denial would just be a waste of time at this point. "I don't even know. All I know is that there was something huge going on in her life, and..."

"And what?"

"Maybe—whatever it was—got her killed."

"You're right. Which is why you need to stay out of this until we know what or who we're dealing with." He passed a hand over his eyes, then looked at me hard. "Elizabeth, you need to understand that this is an active murder investigation, and I need to know that you will stay out of it from here on out."

"I do understand, and I'm not interfering with your investigation. I'm trying to find out what was going on in my sister's life."

"And we don't know yet that they weren't related, so I repeat, stay the hell out of this."

"Okay."

He grunted. "I don't believe you for a second, but it's the most I can hope for at the moment." He got out and slammed the door behind him.

My cell phone rang, Fred was checking in. "I need to see you," I told him.

"Okay. When and where?"

"I'm headed to downtown Minneapolis right now. How about in an hour? Lunch at Valentino's."

"I'll be there."

THE TULLERMAN BUILDING in downtown Minneapolis, where Lee Atwater, my sister's former classmate and Tom rival, had her office, was right off the freeway on Sixth. I parked in the parking lot and took the elevator to the ninth floor.

The receptionist for Dr. Lee Atwater, licensed psychologist, told me that Lee was with a client and had a full schedule for the day. I told her I was an old friend, on my way back home, and was hoping I could say hello before I headed back to Seattle. The woman told me to have a seat and she'd try to squeeze me in.

The reception area was all chrome and leather, and I sat down in a sturdy chair and waited. Twenty minutes later, the receptionist told me I could go in.

Lee was seated behind a large mahogany desk, her back to a wall of glass overlooking the Minneapolis skyline. Her three-hundred-dollar suit fit smoothly over her trim body and told me business was good for Dr. Atwater. The limp hair she'd had in college had been layered and highlighted into a soft cut that framed her small face. The dowdy girl from high school had transformed herself into a swan—or an attractive, successful woman.

I took a seat across from her. "Thank you for seeing me, Lee."

"Well, I didn't want to miss you before you headed back to Seattle," she said with a slight smile on her lips. Then the smile slid away. "My condolences, Liz. I was saddened to hear about Meredith."

"Thank you. I was hoping you could help me with something."

"If I can," she said, but her tone sounded guarded.

"I know that Meredith was seeing you regularly. I'm assuming you were her therapist." I paused and waited for her to jump in. She didn't. "I've been trying to get a handle on what was going on with Meredith these past few months. I know she was struggling with something. I know it was big."

Still no jumping-in from Lee. "I was hoping you might help me," I said.

"Help you what?"

"Help me understand."

She bit her lip. "Meredith was a client of mine, Liz, which means I shouldn't be talking to you about her at all. Even divulging that is more than I should do."

"Even if she's been murdered?"

"Even if."

"Lee, help me. Please." I didn't know where to go with this. "Was there a specific reason she was seeing you? Or the general 'life sucks'?"

"You're putting me in a very awkward position here. I want to help you. I wanted to help your sister, but I am bound by laws and ethics to not discuss her treatment." She stood up, came around the desk, and sat down on it in front of me. "If I can help you through your grief, I'm here for you. Other than that, there's not much I can do."

I wasn't willing to leave empty-handed. I needed some-thing—*anything*. I wracked my brain. "Was there a man in her life causing her trouble?"

"You're not gonna make this easy for me, are you?" She actually smiled. "And I have a feeling you're not going to leave until you have something." She thought for a moment. "We'll have to make this quick because I have a client in ten minutes. I am not allowed to give you any information about why your sister was coming to me, but as a friend, I'll do what I can. You may ask me yes-or-no questions. I'll answer whatever I feel comfortable with—whatever I feel you need to know. Okay?"

"Okay."

"Whenever you're ready."

Without knowing the details of Meredith's life, I wasn't sure where to begin. I'd have to start with the few things I knew.

"Did you know Meredith had been pregnant?"

"Yes."

"Did she give birth to a child?"

Some hesitation. "Yes."

Okay. Now what? "Did she give that child up for adoption?"

"Yes."

"Where is that child now?"

She arched her eyebrows and shook her head. "I can't answer that."

"Because you don't know? Or it's one of those things you don't feel comfortable telling me?"

"Let's move on."

I nodded. "Okay. Did Ruth know Meredith had a child?"

Again the hesitation. "Yes."

"Who was the father?"

She smiled. "Nice try."

I smiled back. "It was worth a shot. Do you know who the father was?"

She looked down at her hands, and her voice was quiet. "No, I don't know for certain."

"Was Tom Martens the father?"

She looked up quickly. "What? Uh, no. Why would you ask that?"

I shrugged. "Was there someone in her life who was threatening her?"

I thought maybe I saw tears in her eyes. The phone on her desk buzzed, and a disembodied voice said, "Dr. Atwater, your next appointment is here."

She stood up. "I'm sorry, Liz, you have to go now."

"You didn't answer my last question."

"I can't. I don't think that's a line I can cross."

I stood and she took my hand in both of hers. "I am so sorry for your loss, Elizabeth. Meredith was a wonderful person, and she loved you very much." She smiled softly, and I had to turn away.

"Thank you, Lee," I said, heading for the door.

"You know, Liz, one thing I was reminded of with Meredith was that our biggest strengths can become our weaknesses if we're not careful."

I turned back. "I'm not sure I understand."

"You will."

EIGHT

I HATE PUZZLES. They hurt my head. I had no idea what Lee meant by her ominous comment.

It was still a mystery why Meredith had sought out her nemesis after all these years, but Lee was a familiar face, and whatever animosity she'd had for my sister when they were younger must have been put to rest.

I stepped into the first available elevator just as Tom walked out of the next one over. He looked in my direction and did a double take; his jaw muscles tightened, and he rolled his eyes toward the heavens.

I made good time getting to Valentino's. Fred was waiting at the restaurant, with a table by the window, sitting across from a drop-dead gorgeous man. Think Tom Selleck in his *Magnum P.I.* days—tall, muscular, and—well, perfect.

As I approached them, Fred looked up and stopped talking. The other man saw me and stood.

"Liz," Fred said, "this is my friend Charlie."

Charlie smiled and took my hand. "It's so nice to finally meet you, Liz." The corners of his eyes crinkled into crow's feet—very charming. "Fred has told me so much about you."

I looked at Fred. I didn't tell Charlie that I'd only just heard about him. "It's nice to meet you too."

My hand was still clasped in his. "I'm so sorry about your sister."

"Thank you." I looked away, determined not to cry.

"I wish I could stay, but I'm due back at the hospital. I just wanted to meet you." He looked down at Fred. "I'll call you later."

Every woman in the place and probably a few men watched as he made his way through the restaurant.

"Wow," I said after Charlie left.

"He's more than just a pretty face." Fred waited a beat. "He has a great body too."

"Good to know you have some depth to your relationship."

He laughed. "I'm kidding, Lizzie. He's the best thing that's ever happened to me."

"I'm happy for you." After we ordered our lunch, I got right to business. "So, what'd you find out?"

"First stop, nada. The photographer was a total ass. Of course, he couldn't remember the family. He takes thousands of pictures a year, and he didn't have any way to easily retrieve the information. Nor was he willing to try, not even for moola. What has the world become, when you can't even *buy* private information? It frightens me."

"Yeah, it's scary."

"I hope you had better luck than I did."

Not much. It didn't take long to catch him up. I told him about Meredith's appointment book, the mysterious man Barb had seen Meredith with, my talk with Lee Atwater, and the fact that Tom Martens was always one step behind me and not the least bit happy about that.

Fred was watching me. "So? What's the deal with Tom?"

"What?"

"He keeps showing up everywhere you go. Is he following you?"

"Well, he did get to Meredith's office *before* me, so I don't think that counts. And I think going to Lee's office was just the logical next step for both of us."

"Uh-huh. And?"

"And what?"

"Is there something else going on that I should know about?"

"Such as?"

"Whenever you talk about Tom, something about you is different."

I looked out the window, not sure how to explain what I felt, not sure I even understood it.

He tapped the back of my hand. "Tell me."

Tears came to my eyes. "Do you remember Darin Silver? The guy I was madly in love with when I was fifteen?"

"What does he—"

"Do you remember him?"

"Yeah. He was a douche."

Yes, he was. "I wanted to marry him."

I looked at Fred. He waited.

"The day he dumped me for my best friend, Maggie, I went home in tears. Everything I'd ever wanted was gone. I was beyond devastated."

"And where are we headed with this trip down memory lane?"

"When I got home that day, Tom was in the living room, waiting for Meredith to get ready to go out. He asked me what was wrong. He let me cry on his shoulder. He told me everything would be okay."

"So, he was a nice guy. So what?"

"Then he asked me the guy's name and where he lived. I didn't think anything of it at the time, but two days later, Darin caught up with me on the way home from school and wanted to talk. He was all nervous about something. Kept looking around. I didn't have a clue what was going on, but he apologized for hurting me and said he wasn't good enough for me."

Fred raised an eyebrow. "And you think Tom was behind that?"

"I do."

"And the point of the story?"

I looked out the window again. "He made me feel safe when I needed it."

Fred was quiet for a long time. "That was a long time ago, Lizzie. We've all changed. Life has changed us."

"I'd like to think some things never change. Nice guys stay nice guys."

"I'm sure Darin didn't think Tom was such a nice guy." Fred watched my face. "I think you need to be careful here."

"It's *Tom*. I've known him since I was nine years old."

"Hey, we've both watched *Dateline*. What do cops do when they don't have any viable leads? They go for the most obvious person to coerce a confession."

"That would never happen—"

"Just be careful. Please."

"Okay." I was quiet for a moment, then looked at Fred. "Did you know Meredith had been pregnant?"

"What? No." He shook his head.

I told him about the autopsy report and what Lee had confirmed.

I could see him searching the recesses of his memory. "That's got to be a mistake. How could she have been pregnant and we didn't know about it? There's no way—we've been in each other's lives too much for her to have hidden a pregnancy."

He was right about that. We'd always been together, the three of us, our lives intertwined. Weeks might pass without seeing each other, but never months. Boarding school was the only time we'd been apart.

"Remember her sophomore year in high school?" I said.

"I was just thinking of that. Ruth packed her off to Chicago. That makes perfect sense in hindsight."

"Lee said that Ruth knew about it. If Meredith had been out on her own, there's no way Ruth would have been her confidante for an unwanted pregnancy."

I picked at a stuffed mushroom on my plate. That had been the worst year of my life. "That whole summer before she left, she was so moody. We fought all the time."

Fred shrugged. "Hormones."

"It might not have been so bad if she'd been the only one who left, but Meredith insisted that I go away to school too, and Ruth bought into it. So they exiled me to Boston. God, I hated that place."

"Maybe Meredith thought it would be good for you, help you grow up."

"Maybe. It seemed more like my punishment. She was so angry with me at that time, and I never understood why— it was almost like if she had to endure a year of purgatory, then so did I."

"Who was she dating then?"

"I've been trying to remember all morning. I think that summer, there was some Mark guy. Ruth didn't much like him."

"And whatever became of the Mark guy?"

"They broke up right before she left for Chicago. Last I heard he was studying to become a priest."

"Curiouser and curiouser."

"Or creepier and creepier."

But very shortly before the Mark guy, there was Tom. I tried to shove the thought away, but chronologically Tom could easily have been the father to Meredith's baby if she'd been pregnant her sophomore year.

There would be no reason for him to lie to me about his relationship with Meredith that I could think of, but now that the thought had made its appearance, I knew it was there to stay.

I looked at Fred. "So, except for the baby, we don't know anything more than we did yesterday."

"Wait." He reached into the back pocket of his slacks and took out a piece of paper. "I haven't had time to look at everything on the flash drive. Charlie stopped by last night, and I got interrupted."

He looked at me and smiled. I didn't even ask. "Actually," he continued, "there were several folders, and I only opened one. Here." He handed me the paper.

It was a bill from a private investigator from last March. I looked at Fred. "What?"

"That folder had a number of bills in it. Look at the invoice details."

The investigator had billed for mileage round trip to Bayfield, Wisconsin, and a five-night stay in the Applegate Motel in Bayfield. "What the hell was going on?" I asked.

"Didn't Barb tell you that Meredith took a trip to Bayfield in May?"

"Yeah. I guess we're going to Bayfield."

UNFORTUNATELY, WE COULDN'T leave for Bayfield right away. It was a four-hour drive, there was a funeral coming up in a few days, and we were due at Ruth's for dinner at six.

Sometime soon I would need to ask Ruth about Meredith's pregnancy, but tonight was not the time. Knowing Ruth, it wasn't going to be an easy conversation.

I got to the house at ten after six, stalling for time, hoping Fred would be there first. I didn't see his car, so it was just me and the old folks until he arrived, or until I went loony tunes.

Ruth and my aunt Rachel sat in the living room. Rachel's red eyes were rimmed with smudges of mascara, and a wad of tissues was clutched in her hand. She jumped off the couch when she saw me, coming at me from across the room with outstretched arms, the deep sleeves of her caftan blouse hanging down like gaping sinkholes threatening to swallow me whole.

She pulled me to her chest, kissed my cheek, and buried my head in her shoulder, rocking from side to side.

When she finally pulled away, she smoothed my hair and clamped her hands on each side of my face. "Honey, I couldn't believe it when Freddie called me. I just couldn't believe it. How're you doing?"

"I've been better."

"I know," she said softly. "Come sit next to me."

I loved my aunt Rachel. She was flamboyant and funny and flashier than her gay son. I could only take her in limited doses, but she was good-hearted and I knew she loved me. Her bleached blonde hair was cut short, and the skin on her face looked tighter than it had the last time I'd seen her—a plastic surgery junkie. *But who am I to judge?* I thought as I made a wide berth of the liquor cart, to make it safely to the couch next to Rachel.

"Where's David?" I asked.

"He and Fred went to the club to hit a few golf balls and go to the shooting range. David isn't handling this well," Ruth said. "I thought he needed some kind of diversion."

My first thought was, the shooting range seemed so inappropriate when my sister had just been shot to death. My second thought was *Poor Fred*. He was about as good at taking care of other people as I was.

"We've been making arrangements," Ruth said. "We'd like your input on the music, Elizabeth. Can you think of anything in particular that Meredith would have liked?"

What Meredith would have liked, I wanted to say, was to finish out her life. To get married and have babies and be a grandmother someday. Meredith would have liked for our family to be more than polite acquaintances who moved through life pretending to do all the right things. Meredith would have liked to have seen us silly and happy and angry when we felt like it. What I said was, "'The Rose.'"

"I'm afraid I'm not familiar with that," Ruth said.

"I'll download it for you. When is the funeral?"

"Saturday morning," she said. "The funeral mass will be at eleven, followed by a luncheon in the church social hall. We will have a private graveside service for the family after that."

Twenty minutes later Fred and David showed up. Fred shot me a glance that told me how enjoyable his afternoon had been. I should have felt sorry for him, I guess.

We gathered in the dining room for a light dinner. I'd always hated this room, with its dark walls and too large table for a family of four. There was nothing to absorb the sound of conversation or clanking silverware, and it bounced off the walls and hung in the air with nowhere to go.

Martha had prepared a cold lobster and pasta salad with her famous creamy dressing, along with a tossed lettuce salad, fresh sliced tomatoes from the garden, and Italian bread.

David sat at the head of the table, refilling his wineglass as soon as he emptied it. I'd never seen him drink so much. None of it was lost on Ruth, who shot him disapproving looks down the long table. He didn't seem to notice, or maybe he simply didn't care.

Meredith's empty chair was the constant reminder why we were all enduring this painful time together.

Martha served apricot compote for dessert, and as soon as the table was cleared, Fred was out of his chair, clearly eager to be gone.

"Come on, Mom," he said to Rachel, "I'll drop you off at home."

"So soon?" Rachel said. "We've barely had time to visit."

"There will be plenty of time in the next few days. I have an engagement tonight, so we should probably be going now."

He looked at me with a certain amount of empathy, knowing that Ruth would expect me to stay the night.

Once Fred and Rachel were out the door, David retired to his study, and Ruth went to the sunroom to listen to music. I found myself heading for the kitchen.

Martha had just finished loading the dishwasher and made me sit down at the table while she brought me a cup of coffee, then took a seat across from me.

"So, how are you holding up, baby?" she asked and placed a large worn hand over mine.

"Okay, I guess."

She reached over and brushed the hair off my face in an old familiar gesture. "I still can't believe she's gone. Not that I'd seen that much of her lately."

"Meredith hadn't been coming around?" I thought I'd been the only one avoiding the home front.

"No," she said quietly and looked down at the table, brushing invisible crumbs into her hand. Something in her face told me there was more to this.

"Martha, did Meredith tell you what was going on that was troubling her so much?"

She looked up at me, her eyes filled with tears. "No. I wish she had. I would have helped her if I could. When she was here in June, she and Ruth had a terrible fight. Meredith stormed out. I didn't know it would be the last time I ever saw her." The tears rolled down her cheeks.

"What was the fight about?"

"I don't know." She dabbed at her eyes with a tissue and drew herself up in her chair. "The police came by here yesterday. That young man, Tom, who used to go with Meredith, talked to all of us. He's a cop now, you know."

"I know."

"Anyway, I don't think we were much help."

"I went to see Lee Atwater this morning."

She shook her head, and then the name must have registered. "That girl from college who hated Meredith for stealing her boyfriend?" She slapped the table as the memory took hold. "She was dating Tom when he left her for Meredith. What did you see her for?"

I guess we all remembered the story.

A rough hand squeezed my shoulder from behind, and

I looked up to see John standing there. He poured himself a cup of coffee and sat down next to his wife.

"I went to Meredith's office this morning," I said. "Lee's name was in her appointment book. She's a very successful psychologist now. Meredith had been seeing her as a client for the past few months."

"Why?" John asked.

"She was upset about something. She needed someone to talk to."

"She could have talked to her family," Ruth said from the doorway.

Her voice took me by surprise. Ruth rarely ventured into Martha's domain. In my whole life, I could probably count the number of times I'd seen Ruth in the kitchen.

She took a seat at the end of the table. "Go on with your talk. What about your sister?"

"All I said was that she was seeing someone."

Martha and John exchanged glances.

"And the someone she was seeing was Lee Atwater?" Ruth asked.

"Yes."

"How do you know this?"

"I was at Meredith's office this morning and saw it in her appointment book."

"Why were you going through her appointment book?" She gave me a look of displeasure that I remembered from childhood.

"Because someone killed my sister and I want to know who."

"Elizabeth," Ruth said, and her voice was hard, "that is what the police are doing. You will not get involved in this in any way. Do you understand me?"

When I hesitated, she said, "I just lost one daughter. I cannot bear to lose another." Her voice shook as she watched my face. "So, I repeat: you will do nothing to jeopardize your safety. I will not allow it." She rose gracefully from her chair, looking down at me. "I'm quite serious about this."

After she'd left, Martha reached out and touched my hand again. "You have to understand how upset she is. Besides, she's right, you know—this is a job for the police."

"I know."

I finally went upstairs to my old bedroom and lay down on the bed. Except for occasional overnights, I hadn't lived in this room since I'd left for college eleven years ago—at Meredith's insistence.

"You have to go away, Ellie," she'd said. "I wish I had. You'll have so much more fun living in the dorm and a lot more freedom than you'd ever have here."

So I moved into the dorm at Hamline, just down the road from home, but far enough away to feel some independence. Meredith had been right: it was a good move, and it felt wonderful to spread my wings out from under Ruth's watchful eye.

It seemed now like it was light years ago.

I stared up at the canopy draping the four-poster bed. Once I crossed the plush carpet and opened the door to Meredith's adjoining bedroom, but I couldn't make myself go in. She was gone, and even the house seemed to sense it. I closed the door and went back to my own bed.

"Whatever happens, please don't hate me." I could never hate you, Meredith.

At nine o'clock, there was a light tap on my door.

I sat up and swung my feet over the side of the bed. "Yes?"

The door opened several inches, and Ruth poked her head in. "I just wanted to check on you before I went to bed."

"Come in, Ruth."

She stepped into the room and closed the door behind her.

She sat on the blue computer chair at the desk and glanced down at her hands, folded in her lap, then looked up at me. "I know how hard this is for you, Elizabeth. It's a loss none of us expected, one nobody could foresee." She took a breath. "I just want you to understand that we *will* survive this. It will make us stronger in the long run."

I wasn't too sure about that—either that we *would* survive or that we would become better people because of it. The one person who would have been there for me was gone, and I didn't know if I could deal with it alone.

"How do you do it, Ruth? How do you cope with something like this? What did you do when your mother died?"

She shook her head. "That wasn't the same at all. She'd been ill for some time, bedridden for two years, and she wasn't happy. Death for her was almost a release. Besides, she was a very old woman, and your father and I were contemplating marriage, so even in my loss, I still had something joyful to look forward to."

"What about when Joseph—uh, Dad—died?"

Ruth was no stranger to loss. "I never imagined myself a young widow with two children to take care of. But as hard as it was to lose my husband, even that was different. I had you girls. I needed to make sure you were okay. I had to postpone my own grief so that I could help you through yours. There was nothing easy about it, but we survived."

"So, the moral is?" I needed to hear something that would help me endure.

She smiled gently. "One day at a time, darling. That's all we can do."

She stood up, crossed the room, and kissed me on the forehead. "Sleep well," she said and left me alone for the night.

I turned off the light and lay in the darkening room, trying with everything in me not to think about Meredith for only a few minutes, if I could.

My cell phone rang. It was Tom. "Are you still at Ruth's?"

"I'm sleeping in my old bed tonight. What's up?"

"Nothing. I just wanted to see how you were doing."

I wanted to read more into his show of concern, but I remembered Fred's warning. "Thanks," I said. "I'm doing okay I guess."

We talked for a few minutes. When we finally hung up, I rolled over in bed and fell asleep thinking about Tom, hoping Fred was wrong and that Tom really was one of the good guys.

NINE

OF COURSE, I dreamed about Meredith. Once again, I was eight years old, and I found her sitting in the hot, dusty attic of our childhood home. It was obvious she'd been crying, and I was more intrigued than upset to find her like that. I couldn't remember ever seeing Meredith cry, not even when we lost our parents.

I sat down across from her, folded my knees up in front of me and watched her face with childish interest.

"What are you doing up here?" I asked.

"Go away, Ellie, I want to be alone."

"Why?" It didn't make much sense to me. It was summer and I wanted to play.

"Ellie, just go away."

"But what are you doing?"

"I'm just sitting here thinking, and I want to be alone." A delicate hand reached up to wipe a tear off her cheek.

"What are you thinking about?"

She sighed. "If I tell you, will you go away?"

It hadn't been a dream as much as a memory; it had actually happened, and I awoke in the early morning light, trying to remember what she'd told me next. I thought it was important, but I couldn't recall what it was.

The bedroom felt hot and sticky. I got out of bed and went to the window, looking out over the lawn. It was browner than I'd ever seen it, and even this early in the morning, there were heat waves shimmering up off the concrete.

Ruth was already heading across the driveway for her morning walk, a ritual she'd kept as long as I could remember.

I opened the bedroom door and made my way down the long hall to the attic. It wasn't so much a conscious decision but came from that deep part of me that was fighting to hold onto my sister. Being in that place that held a memory of her suddenly felt important, however illogical it might seem.

It was an old-house walk-up attic, and the air was stifling at the top of the stairs. I opened a dormer window, which helped about as much as trying to put out a house fire with a glass of water.

On the west side of the large room, pushed up against the wall, were trunks filled with vintage clothing. The adjacent wall was crammed with old furniture and boxes and boxes of books. It was there that Ruth or Martha usually found me on a rainy day, playing house. Occasionally, if I were lucky, I could sometimes railroad Fred into being my reluctant husband. But usually, before the game began, he'd wander off to play with David's old, dismantled guns on the other side of the room.

In the opposite direction were wooden crates with china and Waterford crystal that had belonged to Ruth's mother. I hadn't been allowed to play there, although that hadn't always stopped me.

I wandered toward Ruth's trousseau, pulling the strings for every overhead light I could find.

In the corners of the attic were little rooms with their

own doors, small and impractical. I found myself standing
in the doorway of the one where Meredith used to go to be
by herself, to get away from me.

There was a dormer window looking out over the garden
and a stained mattress on the floor. I lay down on the mattress, trying to pull my sister back into this hiding place,
promising that I would never bother her again if only she
would come back.

It didn't work. I closed my eyes and tried to picture the
thirteen-year-old girl sitting all alone in the hot dusty attic.

"What are you doing up here?" I asked.

*She closed her eyes and her face closed too, all its ex-
pression being tucked away deep inside her.*

"I was just thinking, Ellie," she said.

"About what?"

*"I was wondering what it would be like to live on the
edge of the moon—so far away from the world that no one
could touch you. Where you'd be safe and alone and the
whole place would belong to you. No one could come unless you invited them. And if you didn't want to invite them,
then you didn't have to."*

That's what she'd told me then. The memory was suddenly clear. She'd told me what it would be like to live on
the edge of the moon.

I hadn't understood it then, and I didn't understand it
now—but all of a sudden, I felt very close to Meredith.
She'd revealed a part of her soul to an eight-year-old child,
a child who didn't understand a word of what she was saying but who felt safe just being in her presence.

And that more than anything made me realize that I
needed to know what had happened to her. I couldn't wait for
Tom and his department. They might or might not find the

murderer—there certainly were enough cold cases on the books to show that many investigations were unsuccessful.

But even if they found the person who killed my sister, they would never be able to tell me what had truly been happening in her life. More than anything, I needed to know what had brought her so much sadness.

TEN

I WENT BACK downstairs and climbed into a cool shower, washing away dust and sweat and memories. Then I went to the bedroom, found a pair of cotton slacks and a blouse, and got dressed. I wanted to be out the door before Ruth came back, I knew she'd want me to spend the day with her and Rachel, and that was more than I could endure.

I slipped out the front door and called Fred from my car as I was turning out of the driveway onto the street.

"What's up?" he asked.

"We need to talk to that PI that Meredith hired."

FRED WAS WAITING outside his townhouse in Oakdale when I drove up, and he slid into the passenger seat.

"Where's your car?" I asked.

He looked glum. "Rachel took it." The Jag was his baby, and he rarely let it out of his sight. "I think I'm being punished for something."

I pulled away from the curb, into the traffic. "So, did you get hold of the investigator?"

"I don't think it's going to be so easy with this PI dude," he said. "He can see us in half an hour but said we'd be wasting our time, that there wasn't much he could tell us since Meredith was his client."

We headed south on Hadley Avenue, turned left onto

Tenth Street North and merged onto I-694 South toward West St. Paul and the office of Maynard Edman, private investigator. A red Ford Focus pulled in behind me on the freeway. There was a niggling thought in my brain that I should know that car, but I couldn't place it. I wondered if Meredith's death was making me paranoid. How many red Ford Focuses were there in the Twin Cities metro area? A gazillion maybe? I focused on driving, trying to think how to approach this private investigator and find out what he'd discovered in Bayfield, Wisconsin, that had sent my sister up there weeks later.

Maynard Edman's office was in a strip mall, and a pretty seedy one at that. Fred looked around the parking lot, and I think he was relieved that he wasn't parking his Jag here.

I knew nothing about private investigators except what I'd seen on TV, so I had no idea what to expect in real life. A bell jangled when I pushed open the glass door and walked into the front office.

The vacant desk in the reception area held a computer, a printer, a phone, and a bunch of pens in those crappy little penholders. There were a couple of tall metal filing cabinets up against the wall and ugly stained orange carpet on the floor. I didn't even want to guess what the stains might actually be.

A large man with gray hair, wearing khaki shorts and a polo shirt, stepped out through the doorway of the adjoining office. "Can I help you?"

Fred moved forward and held out his hand. "Mr. Edman? I'm Fred McCallister. We spoke on the phone regarding my cousin Meredith."

It hadn't been that long ago, but Mr. Edman made a show of wracking his brain.

"Oh yeah, right." He shook Fred's hand and looked at me.

"This is Meredith's sister, Elizabeth," Fred said.

Edman nodded in my direction. "Why don't you come into my office?"

His office was about twice the size of the reception area, which wasn't saying much, and the floor was covered with cardboard banker's boxes, overflowing with files. So much for confidentiality.

Fred and I took chairs across from Edman.

"How'd you find me?" he asked.

"We have a flash drive of my sister's that has your bills on it," I said.

He nodded. "And what do you want me to do for you?"

"We'd like to know why my sister hired you."

"Sorry. Not without a court order. Your sister was my client, and I have a contract that binds me to secrecy."

Secrecy? It sounded like they'd formed a club.

"My sister is dead, Mr. Edman. She was murdered. Don't you think your contract is void now?"

He shook his head. "Nope."

"Could you give us an idea what she asked you to look into?"

He shook his head again. "Nope. Sorry."

"You billed her for time and mileage to Bayfield last spring."

"Okay."

"What was in Bayfield that was so important?"

He sighed. "Look, you seem like nice people, and I'd like to help, but I can't. Unless you want to hire me to look into your sister's murder, there's nothing I can do."

"My sister went to Bayfield a few weeks after you did. What was she looking for? What did you tell her was there?"

This time he shrugged. "I went to Bayfield. If your sister went there on her own, I don't know anything about that. Besides, agents from the Bureau of Criminal Apprehension have already been here. *They* will be coming back with a court order and I will surrender my files to them. If you want to know what's in the files, then you might want to talk to the BCA. Otherwise, I can't help you."

He stood up. We were being dismissed.

We walked back out to the parking lot and got in the car. I put the key in the ignition. "Great. Now what?"

"Plan B?"

"Good idea, but we don't have a plan B, remember?"

"Oh yeah."

I looked at Fred. "Edman said the BCA had already been here."

"Yeah?"

"If we have the flash drive, how did they even know to come here?"

"Oh yeah, right. How *did* they know?"

Someone tapped on my window, and I jumped. I looked up to see Tom standing there, looking like his not-happy self. I hit the button to open the window, then looked in my rearview mirror to see a red Ford Focus parked two lanes behind me. Crap!

Tom nodded at my cousin. "Here's the deal, you two. I am not fucking around here anymore. *Stay out of my investigation.* I don't want to have to arrest you, but I will, if you don't stop."

Fred nodded. "Got it."

Tom looked at me.

"What took you so long to get here?" I asked him.

He squinted down at me. "What?"

"You were following me, right? What took so long?"

His jaw clenched. "I had to take a call."

"And how did you know about Edman?"

"I knew about him because I'm investigating your sister's murder, and that's all you need to know." He slapped the top of my car. "Now get the hell out of here."

We headed back toward the freeway. "Where's the flash drive?" I asked Fred.

He patted his shirt pocket. "Right here. Why?"

"We need to see what else is on it."

We were on our way to my apartment when my phone rang. I didn't recognize the number.

"Ms. McCallister?" a voice said when I answered.

"Yes?"

"This is Norma Verhle from Mr. Wainwright's office."

She paused. It took a few seconds to register the name out of context. Mr. Wainwright was our family attorney.

"Yes," I said, not sure why Norma Verhle or Jim Wainwright would be calling me.

"Mr. Wainwright would like to see you in his office at your earliest convenience."

"What for?"

"I believe it's about your estate."

I looked at Fred and shrugged. "I didn't realize I had an estate. When does Mr. Wainwright want me to come?"

"At your earliest convenience."

Yeah, Norma, I got that the first time you said it. "I'm free now—I can be there in fifteen minutes."

"Oh. All right, that would be fine. We'll see you then. By the way, do you have a phone number for your cousin, Frederick McCallister? We don't seem to have a current contact number for him on file."

"He's right here with me. Did you want to talk to him, or should I just bring him along?"

"Please bring him with you. Mr. Wainwright would like to talk to him too." She hung up.

"Well, that was weird," Fred said. "What do you think that's about?"

I shrugged. "The trust, I guess, although shouldn't we be calling them?"

Fred shook his head. "I have no idea."

One of the problems with growing up in a wealthy family is that you don't have to worry about the details of everyday life. Neither Fred nor I had a clue how to function in the world normal people live in, where they always know where their money is and what's involved in their legal affairs.

Traffic was heavy, and it actually took us twenty-five minutes to get to Wainwright's office in an old brownstone in downtown St. Paul. His father had been our family attorney since I was a child, and his son, Jim, had taken over the practice when his father retired. Nice to keep things in the family; it probably saved some start-up money, not having to change the sign on the front of the building or the letterhead on the stationery.

Norma Verhle was a new addition to the office, not that I'd been there often. When I was little, Ruth had sometimes taken me with her when she had legal dealings, but I hadn't been there in many years.

Norma wasn't a real friendly type. She was probably in her forties, rather sexless and dowdy. If there was a Mrs. Wainwright, I was pretty sure she wouldn't have to worry about her husband philandering at the office.

Fred and I sat in the bland waiting area while Norma disappeared into Wainwright's office. The chairs were incredibly comfortable in soft Corinthian leather; the color scheme was mostly brown and earth tones and made me sleepy. Even the artwork was bland.

I felt like I'd been called to the principal's office, and we were about to be scolded for whatever mischief we'd been involved in. Fred looked as out of place as I felt. He bent forward to say something to me just as Norma appeared and ushered us into the attorney's office.

Jim Wainwright, Esquire, was tall, bony, and solemn, nothing like the round, friendly image I had of his father. He stood when we entered the room.

His handshake was warm and strong. "I appreciate you coming over so quickly," he said. "I am so sorry for your loss. Meredith was a lovely young woman."

"Thank you," I said. "I guess I'm not sure why we're here."

"Please, have a seat." He waited for us to be seated across the cherrywood desk from him, and then he sat down. "There are a few business matters that need to be taken care of now that your sister has, uh, passed. I thought we might as well be proactive on these matters."

I nodded. I didn't know what matters we needed to be proactive about.

Jim Wainwright continued, "As you know, the trust established by your grandparents goes into effect for each of you on your thirty-fourth birthdays. Meredith, being the oldest, would have come into her inheritance on her birthday next month. Since she is no longer with us, the terms of the trust state that, assuming there are no legal spouses or progeny, the trust is equally divided between the remaining two beneficiaries."

"And, I assume, that is rolled back into the trust until Fred and I reach our thirty-fourth birthdays," I said.

Wainwright looked a little lost, like I'd cut him off mid-speech and he had to find his place again. "Well, no, not exactly. The wording of the trust states that the two of you—again, assuming there are no legal spouses or progeny—will have equal share to Meredith's inheritance upon her death."

"And what if there was a child?" I asked.

Fred looked at me, with a *shut-up* expression on his face.

Wainwright opened his eyes wide. "*Is* there a child? I had no knowledge of this."

"Neither did I, but my sister's autopsy revealed that she gave birth to a child, and a friend of hers also acknowledged that was the case."

Wainwright scrunched up his forehead. "How old is this child?"

"I don't know."

He cocked his head to one side. "You don't know?"

This felt creepy. "Apparently, my sister had an unwanted pregnancy at some point. We don't know when, but she kept it a secret. The child was given up for adoption."

Wainwright stared at me. He didn't have much of a poker face. Finally, he said, "If that's the case, I will need documented proof of the child—birth and adoption records. And I will need to look into this further to see if a child who was put up for adoption has a legal claim to the estate."

"Well, that might be a problem," I said, "since we only recently learned about the birth and have no idea when it happened or where the kid ended up."

"Would Ruth have that information?" he asked.

"I don't know. You'd have to ask her."

He looked unhappy with my answer. He probably didn't want to ask Ruth any more than I did.

"I think since you have more information on this subject than I do, a question like that would be better coming from family instead of me."

Nice lob back into my court. "I'll see what I can do."

"Good. We will hold off on processing Meredith's portion of the trust until you can get me that information."

Fred and I stood to leave, but Wainwright wasn't finished with us. "Elizabeth," he said, "we will have to change the deed on the house."

"What house?" I sat back down.

"The house on Summit Avenue, of course."

"I'm confused. I don't know what you're talking about."

"The family properties were left to you and your sister."

"You mean when Joseph—uh, my father died?" This was news to me.

"No. It was left to you by your grandparents. Your parents, being legal guardians, merely maintained the properties. When your father died and Ruth became your guardian, she took over that role."

"I had no idea."

"You and your sister were both on the deeds as joint tenants. We should probably update that now that the situation has changed."

I had to think about this. I don't know why, but it felt like a curveball out of left field. "Can we hold off on that for a while, Mr. Wainwright? Until after the funeral, at least? I need some time."

"Of course. No hurry. Just let me know when you're ready."

"Was there anything else?" I asked.

"Not at the moment. Just get me the information regarding the child as soon as you can."

"I will."

Back in the car, Fred said, "You had no idea about the house?"

"No, did you?"

"Not a clue. What are you going to do about it?"

I shrugged. "I don't know. I sure as hell don't want to live in a mausoleum. I'll probably sign it over to Ruth. She loves it there."

I put the car in gear, and we headed back to my apartment. My laptop was perched on the dining room table, and Fred sat down in front of it and popped in the flash drive. Ten folders appeared on the screen, named by dates, beginning with last March.

I sat down next to him as he started clicking. The first folder was invoices. We scrolled through the bills, looking for more information about where Maynard Edman's travels had taken him. There was mileage back and forth several times to an address in Bloomington. Other than that, it was mostly time, copies, and faxes he was billing her for.

The next folder was an electronic copy of their contract.

Folder number three held pictures. Fred clicked on one to enlarge it. There was a fairly large cabin in the woods that looked familiar, but I couldn't place it. Northern Minnesota and Wisconsin are full of cabins in the woods, and after a while, they all start to look the same.

"Do you recognize that?" I asked Fred.

He shook his head and clicked on another picture. It was the same cabin from a different angle.

"Well, this is boring," he said. "How many damn pictures did he take of this place? And what's so special about it that Meredith was paying him a hundred dollars an hour to capture it on camera?"

All twelve pictures in that folder were of the building, the grounds surrounding it, or the woods behind it.

Fred clicked open the next folder. There was a picture of a white Ford Ranger truck parked in front of a small café. I looked closely.

"This must be in Bayfield," I said. "I think I recognize that street scene."

"Still isn't telling us anything."

There was a picture of the truck parked at various locations around town: the grocery store, the hardware store, and then back again in front of the cabin.

Fred opened the next folder and clicked to enlarge the first picture of a man coming out of the post office. I felt my heart stop. Fred looked at me, his eyes wide. I shook my head. The picture wasn't very clear, and it had been taken from a distance.

My voice barely came out of my throat. "Look at the next one."

Fred just stared at me.

"Look at the next one," I told him again.

There was the man—tall, handsome, graying hair, rugged, looking like a back woodsman in his jeans, hiking boots, and flannel shirt, walking out of the bank.

Fred stared at the screen. "Is it him?"

I nodded. Every photograph in that file was a picture of my father.

ELEVEN

FRED DIDN'T BELIEVE IT. "How recent are these?" he asked.

"They're all time-stamped—the oldest one is last April."

"That would probably be easy to fake if you knew what you were doing, to put a false date on a picture."

"Why would Edman do that? And look at him, Fred. That's not the man who disappeared twenty-two years ago—he's older. It's Joseph, but older."

"That would be easy to alter too."

I shook my head. "It's him. I know it's him, and Meredith knew it too. Somehow she knew Joseph was alive, and she sent Edman up there to find him."

"I don't get it. Did he fake his own death?"

"I guess."

"Why?"

"I don't know. To get away from us? From Ruth?"

"Why not just divorce Ruth?"

"He'd still be saddled with two children he obviously didn't want. Oh my God! Do you think your mother knows about this?"

Fred squinted at me, trying that one on for size. "No, I don't believe that."

I stood up and started for the kitchen.

"Liz, don't."

I turned and looked at him. "I can't do this. Meredith is

dead. My father abandoned us. My sister had a child no one knew about. I *can't* do this." I turned back toward the kitchen and the vodka bottle waiting for me over the sink.

He was out of his chair and in front of me in three long strides. "And what the hell is drinking going to do to change any of it? It won't bring Meredith back, and it doesn't make your father any less of a bastard for running out on you."

"I just need to take the edge off."

"Lizzie, I can't stop you. I won't stop you. But I'm asking you again to please try. Please. We'll figure this out. I'm here for you."

I leaned my forehead against his chest, trying to quiet the demons inside me. I was scared—terrified. My coping skills to date had consisted of alcohol, sex, and denial. The three things I'd counted on to get me through were gone. I didn't know if I would make it without them.

I took a breath. "I'll try. But I told you before I'm not making any promises."

"I'm not asking for any. If you like, you can come to a meeting with me."

I looked up at him. "No. I'm not ready for that."

"Okay. When you're ready, let me know."

"I might never be ready."

He smiled. "Or you may be closer than you think."

We sat back down at the table, staring at the pictures of my father. How had he pulled it off? How had he faked his own death and gotten away with it? And why?

"How did Edman find him?" Fred asked.

"Meredith must have known and sent him up there. But how did *she* know? We have to get to Bayfield, Fred. I need to see him for myself."

He thought for a minute. "After the funeral, we'll just

get in the car and drive. We won't tell anyone where we're going. Pack a bag and we can leave straight from the cemetery."

If it weren't for Meredith, I would have left right away, but I needed to do one last thing for my sister, and that was to bury her. Nothing could interfere with that.

Rachel picked Fred up at three. We decided not to talk to her about my father until we knew more. I needed to keep looking but was not sure where to go from here. I opened up the first folder on the flash drive and jotted down the address in Bloomington where Edman had spent so many hours.

IT TOOK ME about half an hour to get there. The house wasn't hard to find. It was a neat ranch style on a typical suburban cul-de-sac with five other houses on the block. The street was quiet, with not much going on at four in the afternoon.

I parked against the rounded curb, two houses away from the address on Edman's invoice. I didn't know what I was looking for, didn't have a clue what to expect. Twenty minutes into it, I was getting discouraged. It would have helped to know who lived in the house and how these people were tied to my sister.

Ten minutes later, a blue Nissan Versa pulled into the driveway. A woman, maybe fifty-five or sixty, got out and opened the back passenger door. Bending into the car, she lifted out two Target bags and headed for the house. A minute later she was back and pulled open the hatchback. She glanced over at me, then took groceries out of the car and carried them into the house. Another minute passed, and she was back for another load. She looked my way again, picked up her groceries, and went back into the house.

What now? Should I knock on her door and ask her about Meredith? And what would I say? I waited another ten minutes and saw her come out of the house, this time heading for my car.

She approached with a hesitant smile, as if to show me she was no threat, and gestured for me to roll down the window.

She was probably closer to sixty, or even on the dark side of it, fit and attractive, but she moved as if her bones ached. She was the woman from the photograph that Meredith had hidden in her album but at least fifteen years older than her picture. So again, why did Meredith have her picture, and why had she hidden it in her photo album?

"Can I help you with something?" she asked.

I shook my head. "No, I'm just waiting for someone."

"Oh? One of the neighbors?" I don't think she believed me, and her guard started to go up.

"Actually," I said, "I was looking at your house. I found your address in some of my sister's things and…"

I was surprised to see tears come to her eyes. "Then you're not here about Dana?"

I remembered now, Meredith had a slip of paper in the book on her nightstand with the name "Dana" and a phone number, the paper that was now in the pocket of my jeans lying on the bedroom floor.

"Who's Dana?"

"My daughter. She left home—again—a few months ago. I've been worried sick about her. The police haven't been doing much to find her, so I have fliers up all over town and friends passing the word along on social media." A tear slid down her cheek, and she brushed it away with the back of her hand.

I almost told her about Meredith, then stopped. I didn't know this woman, I didn't know how she was connected to my sister, but Meredith worked with victims of sexual assault—maybe Dana was one of her clients. Maybe this woman was. There was no way to know. It didn't make much sense that Edman would be tracking down one of Meredith's clients, but I didn't want to put anyone in jeopardy.

She was talking again. "There was a man who came by here a few times and parked right where you are now. I wondered if he knew where my Dana was, but I was afraid to ask. I probably wouldn't have bothered you, but I thought, since you were a woman, it would be safer, and maybe you'd understand if you had children too."

"I'm so sorry, Mrs.…"

"Beckwood."

"Mrs. Beckwood, I can't help you. I hope you find your daughter soon." I started the engine, and she backed away.

"Thank you," she said and turned toward her house.

I felt sorry for her. I felt sorry for me. Another dead end on a whole roller-coaster ride full of them.

I MADE IT home by six. Tom showed up a few minutes later, looking exhausted and not bearing food.

I motioned him into the living room. "You okay?"

He dropped onto the couch. "Long day."

"Something new happening with the case?"

He shook his head.

I sat down next to him. "Then why are you here?"

He raised his eyebrows. "You want me to go?"

"No. I'd just like to know what's going on?"

He shrugged. "Just checking on you."

"That's it?"

"That's it."

"And do you do this with all the victims' families?"

He looked uncomfortable. "No."

"Then why me?"

He didn't say anything.

"Is it because I'm a suspect?"

He still didn't say anything.

"Tell me."

"I'm not sure how to answer the question."

"Simple yes-or-no question. Am I a suspect?"

"Until we find Meredith's killer, everyone is a suspect. But that's not why I'm here."

It was my turn not to say anything. I waited.

He looked at me. "I'm here because I want to make sure you're okay. Simple as that."

I wanted to believe that, but it felt like he was holding something back.

"Am I in some kind of danger?"

"No. Why? Did something happen?"

He was pissing me off again. "Nothing happened. I just don't understand all this personal attention."

He closed his eyes and rubbed his forehead. When he opened his eyes again, I could see the cop was gone, and he was suddenly just Tom. "I'm sorry if I'm scaring you or making you mad. It's just that your whole family was a huge part of my life. I feel like…"

He paused. I waited for him to go on.

"Like I owe you something."

"More than finding my sister's killer."

He thought about it. "Yeah. More than that."

"Why?"

"Because, I'm not just a cop—I'm a friend. And that's what friends do. They take care of each other."

I wasn't totally convinced that was all there was to it, but he sounded so sincere, like it really was important to him. "Okay," I finally said.

He looked relieved. He stood up. "You mind if I get something to drink?"

"Help yourself?"

"Can I get you anything?"

"Just water."

He came back in the living room and handed me my water. "So, what did you do with the rest of your day? Or do I even want to know?"

"Fred and I were called to Jim Wainwright's office."

He took a long drink from his beer. "Who's that?"

"The family attorney."

"What did he want?"

"To talk about the trust."

"What about it?"

"If there are no legal spouses or children, then Meredith's portion of the trust is divided between Fred and me." I left out the fact that we didn't have to wait until we turned thirty-four, I knew that wouldn't look good for either one of us.

Tom nodded. "Well, that one was obvious. Did you tell Wainwright about Meredith's child?"

"Yes. He didn't know anything about it and wants me to get him a birth certificate. How do I do that when I don't even know when the baby was born? Or where?"

"You'll figure it out."

"So, what's going on with the investigation?"

"We're still waiting on a few things right now."

"Did you get Edman's files?"

He looked me in the eye, and I braced myself for a lecture. "Yes."

"And?"

"Haven't had time to go through them yet. Probably tomorrow." He was watching me. "Do you want to tell me how you knew about Edman?"

"No."

"Let me rephrase the question: *How* did you know about Edman?"

"I'm not sure I have to answer that, do I?"

"Withholding evidence is a criminal offense. So? Want to try again?" The cop was back.

I hesitated. I couldn't let him stop me from doing what I needed to do.

"I found a flash drive of Meredith's," I finally said.

He arched his eyebrows. "Where?"

"She'd hidden it in her bedroom."

"Where's the flash drive now?"

"Fred has it," I lied.

"What was on it?"

"Just a bunch of invoices from Edman."

The look in his eyes said he didn't believe me. "Dammit, Liz, what the hell do you think you're doing? You shouldn't have been going through her house, and you should have given it to me as soon as you found it." He took a breath. "So, I repeat, *what* do you think you're doing?"

"I'm trying to find answers. I'm trying to find out what was happening to my sister. You're looking for a murderer. I need more than that. I need to know *why* someone wanted to kill her, what she was running from."

"Please trust me to do my job. I'll find all the answers you need, but you have to trust me."

Yeah, I got that, but I wasn't big on trust. It had let me down too many times, and I felt too vulnerable to give it another go.

I COULDN'T SLEEP. I lay in bed, staring at the ceiling. All I could think of were the pictures of my father.

I made my way downstairs in the dark and booted up the laptop.

I don't know what I expected to feel when I looked at my father's face. I'd known him longer and better than I had my mother. He took more time to develop a relationship with me than she ever had. I remember going places with him. He took me to school sometimes and out on errands. We went fishing and he loved to swim, so we were often at a lake or pool. He was charming and funny, and I liked him. Maybe I loved him, but even as a child, I knew he wasn't a part of my life the way my friends' fathers seemed to be.

Looking into the pictures of his handsome face, I wondered if I missed him. I wondered if I ever had.

What a strange fucked-up life my sister and I had led.

I know that, at that moment, I felt betrayed. How could he have left us? What was so terrible about his life that he needed to run away and leave his family behind? And how had Meredith known that he was out there somewhere?

Meredith's house seemed to hold all the answers. There must be something there that I'd missed.

It was just after five when I pulled into my sister's driveway, the crime scene tape still draped across the front door, the sun just a glimmer on the horizon. I had my key in the lock when something moved behind me. I turned quickly, expecting to see a bear meandering across the lawn.

There was no bear, but the girl I'd seen across the lake that first morning—the one who'd stood there staring at me—was maybe a hundred feet away now.

There was something familiar about her, and now that she was closer, it was obvious she wasn't a young girl at all, just small, maybe in her late teens. Hard to tell in the hazy morning light. I made a step toward her, and she turned and ran into the woods.

What the hell! I took off after her, like a linebacker running defense.

She was younger and had a head start, but despite all the drinking years, I was still in pretty good shape, and I knew these woods better than anyone. Meredith and I had often taken long walks through the trees on autumn afternoons.

My breath caught in my throat in the heavy morning air. I kept running. Branches slapped at my face and grabbed my shirt, and tree roots stuck out of the ground, trying to trip me up. I felt a stitch in my side. I kept going. Three hundred yards into the woods, we came to a small clearing, and I saw my chance. I dove for her—my feet left the ground and I was in flight.

I miscalculated the dive and hit the ground. Hard. All the air whooshed out of me. What linebackers never have to worry about—and if they did, would probably end professional football as we know it—are boobs. My ribs scraped across a rock, tearing the skin, and then I hit. Breasts first. Oh God, it hurt like hell. I wanted to cry.

My hand clipped her ankle. She fought to stay upright and lost. She went down in slow motion, not the bone-crushing impact that I had taken. I held onto her ankle as if it were a prize for the least-graceful-fall contest.

What I hadn't expected—what you *never* see in football—is the kick. She pulled her free leg up to her chest and kicked as hard as she could at my face. Her shoe glanced off my cheek. I yelled out in pain. I saw stars, but I didn't let go. I hung on.

Her free leg was cocked and ready to go again. A split second before she came down on the top of my head, I rolled hard to the right, twisting her bottom leg with me. Something popped and she screamed.

She was flipped over onto her back, breathing heavily, moaning softly.

I scrambled up her legs until I was straddling her chest, pinning each of her arms with one of my knees, my breath ragged.

Her face was turned to the side, searching for something. She arched her lower body, trying to buck me off. I sensed her legs moving into some kind of scissor kick behind me.

There was a rock by her head. I grabbed for it and held it over her face.

"Don't!" I yelled. "Don't even!"

The rock aimed at her head stopped her.

She looked at me, and I saw, up close—through the sweat and dirt and scratches on her face—I was looking into the face of my sister.

TWELVE

It took my breath away. My brain did one of those "this does not compute" things.

"Who are you?" I said.

She looked at me.

"Who *are* you?" I yelled in her face.

She smiled. "Don't you know me, Auntie Liz?"

I fell off her and scooted toward a tree, pressing my back up against it, trying to distance myself from something I couldn't process. She even sounded like Meredith. She sat up. I thought maybe she'd take off running again, and I didn't care.

She cocked her head to one side. "What? No hug? No 'welcome to the family'? No questions?"

My sister was dead. I'd thought I'd never see her again, and this girl—she was wearing Meredith's face. I blew air out of my lungs, trying to gain some perspective, trying like hell to put this all together.

There was no warmth in her eyes. "I'm Dana."

"And Meredith was your mother?" I couldn't stop staring.

"My birth mother."

"How…when…"

A twig snapped. I turned to my left and someone sucker-punched me hard on the side of my head. I felt the impact, registered the pain, and then I was gone into a deep black pit.

SOMETHING COLD WAS being pressed against my face when I came to. I could hear people talking. I opened my eyes, Dana was standing over me, a young man sat beside me, holding that cold thing against my cheek. We were inside a house.

"Who are you?" I asked the young man.

"I'm Scott," he said. "Scott Pederson. Sorry for the smack, but with all that's been going on out here… I didn't know if you'd come for Dana."

What had Tom said about Scott Pederson? Oh yeah, the sex offender.

I looked around. We were in the guesthouse on Meredith's property. I hadn't been in it since she bought her house.

The cottage was small—a living room, dining area, kitchen, and two small bedrooms. Well, one of the bedrooms was more like a large storage area with a window; you could barely fit a single bed in it. A short hallway ran from the kitchen, past the bedrooms, to a door at the end of the hall that led down to the lake.

I was lying on the couch in the living room. Scott sat on the edge of the cushion, holding that cold thing against my face. Dana watched, a guarded expression on her face.

I tried to sit up, got a little woozy but pushed through it.

Scott handed me the compress, which turned out to be a bag of frozen corn. "Are you okay?"

The skin on my cheek was tender when I pressed the bag of corn against it, but the cold felt so good. "I don't know," I said.

Scott was nice looking, about twenty, kind of lanky, with dark curly hair and gorgeous thick eyelashes. Dana had my sister's delicate beauty, but there was an edge to her that Meredith never had.

Scott scooted down the couch, and I swung my legs over the side.

He looked me in the eye. "You don't have to be afraid of me. I won't hurt you. And the police already questioned me about Meredith. I was out of town when it happened. I would never have hurt her if that's what you're thinking. I wish I'd been here, though." His voice started to shake and his eyes filled with tears. "I would have protected her."

"It wasn't your fault, Scott," Dana said. "You didn't know." She put her hand on his shoulder.

Scott wiped away the tears. "I know. It's just that...after all she'd done, she deserved better."

I didn't know what to make of these two and I didn't know if I really shouldn't be afraid. The only reassurance I had was that Tom had already talked to Scott, and Scott wasn't in jail.

"How did you find Meredith?" I asked. "Or did she find you?"

Scott looked up at Dana as she walked over to the club chair in the corner and sat down.

"Dana found *her*," Scott said.

"When? How?" I looked at Dana. She met my gaze with a sullen glare.

"Go on, Dane," Scott said to her. "Tell her what happened. She has a right to know."

"As you know, I was adopted when I was three days old." She shot me a defiant look as if that were somehow my fault.

"I didn't know," I said. "I only found out about you a couple of days ago."

That seemed to take some of the wind out of her sails. "Really?"

I nodded. "How old are you?"

"Eighteen."

I did the math. "Meredith wasn't even sixteen when you were born. Apparently, she and my stepmother thought it best to keep all that a secret."

"Yeah, that's what Meredith said. I guess I didn't really believe her. Anyway, my adoptive parents live in Bloomington."

"I met your mother."

She sat forward, surprised. "When?"

"Yesterday. I found the address in some of Meredith's things. I didn't realize it was your mother. I was parked across the street from your house, and she came out to see who I was. She's worried about you."

"See, Dane," Scott said. "You *have* to call her."

Her look softened. "I know."

I tried to wrangle Dana back. I didn't want to get sidetracked here with some other family dynamic. "So? Meredith? How did you find her?"

"My parents were pretty open about my sister and me being adopted. They always tried to make it sound like a special thing—like *we* were special because they chose us. I don't know—I guess that was a good thing. But when I got older, I wanted to know who my real mother was, and I started digging around in my mom's files, and one day I found my birth certificate and adoption records."

I had to ask. "Who was the father listed on the birth certificate?"

She shook her head. "It said 'Father Unknown.'"

Well, that didn't help. "So, you found Meredith's name and you tracked her down?"

She rubbed her hands across her jeans. "Not right away. At first, I was scared, 'cause I thought she probably didn't want to meet me since she'd given me up. I was kind of fucking up in school, and my parents made me go see this shrink. She kept telling me I should call my birth mother, that maybe it would help me work things out. But it wasn't until my dad started to get all weird about Scott that I made a point to find Meredith."

I glanced at Scott. He looked away. "Why did your dad get all weird about Scott?"

The defiant look was back in her eyes. "You know, because they thought we were too young to be in love and be serious about each other, and then when my dad found out we were sleeping together, he just went nuts."

I looked at Scott again, and this time he met my gaze. "The statutory rape thing?"

He nodded.

"I left home then," Dana said. "I was living on the streets for a while, kind of doing drugs—not the hard stuff, but Scott said if we're going to have a future, I had to get myself clean and figure out what I wanted. That's when I looked up Meredith. I thought maybe if I made some connection with my birth mother, it would help me figure out who I was."

There was still an edge to her voice, but it was a surprisingly mature insight.

"When was that?" I asked.

"I don't know. Last spring, maybe March."

So, Dana looking up Meredith last March started something in motion? That didn't make much sense. Knowing my sister, I'd think finding her daughter after all these years would have brought her joy. Why did it send her to a therapist? And then why did she hire Edman to find Dana's mother?

"How was it when you finally met her?" I asked Dana.

She looked down and then back at me. "It was okay. I mean, I guess it was good. She said she'd always wondered about me and hoped I was okay and everything." She looked at Scott.

"Meredith was good to both of us," he said. "She let me live here while I looked for a job, and she talked Dana into going back home and finishing school."

Dana started to cry. It took me by surprise that the girl had any emotion besides anger. The initial tears turned to sobs. Scott got up, walked over, and sat down on the arm of the chair, pulling her into his chest until she was quiet again. A small, sweet gesture.

When she regained her composure, she pulled a Kleenex from her pocket and dabbed at her eyes.

"You okay?" I asked her.

She nodded. "It's just that I—I guess I fucked everything up for everybody. My dad still hates Scott. And when I finally meet my birth mother—she gets killed." Her eyes filled with tears again, and she laid the side of her head against Scott's arm.

There were too many threads to follow. I thought of my fifteen-year-old sister being sent away to deal with the biggest thing in her life all alone, and I wanted to cry. I closed my eyes and took a breath. I had to stay on track. I had to do this for Meredith.

"Dana, did you know Meredith hired a private detective to track down your adoptive mother?"

She lifted her head from Scott's arm. "No."

"Why would she do that if she already knew you?"

She looked at her hands. "I don't know. I mean, I guess in the beginning I wasn't real honest with her. I told her my parents were mean and used to beat me and stuff, but when she wanted to call the police, I wouldn't tell her where they lived."

"But they didn't beat you, did they?"

She shook her head.

My head was throbbing, and I don't think it was all from being punched in the face. This young woman sitting across the room from me was my niece. Meredith's daughter. And Meredith had known about it and never even told me. In a matter of a few days, my entire life had changed. My sister was dead, and nothing would ever be the same again.

I felt as if I'd fallen down the rabbit hole, and I didn't know how to get out. I needed to get out of that house. I needed to talk to Fred.

My ribs had really taken a beating when I tackled Dana in the woods. Spasms of pain radiated throughout my midsection as I got up off the couch.

Scott started to stand, but I waved him back down. "I have to go."

"Will we see you again?" he asked.

"Definitely." The part left unsaid was, *Possibly in court if you were involved in my sister's murder.*

Dana had withdrawn into her sullen state. I think Scott didn't want me to leave, but I couldn't stay there anymore. I couldn't look at Dana, her pouty face so incongruent with my sister's features.

THIRTEEN

TOM'S RANDOM APPEARANCES were becoming as predictable as my dreams about Meredith. He was leaning up against the driver's door of my car, arms folded across his chest.

He looked at my face, my blouse, and then back at my face. "What happened to you?"

"I took a tumble." I moved closer to my car. He didn't budge. "What are you doing out here?" I asked.

"Well, that was my next question for you."

I edged closer to the car. It was obvious he wasn't going anywhere. And apparently, neither was I.

"I came out to examine *my* crime scene," he said, "and guess what? Your car was here. Again."

"It looks like you're following me."

"It looks like you keep ending up places you shouldn't be."

"If you came out to examine your crime scene, shouldn't you be…examining your crime scene?"

A woman appeared in the doorway to Meredith's house. "I found the key," she called to Tom.

"What key?" I asked.

He started to say something, then stopped. "You might as well come and look. But don't touch anything." He shrugged again. "Not that you haven't contaminated evidence already."

I followed him into the house. The small black strongbox that held Meredith's pistol was sitting open on the coffee table.

The woman picked up the gun with her gloved hands, sniffed it, checked to make sure it wasn't loaded, then slipped it in an evidence bag and handed it to Tom.

He took it in his gloved hands and turned it over, felt its weight, then looked at me. "Nice gun."

The tone held some accusation, although I wasn't sure what I was being accused of. "It belonged to our father. Ruth gave it to Meredith when she bought this house. For protection." The irony of that last part hung in the room, hovering over the police outline on the carpet of my sister's body.

The woman had been watching me. She slipped the glove off her right hand and reached toward me. "I'm Sherry."

"This is my partner, Sherry Bradford," Tom said. "Sherry, this is Liz McCallister."

I reached out to shake her hand. Sherry was almost as tall as Tom, with shoulders as broad as his. She shook my hand with a grip that made my fingers tingle.

"Sorry about your sister," she said.

She looked at Tom. "Are we done here? If so, I'm heading back to the office."

Tom handed her the gun in the evidence bag. "Go on ahead, I'll be a few minutes behind you."

Sherry nodded toward me, then headed toward the door.

I waited for some kind of remonstration. Instead, he said, "How'd you get those bruises and scratches."

"I found Meredith's daughter."

"Next door?"

"Yes. How did you—"

"I interrogated her yesterday."

"Why didn't you tell me?"

"I don't report to you."

Oh. We were playing that game. I didn't respond.

"You still didn't tell me how you got all those scratches."

"I tackled her in the woods."

He actually laughed. "That must have been quite a sight."

"Yeah, well it wasn't so funny at the time."

"And what were you doing out there?"

I didn't know what to say. How could I explain any of this to anyone? I couldn't even explain it to myself. There was no logic—no reason—just a driving need to...not let go.

"I just...want her back."

He was quiet. We both were.

Some time passed. Thirty seconds. Five minutes. I don't know. His cell phone buzzed and jolted us both.

I'm not sure, but I think he sighed. "I have to take this," he said, looking at the screen.

He turned his back to me and bent into the call. "Martens." Pause. "Yes, sir."

He looked at me over his shoulder, then walked out the back door to the patio. I could see him moving toward the lake and out to the end of the dock.

There wasn't much of the house that I hadn't searched the other day, so there seemed no point in poking around. I'm sure whatever I missed, Tom and Sherry found.

I turned toward Meredith's desk. A fat red folder, about two inches thick, that hadn't been there on Sunday sat in the center of it. I moved closer. The printed tab read, "McCallister, Meredith" with her date of death. Tom's investigation.

I looked out the glass door leading to the lake. He was still standing at the end of the dock, talking on his phone.

I opened the folder.

The first batch of pages were interviews with my family, Fred, and me. I passed over those. Edman's files had been printed out and clipped together. I'd already seen those. I moved on.

Fred's bank statements. Nothing remarkable if you knew Fred. Every month had bounced checks and overdraft fees. He had two automatic monthly deductions for his condo and the Jag. Fred lived off an allowance that his father had set up for him when he turned twenty-one. According to my cousin, it wasn't enough to support a young man with expensive tastes. It probably was, if the young man would quit bouncing checks.

There were financial statements on all of us, including John and Martha and my aunt Rachel. Meredith's bank statements showed images of all the cancelled checks she'd written in the past six months. Her checks to Edman, the private investigator, must have been how Tom had found him.

U.S. Bank in St. Paul had always been the family bank. Meredith and I had both had accounts there from the time we were children. Meredith also had an account at a credit union in West St. Paul and a local bank in Lake Elmo, not far from her house.

The cell phone log for Meredith's number showed all incoming and outgoing calls for the previous month—everything from last Friday night highlighted in yellow. I scanned it, looking for familiar numbers: the night of her murder, shown in black and white; her desperate calls to Fred and me; and an early evening call from Ruth. My eyes filled with tears. Where had her family been when she needed us? *"Whatever happens, please don't hate me. Please."* I'm sorry, Meredith. I should have been there.

I blinked back tears. Four or five incoming calls were from a number I didn't recognize. I took a picture of the number with my phone.

I rifled through the extensive background checks on our family until I came to a police report from Bayfield County in Wisconsin—copies of the official investigation of my father's disappearance in the boating accident on Lake Superior when I was a child. I skimmed the information and stopped when I came to the name of the surviving crew member on the boat: John Netze. John of John and Martha. John, who had worked for my family for almost four decades, had been on my father's sailboat with him when it crashed against the rocks in the Apostle Islands. John? Why didn't I know this? I felt sick.

John was found unconscious on the beach and was in the hospital for twenty-seven days. His only recollection of that night was the gale-force winds, but nothing of what happened or how the boat ended up on the rocks.

If John had been there when my father disappeared, had he been part of the deception too? Did Martha know? More secrets. It seemed we were drowning in them.

I hadn't heard Tom come back. "Anything interesting?" he asked from behind me.

I turned. I don't know what look I had on my face. Tom blanched when he saw me.

He moved closer and took hold of my arm. "Liz? Are you okay?"

I pulled away. He moved toward me again. "Liz?"

I took another step and was up against the wall.

"Tell me what's happening," he said.

"I don't know." It came out in a whisper.

He bent in close. "What did you see in the file that's upset you so much?"

I finally looked up, met his gaze. "John."

It was obvious he didn't understand, but then why would he? His childhood hadn't been one lie after another.

"What about John?"

"I didn't know he was with my father when his boat crashed."

He seemed to relax a little, but I'm not sure he completely trusted my stability at that point. The expression on my face must still have been disturbing to him.

"You were a kid," he said. "It's understandable that they didn't give you all the details of the accident."

"Maybe."

"But?"

"After almost two and a half decades, why didn't anyone ever mention it?"

"I'm sorry, Liz. I don't have an answer for that."

He moved back a couple of steps, giving me some room. Giving me some air. He leaned his backside up against the desk.

Tears filled my eyes. "What the hell is wrong with my family?"

"I don't know. But everything about your family isn't bad."

A half laugh that held no joy bubbled out. "Name one thing."

"I'll name two. You and Meredith."

The tears slipped down my cheeks. "Thank you, but I'm not so sure about that."

"You don't have to be. I am."

I wiped my eyes and pulled myself together. "I should be going."

He walked me to my car.

I opened the driver's door, then turned to face him. "Is this hard for you?"

"Is what hard for me?" he asked, but I was pretty sure he knew what I was talking about, and he was stalling for time.

"Investigating Meredith's murder."

He looked away.

I waited.

Eventually, he looked back at me. "Yes."

I'm not sure why that surprised me, but it did.

He cleared his throat. "When I got the call on Saturday, when I found out it was Meredith, I thought about excusing myself from the investigation."

"Why?"

"In case it felt too personal—in case I couldn't be objective. But I thought I could handle it."

He stopped. I waited.

"At first, I thought I was okay. It was hard to see her body, but I still thought I could do this. And then..."

I waited again.

He rubbed his forehead. "It got harder."

"In what way?"

It took him a long time to answer. "You."

"Me what?"

He looked me in the eyes, and I saw the young man he used to be. The college boy who used to have Sunday dinner at our house. The handsome boy I'd had such a crush on. "Meredith was a big part of my life, Liz. Your family was a big part of my life. And you..."

It felt like my heart stopped. I'm not sure what I wanted or expected him to say.

"Everything about this is right there in your eyes—

your loss—your sadness. Every time I look at you. And I know your family is feeling the pain just as deeply. I almost walked away Saturday morning when I saw you. I almost handed the case over to someone else, but then I realized I didn't want to. I wanted to be the one to find Meredith's killer. For her. For you."

I WATCHED TOM in my rearview mirror, all the way down Meredith's driveway, until I couldn't see him anymore. He was watching me drive away like he had the other day, but I'm not sure he was seeing me at all. His thoughts were somewhere else.

I wish I'd been paying attention these past few days to all that he might be feeling. But, then, that wasn't me. That was Meredith, and I didn't think I could ever be who she was.

I was out of Tom's line of vision and almost to the county road when I steered off into the trees, pulled out my phone, and opened the picture I'd taken of the number from Meredith's phone log. A reverse search showed the number was Lee Atwater's. Well, I guess that wasn't surprising that my sister would be talking to her shrink, as distraught as she had been. But it made me sad all over again to think of her reaching out in desperation to the people she thought would be there for her, and then we weren't.

I knew those thoughts would derail me, and pushed them aside. What I wanted—needed—to do was find out more about John's involvement in my father's disappearance and if that was somehow tied to my sister's murder.

Rachel seemed like the only reliable source. There's no way Ruth could have known what my father was planning to do. For all she knew, she was a widow left with two step-children to raise. Martha would protect her husband if he had been involved in the lie. Rachel was the only one left from that generation who would be able to tell me what really happened.

I called her condo, hoping she was there, hoping like hell she wasn't already at the house on Summit Avenue.

She answered on the fourth ring. "Hi, honey," she said when she heard my voice.

"I need to see you, Rachel. Can I come over now?"

She hesitated. "I was just heading out to meet some friends for lunch."

"Please, Rachel, it's important."

She hesitated again. "Sure, honey, come on over."

I pointed my car in the direction of the freeway. Rachel had a townhouse in Oakdale about a mile from Fred's condo, but she was rarely there. She had a home in Aspen, one in the Florida Keys, and one in Cabo San Lucas. She traveled most of the year and came home to the Twin Cities for two weeks at Christmas.

She and my uncle Alex divorced when Fred was ten. My uncle was the CEO of some big-ass investment firm and re-married as soon as the ink was dry on the divorce decree—a cliché office romance with his young, pretty secretary. But maybe it had been a good match; they'd been together for twenty years, almost twice as long as he'd been married to Rachel, and they had two children together. Wife number two was a nice woman, a little too Suzy Homemaker for me, but Alex seemed happy, so maybe that's what he'd been looking for after living for over a decade with my flighty, flamboyant aunt.

After the divorce, Rachel had her and Fred's last name legally changed back to McCallister. I still don't know how she convinced my uncle to allow it. I know Rachel dated, and there'd been a series of men over the years—none of them up to Fred's standards.

As soon as my cousin graduated from high school, Rachel was out the door, living the life of a gypsy.

I loved my aunt—she was crazy and fun and had the most interesting stories—but as I said before, I could only take her in small doses. I think her son felt the same way.

I stopped in front of her townhouse and walked up the front walk. She must have been watching for me, because the door was pulled open before my foot hit the first step on the stoop. She was dressed in beige slacks and a yellow cotton blouse, which seemed a bit conservative for my aunt.

Her arms went around me in a tight hug, holding on longer than usual. She finally stepped back and brushed a few tears off her round over-blushed cheeks. "This is so hard. You and Meredith were like my own daughters. I still can't believe she's gone."

She looked at me closely. "You look like hell. What on earth happened to you?"

I'd forgotten about the scratches and the bruises and my dirty clothes. I looked down at my blouse. "Long story."

"I cancelled my lunch date. We've got all afternoon."

I moved past her into the living room, cluttered with mementos from all her travels.

"Do you want a drink?" she asked from behind me.

"Coffee?"

"Sure." She was back in a couple of minutes with two mugs of black coffee. Handing one over, she settled herself on the couch next to me.

She took my hand in hers and rubbed the back of it with her thumb. Sometimes when I hadn't seen Rachel for a while, I forgot that, unlike the rest of us, she was a toucher, and I realized that I found comfort in that and missed it when she'd been away too long.

"What did you need to see me about that was so urgent?" she asked. "Or do you just need to be with family right now?"

All of a sudden, this mission I was on seemed secondary to the fact that I was with my aunt and she loved me. I put my head against her shoulder and started to cry. She held me and stroked my hair and told me it was okay, which made me cry harder. I missed my sister. I missed my father. And I missed the family we had never been.

Rachel held me like that for a long time, long after I was all cried out. She kissed my forehead and brushed the hair back off my face.

I finally pulled away from her and sat up.

"Let's get you cleaned up, and then you can tell me your story," she said.

Half an hour later, I'd washed my face, brushed my hair, borrowed a clean blouse from Rachel, and we were sitting in the shade on the patio.

"So, tell me," she said.

"Did you know that Meredith had a child?" I watched her face. It felt like my entire life had been one big lie, and I was reluctant to trust people's words anymore. It was their faces that gave them away, their eyes that told me more truth than anything they said.

Unfortunately, her face was a blur of emotions that I couldn't read. She looked off into the distance. I waited. Nothing.

"Rachel? Did you know that my sister had a child?"

This time she looked me in the eye. "No," she said, but still her face was clouded with many things. "I wondered, but I never knew."

"What do you mean you wondered? Tell me what you know."

She looked off into the great beyond again, then back at me. "We're talking high school, right?"

I nodded.

"Sophomore year, I think, when Ruth packed her off to boarding school?"

"Yes."

"I wasn't sure what was going on, but I wondered if that was the reason. Meredith was getting pretty moody—hormonal—which was so unlike her. And she and Ruth were so secretive."

"Didn't you ever ask them what was going on?"

She cocked her head to the side as if I'd asked the stupidest question like *ever*. "Liz, honey, think about it. Ruth and I were never close. She's got that old-school, family-name crap going on. I was never into that. I have nothing against Ruth, but we have nothing in common except you two girls. I tolerated a lot because I wanted to be in your lives, but if it hadn't been for the two of you, she and I would have drifted apart."

She chewed on the inside of her cheek. "Ruth would never have told me if Meredith was pregnant, even if I'd asked. She would have thought it was a disgrace to the family, like we were living in the fifties or something. Nobody gives a crap about that stuff anymore—it happens all the time. And Meredith…" She stopped.

"Meredith what?"

Her eyes filled with tears. "Meredith was too much like Ruth. If I have any regrets in my life, it's that I didn't fight for custody of you two girls after your father died."

Died. She'd said *died*. Did that mean she really thought he was dead?

She patted my hand. "I know that Ruth loves you and she did the best she could, but she's too damn serious, and again, that whole thing about family name and family honor—what a bunch of BS. I saw, through the years, how much influence she had over you girls, especially your sister. You were always hell-bent on doing your own thing, but Meredith…" She shook her head. "Meredith took on Ruth's serious side. It made me sad."

"And you never asked Meredith either?"

"I think she would have shut down. I'm sure she was embarrassed."

"Do you know who the father might have been?"

"Oh geez." She rubbed her forehead. "I don't even remember who she was dating then."

"I think it was some dude named Mark."

She laughed. "Oh yeah, that's right, Mark Dutton. Father Mark—he's the parish priest over at St. Ignatius. Wouldn't that put the congregation on its ear?"

"So you think that's what the whole boarding school thing was about?"

She nodded. "Probably. What brought this up after all these years?"

I told her about the autopsy and then about chasing Dana through the woods. "I met her, Rachel, and she looks exactly like Meredith."

She took a breath as if I'd poked her in the ribs, and then her eyes filled with tears again. "I'd love to meet her sometime."

"I'm hoping she'll be at the funeral." Which brought us now to the subject of my father.

Rachel picked up the pack of cigarettes from the table and took one out. I waited until she had it lit and had taken a couple of deep drags before I jumped in with the next round of family skeletons.

"Tell me about when Joseph disappeared," I said.

She cocked her head again. "Oh, honey, you don't want to go there right now. We can talk about your father some other time. You have too much else going on."

I reached out and touched her arm, watching her face. "Please, Rachel, it's important."

"You're sure?"

"Yes, please tell me."

"Okay." She took another long drag from her cigarette, searching her memory. "Your father loved anything and everything outdoors. Fishing, boating, hiking, swimming—you name it, he was all over it. He'd been like that since he was a kid. I think Ruth tried to keep him tied down, but with no luck." She stopped talking and looked down at her hands, twisting the rings on her finger.

"The accident?"

She looked up at me and nodded. "Every spring he'd plan a big trip. That year it was to take the sailboat out on Lake Superior and cruise the Apostle Islands. He was supposed to be gone a month. A week into the trip, we got word from the Coast Guard that his boat had been found smashed against the rocks. They never found his body. It was so strange since he was such a good sailor and swimmer, but the lake is big and cold, and he must have finally met his match." She looked down at her hands again. "It's probably how he wanted to go, though."

"Was he alone on his trip?"

"John was with him."

"Did they usually go on those trips together?"

She thought about that. "No, I don't think so. In fact, that might have been the first time they went on an adventure together."

"Didn't you think that was odd?"

She shrugged. "I guess I didn't think about it at all. Maybe John thought it would be fun and asked if he could go, or your father needed an extra hand on the boat." She squinted her eyes at me. "Why?"

"I was just wondering. I just found out that John was there, and it surprised me."

She nodded as if she accepted that.

"So, what did John ever say about the accident?" I asked.

"Not much. They found him unconscious on the beach, and I think he had amnesia—he didn't remember the accident at all. He was in the hospital for almost a month afterward. He never talked about it much; maybe he had survivor's guilt since he lived and your father didn't."

We were both quiet while Rachel lit another cigarette. There seemed so much I didn't know about my family, so much I needed to understand.

"How did Joseph and Ruth end up together? She's so different from what I remember of my mother."

Rachel smiled. "Do you want the honest answer?"

I wanted lots of honest answers for a change. "Yes."

"Money."

"Whose money?"

"Ruth's. Your father was pissing away his inheritance faster than—well, I don't know what, but he was getting pretty close to the end of what our parents had left him. Ruth had money and wanted to get married."

"That simple?"

"I'm sure Ruth would give you a different story, and your father probably would too if he were here, but I'm pretty sure that's how it went down. It's not rocket science, but it is real life. People will do almost anything to get what they want."

"So, Ruth married a man who didn't love her, just to have a husband, and Joseph had the money he wanted so he could play? Sounds lovely."

"Well, you know Ruth—definitely old-school about everything. In her mind, it would be more honorable to be in a loveless marriage than to be an old maid."

"Couldn't Joseph have just borrowed money from the trusts that Grandma and Grandpa set up for us?"

She raised her eyebrows. "I guess you don't know that part of our family history either."

"Do I want to?"

She shrugged. "It's probably not as bad as it sounds. Your grandparents were less than enchanted with your mother. They thought she married your father because of the money behind his name."

"Did she?"

She shrugged again. "Maybe. I don't really know. I think they were in love. I know your father was. He was crazy about her."

"So, what happened?"

"Your grandparents had already formed their opinion of your mother by the time the two of them got married, but your mother didn't help the situation much either. She never tried to form a relationship with them or smooth the waters."

"And?"

"When they made their will, they completely sidestepped

your parents. Your father's trust had already been established, but they didn't want your mother to get her hands on anything else."

"They must have really hated her."

"Yes, I think that's the statement they were trying to make. I was married by that time and your uncle was doing very well, so they weren't worried about Fred and me. They left the family properties to you and Meredith so you would always have a home. And then they set up the trusts for you and Freddie and your sister, but they made sure it was all so ironclad that no one could touch any of it except the three of you."

One more layer added to our dysfunctional family. Nothing surprised me anymore.

"I don't understand all the legal ins and outs of it," Rachel said. "Wainwright could explain it better if you wanted to know."

"So my mother was the reason behind the way it was all set up?"

Rachel stubbed out her cigarette. "She was the reason behind it, but she really can't be blamed for all of it. Your father would have pissed away all his money, regardless of who he married."

"Joseph sounds like a spoiled child."

She looked down at her hands and up at me. "We were both spoiled children, Liz. I wasn't a very good mother or wife. I always wanted things my own way—that's what I was used to, and my son paid a very high price for that. I was just lucky that I had a husband who did well financially and taught me how to handle money to make it last."

"And David? How did he come into the picture?" Now that I had her talking, I was going to push this as far as I could. Maybe somewhere in the mystery of my past I would find answers to quiet the demons that kept everything in my life off-kilter.

"I think Ruth and David had known each other for years, through church and the country club. They seemed to get along well, but I don't know if that match was any better than the one with your father."

"Then why marry him?"

"The same thing that always drove her—being a Mc-Callister. Your father went through much of Ruth's money in the year they were together, David could replenish the coffers. He was pretty well-heeled himself, so she could keep on living the life of the landed gentry."

So, Ruth had her own demons.

"You know, between Ruth and David, your sister never had a chance."

"What do you mean?"

"Well, she got Ruth's serious side, and then David had her schlepping around doing all that volunteer work with him with the youth group. Not that any of that was bad, but she needed to be a kid herself, she needed to have some fun in her life."

"I must have been a great disappointment to Ruth and David."

"I hear there's dissention at the church, and David might be usurped as president of the church council," she said with a smug grin.

"I hadn't heard, but then I don't hang around the manor much these days."

FOURTEEN

I LEFT RACHEL'S with more information, I guess—not that much of it helped me now. I started for home, then took an unexpected exit that led me straight to St. Ignatius's Church.

It was a beautiful building over a hundred years old, with the original stained-glass windows. Our family church, St. Bartholomew's, was considerably larger, but St. Ignatius seemed more welcoming.

I climbed the steps to the front door and found it unlocked. The narthex was vacant and cool, and I looked around on a table until I found a bulletin from last Sunday and the calendar for the week. Tonight, the Confirmation class was meeting in an hour with Father Mark. I walked into the sanctuary and down the aisle, then slid into a pew about halfway to the altar.

Except for weddings and funerals, it had been a very long time since I'd been to church, but something in me wanted so much to be here right now. I needed to know that my sister was finally safe, and nothing bad could ever touch her again. I needed that assurance.

I don't know how long I sat there in the cool, quiet darkness, but for the first time since Meredith's death, I felt a faint glimmer of peace poking through the grief. I closed my eyes and breathed it in, trying to capture it, hoping it would carry me through whatever lay ahead.

When I opened my eyes, I was surprised to see Father Mark standing there.

"I didn't mean to interrupt," he said with a gentle smile as he slipped into the pew in front of me and turned so that we were looking at each other. "I don't think I've ever seen you here. I was wondering if I could help you with something. I'm Father Mark."

He looked almost twenty years older, of course, but he still had a boyish face and clear, penetrating blue eyes.

"I know who you are," I said.

"Have we met?"

"I'm Elizabeth McCallister."

The recognition was sudden, maybe because Meredith's murder had been on the nightly news and in the papers. "Elizabeth, I can't tell you how sorry I am about your sister's death." He placed a comforting hand on my arm.

"Thank you. I was hoping I could talk to you about Meredith if you have a few minutes."

"Of course. Let's go back to my office—it's more private there."

We were seated in the small, cluttered office behind the sacristy, and as usual, I didn't know where to start. Mark waited quietly.

I took a deep breath and asked, "Meredith had a child when she went away to school in Chicago. Were you the father?"

Of all the things I could have said, I could tell by the look on his face that he hadn't expected that.

"Uh, no."

Well, this was uncomfortable for both of us now. It was different with Tom; between the time he and Meredith had dated in high school and then again in college, he'd been in our lives for well over two years, almost a part of the family. I didn't know Mark that well. His time with Meredith had encompassed a couple of months one summer nineteen years ago.

"Look, Mark, I'm sorry. You haven't seen me in almost twenty years, and I don't know you very well, but so many questions have come up this week since my sister's death, and I need to understand…"

He shook his head. I don't know if he was thinking about the possibility of having fathered a child or if he was trying to figure out how to make his escape from the crazy lady sitting across from him. "I'm not really comfortable discussing this with you."

"I appreciate that, and again, I'm sorry, but it's important."

"How important?"

"Very."

We were both quiet for a while. Finally he said, "Elizabeth, this is very awkward."

I didn't say anything.

He looked around the small room before his gaze finally settled back on me. He took a breath. "I'll try to explain to you what happened back then. The reason we started dating in the first place was because Meredith asked me out. We didn't exactly run in the same circles, and I was surprised when she did. I didn't think she even knew who I was until she stopped me at school one day and asked if I wanted to take her to a movie. I certainly didn't expect it, but the truth is that I was flattered. Meredith was a very pretty girl, and lots of guys wanted to go out with her. I was surprised that she chose me."

My very reserved sister, who would rather stay home

on a Friday night, asked a boy out? That in itself was odd. "And then you dated all summer."

He nodded. "Well, we did things together, but it was no big romance. I think I kissed her a few times—or tried to. I wasn't very experienced in that department."

"So, there's no way the child could be yours?"

He scrunched up his face. "I suppose it's possible, but not likely."

"Meaning?"

He was quiet for a long time. "I'm not sure this is something we should be talking about."

From his perspective, it clearly was none of my business, and awkward as hell. But I needed to know.

"Please, Mark. I wouldn't ask you this under any other circumstance, but there seems to be some connection between Meredith's pregnancy and her murder. I can't explain it…"

There seemed to be some inner debate taking place that took forever, but I didn't think I should push him. I'd already taken him down a path he clearly didn't want to be on.

Finally, he said, "About a week before Meredith was supposed to leave for Chicago, we were out one night and went for a drive. We ended up by a small lake on some deserted back road." He stopped.

I waited.

"This is very uncomfortable." He looked down at the floor. "Meredith got a little, uh, *forward*."

"Forward?" It sounded like something Ruth might say about a disreputable young lady.

"You know what I mean." He was actually blushing. "She started to take things to a level we'd never been to before. I'd had thoughts, by that time, of joining the priesthood, so I was very confused. But I was also an adolescent boy, alone on a deserted road with a beautiful girl."

Now I felt the need to hurry this along, or we'd be here all night. "And?"

"I didn't know at all what I was doing. There was a lot of fumbling and choreography, but I never thought we fully consummated things, if you know what I mean."

"I don't think I do."

He rubbed a hand across his forehead. "I'm not sure how to say this, but it happened much more quickly than either of us expected, I don't know if I ever actually, uh, entered her before I, uh…"

Oh. Now I got it.

"So, I suppose it's possible I could be the father—I've heard of people getting pregnant in some unconventional ways—but I really don't think I am."

"And then Meredith left for Chicago and you never saw her again?"

"I saw her at a few parties when we were in college, but other than that, I don't think I saw her again until last April."

That got my attention. "Wait. What? Did you run into her somewhere?"

"No, she came here to see me. She wanted some spiritual counseling, and we met here a few times. She sat right where you're sitting now."

"What did she want to talk about?"

"I'm sorry, I can't tell you that. But I can assure you, it wasn't about, uh…this. She never mentioned a child to me." He looked at his watch. "I have a Confirmation class in about five minutes."

He walked me to the front of the church and took my

hand in both of his. "I truly am sorry for your loss, Elizabeth. Meredith was a lovely person, and I know this is a difficult time for you. I hope our discussion tonight wasn't too disconcerting."

"No, Mark. I appreciate your time and your honesty."

Minutes later, I was in my car, thinking that if it had been any other time—if my sister hadn't just been murdered—the story of Mark and Meredith would have made me laugh. But it wasn't any other time. It was now, and the story was just one more sad episode in a tragic tale.

So, IF MARK wasn't Dana's father, then who? Unless Tom was lying, but why would he lie about that? With DNA, it would be easy enough to prove. I couldn't think of anyone between the time she broke up with Tom, at the end of her freshman year, and when she started dating Mark. But the whole Mark thing was so out of character for Meredith. Maybe she'd had a secret life I never knew about—some mystery boy in between Tom and Mark.

I was almost to the freeway when my phone rang.

"Hi," Tom said. "Where are you?"

"On my way home."

"From?"

"If it's any of your business, I spent the afternoon with my aunt Rachel."

"Sorry. It isn't my business."

I was starting to feel pissy. "Was there a reason you called?"

There was a brief pause. "Not really. Just checking in. I wanted to see how you're doing."

It was my turn to take a beat. "Thanks. I'm okay I guess. Can we talk about something else other than the state of my mental health—which is usually questionable on a good day."

"Sure."

"Are you still at work?"

"Just heading out. I'm on my way to my nephew's fifth birthday party."

"That sounds fun." And normal. I envied him.

He was quiet for a minute. "Call me later if you want to just…talk."

For some reason that made me want to cry. I cleared my throat. "Thanks. Have fun at the party."

I hung up before he could say anything else.

I wasn't in the mood to be alone, and I think I'd been half hoping Tom would stop by again tonight.

I called Fred. "Do you want to meet me for dinner?"

"Can't. Sorry. It's Charlie's first night off in two weeks, and we're going out. You want to join us?"

"That sounds romantic. I'm sure Charlie would love having me tag along."

"I don't think he'd mind. I heard you spent the day with my mother. Trying to gain points over me?"

"That wouldn't be hard to do. Did she tell you I met Meredith's daughter?"

There was only the sound of dead air. I thought we'd been disconnected.

"Fred?"

"Yeah, I'm here. No, Rachel didn't mention that. What's she like?"

"An angry teenager, but it's so weird to be with her—she looks exactly like Meredith."

He let out a breath. "I want to hear all about her. Can you meet me for breakfast tomorrow?"

We made arrangements and hung up, and I took the next exit for West St. Paul. I didn't expect Edman, the PI that Meredith had hired, to be in his office, but it was worth a shot.

The parking lot at the strip mall where Maynard Edman had his office was almost deserted when I pulled in. The front door to his office was unlocked, and the bell rang to announce my arrival. Still no receptionist on duty, but it was after hours, so maybe she'd gone home.

"Back here," Edman called.

I poked my head through the doorway. "I didn't expect to find you here so late."

He looked up from his desk. "I thought you were the delivery guy with my dinner."

He waved me in. "Have a seat," he said, and then, seeing the scratches on my face, "Who'd you tangle with?"

I kept forgetting what I must look like. "Long story." I sat down across from him.

He raised his eyebrows. "Well, I hope you won. I've been expecting you."

I looked at him sideways. "What do you mean?"

He leaned back in his chair. "You need information that you think I have. I was pretty sure you'd end up here again."

I met his gaze. "*Do* you have information I need?"

"Maybe. Tell me what you're looking for."

"You weren't very helpful the last time."

"I know, but I had the cops breathing down my back for my files. So, what is it you need?"

"My sister sent you to Bayfield to find someone. Did she tell you why?"

"Nope."

"And you didn't ask?"

He leaned forward and put his elbows on the desk. "Sometimes I do, if I don't think the job is on the up-and-up. Like if someone wants me to be the front-runner for a hit. Most of the time, I don't ask. It isn't my business. Your sister was a nice lady. I don't know what was going on in her life, but it seemed important to her, and she was paying my fee, so I didn't ask."

"What did she tell you about the man she sent you to find? She must have given you some information."

He opened the bottom drawer in his desk, pulled out a manila folder, and spread it open in front of him. "She told me the man's name used to be Joseph McCallister, so I assumed some relation. He currently goes by the name of Andrew Zimmer."

"Why didn't you tell me this the last time?" I kept watching his face, trying to figure out if he was jerking me around. That wasn't the sense I got, but I couldn't be sure.

"The cops were coming, and I didn't want to get in the middle of that. Look, I liked your sister—she really was a nice lady. You might think that I'm just some washed-up PI, but the truth is, there are times I honestly feel like I'm helping people. I wanted to help your sister. I'm sorry about what happened to her. Whatever was going on, she didn't deserve that. I'd like to help you if I can." He shrugged again.

"I'm assuming you'd like to help me for a fee."

"Look, honey, I'm not gonna pretend here. That's how I make my living. If my time is involved, it's gonna cost you. If you want to sit here and chat and watch me eat my dinner, then it's on the house."

The bell on the front door jangled. "Back here," Edman called.

The delivery boy from the pizza place across the street came in. Edman paid him and plopped the box on his desk. "Help yourself," he said as he grabbed a slice with sausage, mushrooms, and ripe olives.

I didn't think I'd eaten all day, but couldn't remember, which was not a good sign. Now I realized how hungry I was. I reached for a piece, then slid back in my chair.

"Okay. Whatever your fee, you're on the clock. Help me."

He got up, walked over to the mini fridge on the counter in the corner, and came back with two cans of Diet Coke. He handed one to me and sat back down, closed the manila folder, and put it back in the drawer. "Here's what I know. Joseph McCallister is your father."

"I thought you didn't know…"

He raised an eyebrow. "I'm not stupid. Your sister gave me the name, and I did my homework. Your father disappeared in a boating accident over twenty years ago—presumed dead. Meredith had the name he's currently using, the Andrew Zimmer thing. That's who she sent me to find. She had a couple of old pictures and the name of the bank he uses."

"How did she know his current name?"

"She didn't tell me that part, but my guess is—and this is just a guess—that she found some documents that led her to him. Like where he does his banking."

"I don't get it. Why would she even wonder after all this time? We grew up believing that our father was dead." I was thinking out loud, and I didn't expect Edman to have any more answers than I had, but he surprised me.

"Someone has been supporting him all these years. Whoever it is, your sister found the documents, probably checks made out to Andrew Zimmer."

"But why would she question that? Andrew Zimmer—Joseph McCallister—how would she ever make that connection?"

"She must have been looking for it. And if your father disappeared up by Bayfield, and the checks to Zimmer were going into a bank account there, then she must have put two and two together."

I reached for another slice of pizza. "That's still a stretch."

He nodded. "But something must have clicked for her."

"And she gave you old photographs of Joseph?"

"Yes. It wasn't hard to identify him from those. He still looks pretty much the same, just older."

"Did you talk to him?"

"That wasn't my job. She just paid me to find him."

"What does he do?"

"You mean, like a job?"

"Yeah."

"As far as I can tell, nothing. Whoever's supporting him must be supporting him very well."

What the hell? Who was in on this with my father?

"One more thing," Edman said, looking me in the eye.

"What?"

"He has another family."

AFTER I LEFT Edman's office, I drove around aimlessly, trying to think, trying to get a handle on all this information that was coming at me like sniper fire. Apparently, it wasn't enough that someone had murdered my sister; it felt like some giant cosmic hand had shaken the hell out of my snow globe, and my entire world had been turned upside down.

Eventually, I ended up at home, exhausted. I took my laptop upstairs, lay down on my bed, and popped in Meredith's flash drive, pulling up the pictures of my father—looking at his face—trying to understand why he would leave his children behind to start a new life.

The next thing I knew, a warm hand rested on my shoulder. I opened my eyes to see Tom standing there.

"What are you doing here?" I asked.

"Checking on you. I rang the bell, but you didn't answer, and the front door was unlocked."

"Is the birthday party over?"

"Uh-huh." He watched my face. I don't know what expression I was wearing, but it prompted him to ask, "You okay?"

I shook my head and put my hand on his chest. "Could you just be here with me tonight, please? You know…just *be* here? I don't want to be alone."

He hesitated. "Liz, I…my job…"

"Could we put that aside, for right now? Please? No Special Agent Martens. No Elizabeth McCallister, family member of the deceased. Just a friend helping another friend through the night."

Even in the darkening room, I could see him struggling for an answer.

"Please?"

He put the laptop on the floor, slipped off his shirt and shoes and crawled into bed beside me. I curled into his arms.

"Are you okay, Liz?"

"I don't know."

"I saw the pictures on your computer. Do you want to talk about that?"

"I don't think I can right now."

His arms tightened around me. "Okay."

"Tell me about the birthday party."

I fell asleep listening to the sound of his voice and thinking about a little boy on his fifth birthday and what a magical night he must have had.

FIFTEEN

THE NEXT MORNING, I found Tom tucking in his shirt as I emerged from the bathroom. "All the guys are going to see that I'm wearing the same shirt and pants I had on yesterday."

"The guys at work pay that much attention to your wardrobe?"

"Sure. We're very competitive that way—you know, who has the latest designer fashions and who looks like they've gained five pounds." He smiled at me. "So, how are you today?"

I shrugged. "It's a roller coaster and I'm not enjoying the ride all that much."

"It'll get better. I ran a check on Dana. Do you want to hear about it?"

"Okay."

"She's been picked up a few times for vagrancy and possession. There was one arrest for solicitation, but she cut a deal."

"None of that surprises me except for the solicitation. She'd alluded to the rest of it."

"Alluded?"

"Well, she didn't actually say she'd been picked up, but she was honest about living on the streets, and the drugs."

"Meredith's bank statements show a number of checks written to Dana and Scott."

"How much are we talking about?"

"Total? Probably six grand spread out over three or four months." He sat down on the edge of the bed and bent over to put on his shoes.

"That's not a lot of money when you think she was probably trying to help them get back on their feet."

He looked up at me. "Maybe."

"You think there was more going on?"

"I have no idea, but it's certainly possible." He was quiet for a minute. "Do you want to talk about the pictures on your laptop?"

"No."

He watched me for a while. "Were those pictures on Meredith's flash drive?"

I pulled a pair of tan shoes out of my closet and slipped them on.

"Liz, did you get those pictures off Meredith's flash drive?"

I finally looked at him. "Yes."

"So, there was more on the flash drive than the invoices from Edman that you told me about."

"Uh-huh." Looking at him was a mistake. I could see the disappointment in his eyes, knowing that I'd lied to him.

"Do you know who the man in those pictures is?"

"Tom, I don't want to talk about this right now. Please, can we do it later?"

He waited until I met his gaze again. "Okay," he said, and then he was gone.

I made it to the Blue Door Café on University Avenue

five minutes before Fred arrived, and grabbed a booth in the back.

"You look like hell," he said as he slid into the booth across from me.

"I feel like hell." It wasn't just the scraped ribs from yesterday. I felt raw and vulnerable.

The waitress came over and we ordered. While we sipped our coffee, I told him about Dana and Scott. I think he wanted more, but there was nothing more to share. I understood what he was looking for, though. We were grasping for any thread that kept us tied to Meredith, no matter how tenuous.

After breakfast, Fred walked me to my car. "The visitation's tomorrow night. You want me to pick you up?"

I leaned into his shoulder. "I don't know how to do this, Fred. I don't know how I'll get through it."

"There isn't a playbook for this, Liz. We do what we need to do for Meredith. That's all we've got."

"I know."

"I'll pick you up at six."

I watched Fred drive away, and I suddenly realized what I needed to do. It was almost nine o'clock. I called Edman at his office. "Want to take a drive up north?"

"Bayfield?"

"Yes. You know how to find him. I don't."

"When?"

"Now."

He didn't even hesitate. "Your car or mine?"

"I'll pick you up at your office in twenty minutes."

Four hours later we pulled into a Holiday Station in Bayfield, Wisconsin. Edman got out and filled my car up with gas while I walked to the corner and looked down the street at the familiar scenery. In college, I'd dated a boy from Cornucopia, a little town about twenty-five minutes west of Bayfield. There were memories—or partial memories—of several drunken weekends up here. I wondered if I'd gotten drunk in the same bar where my father might hang out. I wondered if I'd been that close to him and never even known it. Would he have recognized me? And would he have even cared?

I paid for the gas, and we both used the restroom. Ten minutes later we pulled out of the gas station, with Edman driving.

There hadn't been much chitchat on the drive north. Now he turned his head slightly toward me and asked, "Are you ready for this?"

I returned his gaze. "I don't think I have a choice."

He drove down the main street of town, then headed northwest to the Meyers-Olson Road. Suddenly things started to come back to me as I watched the scenery fly by. I remembered now that we had a family cabin, but I hadn't been there since I was four or five and had only vague recollections of the drive out of town. Funny, when I saw those pictures on the flash drive, the cabin hadn't triggered anything. It was almost like a jagged part of my childhood that had broken loose and floated off with the tide.

"Isn't it curious that my father held onto the family cabin?" I asked Edman. "I mean if he faked his own death, it was pretty ballsy of him to stay in this area and then to live in the cabin people knew belonged to our family."

Edman snorted a laugh.

"What?"

"You keep calling it a cabin, kid. It's not really a cabin—more like a lake home. Pretty fancy cabin when a lot of people around here don't even have indoor plumbing at their cabins."

"I know. Still, why would Joseph put himself in such an obvious place if he was trying to hide or start a new life?"

Edman scratched his jaw with a big, meaty hand. "I wondered that too when your sister sent me up here, so I did a little more research. Far as I could tell, your father disappeared for about five years, headed for San Diego. When he finally came back, the story had died down, and the *cabin* had been vacant all that time, so Andrew Zimmer bought it from the McCallisters. I don't think enough people around here knew Joseph very well, so when he came back, they may have recognized the face as someone who looked familiar, but they didn't put it all together."

"It still seems like a gamble to me."

"Nothing personal, but I think your father's an arrogant son of a bitch. I don't think he ever expected to be found out."

"How hard is it to come up with a new identity—to start over as someone else?"

Edman glanced over at me, then back at the road. "Not as hard as you might think, especially twenty-some years ago before everything was so computerized. And"—he looked at me sideways again—"your father had all the ID he needed to get started."

Warning bells went off in my head. "What does that mean?"

Edman slowed the car, pulled off to the side of the road, and we came to a stop. He switched off the motor and struggled to turn sideways in his seat to face me. "I've got to tell you up front, honey, that I'm a pretty straight shooter. If you don't want to know what I know, then you'd better tell me now, because you might not like what I'm about to say, and I'm not going to water any of this down for you." He looked me in the eye.

Those warning bells in my head were getting louder, or maybe it was me, trying to halt this momentum that had started with my sister's murder. Whatever it was, I felt like there was nothing I could do to stop it, and if I was going to find what I needed for Meredith, I had to take it all, no matter what.

"Tell me." The words came up my throat in a strained whisper.

"You're sure?"

I shook my head. "No, but I need to know."

His gaze didn't waver when he said, "According to the Coast Guard report, there were three men on your father's boat when it went down: Joseph McCallister, John Netze, and Andrew Zimmer."

Apparently, I hadn't read the report in Tom's file closely enough. Knowing that John had been on the boat with my father threw me for a loop; I must have stopped at that point. Not that Andrew Zimmer would have meant anything to me at the time, since Edman hadn't given me that information yet.

"And who was Andrew Zimmer?" I managed to ask.

"Just someone he hired to help on the boat. He was about your father's age and build, so it was pretty easy to slip into his identity. Zimmer's body was found on the beach not far from where John was, but it took a while for authorities to identify him since he had nothing on him."

I looked off into the trees. Who was this man I'd known as my father? Had he murdered Andrew Zimmer or just taken advantage of the situation that presented itself? And had he murdered his own daughter when his new life was being threatened to be exposed? I thought I'd moved past caring, but maybe I hadn't.

Edman gave me a minute to digest this new information, then said, "We need to talk about how this is gonna go down. I need to know what you expect to happen here today."

On the four-hour drive up, I hadn't even thought of that. Part of me wanted to finally meet my father face-to-face—to confront him, scream at him, tell him that my sister was dead, and how could he have left his children? Part of me wanted to know that there was some reason he'd had to leave, like he was in the Witness Protection Program and he missed us and thought about us every day. I wanted him to say he was sorry.

"I don't know," I told Edman.

He looked out the front window, thinking. "Okay, my advice: You've got a lot going on right now, and you have to be back in St. Paul tomorrow. I think we should approach the house from the back—see if anybody's home. There's a woman and a teenage girl that live there too. Whatever you have to say to your father, whatever questions you want to ask, you probably should be alone when you do that, and prepared for whatever his answers might be. Right now, we just go in and see what's going on."

"Okay."

He stared at me without blinking. "Or," he said, "we can turn back now if you want."

I looked straight ahead. "No. We're going to do this."

WE WERE THERE in less than ten minutes. Edman pointed out the main drive to the house as we passed it and swung onto a dirt logging road about half a mile farther down. The logging road was rutted and bumpy, and he took his time maneuvering my car farther into the woods.

I opened my window and smelled the cedar trees and warm summer air. *It shouldn't be like this,* I thought. *Meredith should be here. We should be going to the family cabin together for a long relaxing weekend.* We would never do that now. I pulled my thoughts back, concentrating on the road ahead.

The logging road wound around behind the house. Another ten minutes in and Edman pulled the car off the dirt track, as far into the trees as he could get.

"We hoof it from here," he said.

I got out first and walked around to the driver's side. Edman's pants' leg slid up as his left foot came out of the car, and I glimpsed a small-caliber gun strapped to his leg. He saw me notice it.

"Does that bother you?" he asked.

"No." It made me feel safer knowing he was prepared for anything.

There was a hard-packed dirt trail through the woods that he seemed to know well. It would have taken me an hour to find it, but he headed straight for it, with me bringing up the rear.

It wasn't that far from the road to the hill behind the house. It was easy to spot where he'd sat when he watched them come and go. He stopped and put his hand up. We listened, but there was nothing except the sound of the woods behind us.

We moved in closer and positioned ourselves at the edge of the tree line. Not that we were camouflaged, but someone would have to be looking directly at us to notice we were there.

The cabin, as I'd been calling it, really was a lake home—large with lots of windows, a mammoth fireplace on the west wall. My memory of the inside was sketchy, and we were looking at it from the back. Maybe a front view would have brought a clearer recollection.

Fifteen minutes passed. Then a door slammed on the other side of the house, and seconds later a teenage girl came into view as she stalked her way to a white Ford Ranger pickup. What was it about pouty teenage girls? I suppose I'd been one once myself, but a whole new generation had blossomed since then, and they seemed moodier than I remembered.

The girl was tall and blonde; probably pretty, but I couldn't get a good look at her face. She was barely to the truck when the door slammed again, and a woman bearing a strong resemblance to the girl walked over to the vehicle. She grabbed the girl by the upper arm, turned her around, and then they both started yelling. Less than a minute later, another door slammed, and within seconds my father strode into view.

Edman must have heard my intake of breath or sensed my body stiffen. He placed a warm hand on my arm and looked me in the eye. With just the slightest movement of his head he was telling me to keep quiet.

I stared at my father. Even from a distance, I recognized him. He was still so handsome.

He stepped between the two women, his deep voice low, calming. He put his arm around the girl's shoulders, and I felt something stab right into my heart. All the years I—

we—needed a father, where had he been? He'd been with the family he wanted, I guess, not the one he'd left behind.

I bit my lip and knew at that moment that he could never make right what he'd done to us.

After a brief discussion, the girl kissed him on the cheek, then climbed into the passenger side of the pickup truck. He kissed the woman on the lips, got into the driver's seat, and drove out of view—a charming little family vignette.

The woman went into the house and came back out with her purse, got into a Jeep Cherokee, and followed them down the driveway.

Edman looked at me. "Well? Do you need more?"

"Oh yeah—I need a helluva lot more." I stood for a minute, the pain of loss replaced by the anger of betrayal. "We're going in," I said.

He raised his eyebrows. "You sure?"

"I'm damn fucking sure." I took a step toward the path that wound through the rocky hillside.

He reached out a hand and stopped me in my tracks. "I go first," he said with a voice that told me there was no room for debate. "And you listen to *me*. We don't know that the house is empty, and there's a very good chance we could get caught. So, if I say we're leaving now, I mean it. And if you're not five seconds behind me, I leave without you."

"What about 'no man left behind'?"

"This isn't the fucking Marine Corps, honey. This is more like we could get shot or arrested or I could lose my license. You get it?"

I nodded.

He moved in front of me and led the way down the hill. "There's an old cellar storm door on the other side," he said.

"Have you been in here before?"

He looked at me over his shoulder but didn't answer.

The hill wasn't very high, and we were at the house in barely a minute, Edman walking up close to the white clapboard building, trying to be as inconspicuous as possible. I reached out and touched the siding, trying to resurrect a memory, hoping the house could return part of my childhood to me. It didn't. I followed Edman around to the east side of the house and a cellar door that jutted out of the ground. He fiddled with a padlock, unhooked it, and slipped it into the pocket of his jeans, then pulled the door open, revealing a dark chasm with stairs leading into the cellar.

It was obvious he'd been in here before as we climbed down the wooden stairs into the basement. He had a penlight and pointed it at the floor so I could see where I was going. In the middle of the room, he reached up and pulled the string, which illuminated the single naked lightbulb hanging above us. He put his finger to his lips and cocked his head in the direction of the interior stairs leading to the house.

The old cellar was filled with stuff, probably accumulated over a hundred years in the old family home. Ladders, old paint cans, spools of colored wire. There were a few steamer trunks covered in dust and filth, broken and discarded toys, and furniture crammed into corners.

We climbed the stairs slowly, stopping at each creak along the way on the old wooden risers. At the top Edman paused, reached down, and pulled the gun from the holster above his ankle. He took a quick look at me, then turned the knob slowly and eased open the door onto a hallway.

Adrenaline coursed through my veins, pumping my heart in a frightening rhythm as I stepped into the house for the first time in probably twenty-five years. I wasn't sure what I expected to feel or remember.

The hallway was part of a butler's pantry between the large kitchen and a swinging door that led to the dining room.

The kitchen was a combination of the original room, with its deep farm sink and large window and new stainless-steel appliances, with a gas range and a large white island in the middle.

I walked over to the table by the window and ran my hand over the wood grain, a small memory struggling to make its way to the surface of eating there on summer mornings after we'd been out fishing with my father—another stab to the heart.

Edman cocked his head again toward the swinging oak door leading to the dining room, and I followed him in. This room I remembered, a clear picture in my head of our family, when my mother was still alive, eating dinner at the large table; Martha coming from the kitchen, carrying a platter of roast beef; my father at the head of the table, saying something that sent Meredith and me into fits of laughter. I stopped and looked around. The dark wooden built-ins were still there, along with the table and chairs. There were new curtains hanging from the windows, and a small desk with a laptop in the corner of the room.

Each room after that—the living room, the sun porch, even the front hallway—was a mixture of the old and the new and triggered a long-forgotten picture of what life had been like for one very brief part of my life.

When it seemed that no one else was in the house, Edman holstered his gun and asked, "Where to now?"

I had to think. What was it I was looking for? What about my father's life did I need to find?

"There's an office over there." I pointed to two large pocket doors. "I want to find out who's been sending him money or what kind of paper trail he has."

"You think he's stupid enough to have evidence lying around?"

"No, probably not stupid, but you did say he was arrogant, and after all he's living right here in plain sight."

The heavy doors creaked when I pushed them open. A mahogany desk sat directly across the room, with two small, wooden, two-drawer filing cabinets up against the wall behind it.

I had a picture of this room, of someone sitting behind the desk, but I don't think it was my father. I tried to force the memory into focus, but it eluded me, and I finally pushed it away.

I walked over to the desk and started opening drawers while Maynard Edman rifled through stacks of mail.

The drawers were crammed with piles of unorganized papers that someone had randomly thrown in. There wasn't much worth looking at—just a bunch of receipts from local businesses, and coupons. The middle drawer had pens and envelopes and stamps. One of the deep bottom drawers had a small black cash box with probably ten thousand dollars in hundred-dollar bills, along with Andrew Zimmer's Social Security card and a hunting license from the previous year. I placed the metal box back into the drawer, and my hand bumped a slat of wood that looked like the back of the drawer, but wasn't far enough back for a drawer so deep.

The board wiggled when I pushed on it, and I was able to slide it loose. Back in the recesses of the drawer were documents and a handgun. I took out the papers and found my mother's death certificate and a picture of her and my father dressed up like they were going to a wedding, my father's passport as Joseph McCallister, and his old driver's license with the address on Summit Avenue.

I pulled out the gun, pointed it at the floor, and popped out the clip to see that it was loaded.

"Whoa," Edman said.

I put the magazine back in the gun, replaced it, and slid the wooden panel back into place. "Find anything?" I asked him.

"Nope. No credit card receipts, but there is a debit card tied to their bank account, so they're pretty much living on cash. And they piss away a lot of money."

I opened a drawer in one of the small filing cabinets. Someone had taken more care here, and everything seemed organized in neat folders, but as far as I could see, it was mostly paid bills, car and health insurance, and property tax statements. I kept going. I found a file with their cell phone information, grabbed a random bill, folded it, and put it in my pocket.

In the bottom drawer of the second filing cabinet, there was another false wooden back, and I pried it loose to see what was back there.

There were bank statements from the Chippewa Valley Bank in Bayfield, with monthly deposit slips ranging from one to ten thousand dollars. Clipped to each slip was the carbon receipt of a cashier's check from a bank in downtown St. Paul, the signature scribbled in a fashion that made it impossible to read.

I handed them to Edman. "I can't read who they're from."

"I think that was done on purpose." I shoved the most

recent ones in my pocket with the cell phone information and looked into the hidden space again. Nothing more of interest there. I slid the panel back into place and closed the drawer.

"We don't know how long they're gonna be gone," Edman said. "We should probably head out now."

"There's just one more thing I need to see." I started for the hallway.

SIXTEEN

"I'M NOT KIDDING," he said behind me. "We don't have any idea when they'll be back."

"I'll hurry." There was a wide main staircase in the front hall, and I took the stairs, two at a time, until I was in the long upstairs hallway, Edman close behind me. One quick look around, and I took a right, went to the last door at the end of the hall, and pushed it open.

I sucked in my breath. This had once been my bedroom. It faced the front of the house, with an old oak tree probably at least a hundred years old right outside the window. Almost everything was the same: the single bed with the pink comforter in the same corner where I'd slept—where my father would tell me stories before I fell asleep in his arms, and where Meredith would crawl into bed with me when I was scared by a storm and the tree branches that scraped against the window every time the wind blew. This was the room that held the childhood I'd lost so many years ago.

"Your room?" Edman asked.

I nodded.

"Long time ago, kid," he said softly.

"Yes, it was."

A car door slammed, and he moved quickly to the window. "Fuck!" he said and crossed back across the room, grabbing me by the arm. "She's back. We're going down the rear staircase. Do *not* make a sound—just follow me."

He hadn't loosened his grip on my arm, and I had no choice but to follow him as he pulled me along toward the other end of the hall. We were at the top of a dark staircase that I knew ended in the kitchen. I heard footsteps on the front porch. One quick look at me, then he was descending the narrow stairwell, with me only steps behind him.

The front door opened and I could hear someone moving through the front hall, the living room, into the dining room. Edman was already in the cellar when I slipped on the last step going into the kitchen. I don't know if he didn't hear me fall or if it really was every man for himself now. He kept going.

I landed hard on my ass, a ripple of pain shot from my tailbone up my spine and into my neck. For a second, I lost my bearings, then scrambled to my feet.

She, the woman, must have heard the thud. I was barely upright again when the kitchen door flew open, banging against the wall.

For a moment, we were like two cartoon characters: we both jumped.

"What the..." she started and stopped. There was a maniacal look in her eyes. "Why don't you people leave us alone!" She came at me quickly and grabbed me by the throat.

She was very strong. She pushed me up against the wall, her face too close to mine. The first thought that flashed through my mind was that she was very pretty, then her hands tightened, and I clawed at her face and kicked her shin and struggled to breathe. Her hands loosened, and then she got her grip again.

"Stay away from us," she hissed in my face. "I will tell you the same thing I told your sister when she came up here: I know who you are and I know where you live. You will not ruin our lives, do you understand?"

Neither she nor I had noticed Edman's return. His arm went around her throat and squeezed with enough force that she let go of me and grabbed hold of his forearm. He pulled one of her arms behind her back and moved her into the dining room, the door swinging erratically behind him. He released his grip and pushed her hard, so that she skittered across the floor and banged her head into the wall on the other side of the room.

The next thing I knew, he was in the kitchen, pulling me toward the cellar door and down the stairs. We ran through the basement and up the stairs to daylight, Edman running at the speed of light, dragging me along behind him. We didn't stop until we were breathless, next to my car at the side of the road.

"Get in!" he yelled.

I jumped in the passenger seat and barely had the door closed when he gunned the motor, swung the car hard to the left in a tight U-turn, and flew down the logging road at brain-jarring speed.

We were almost to the highway. Edman pulled the car to the side of the road and blew air out of his lungs. He turned and looked at me. "You okay?"

I was pretty shaken. "I think so."

"You know people get really pissed when you start messing with the status quo."

"So I gathered." I reached up and rubbed my neck.

He moved my hand away and pushed open the collar of

my blouse, probing my neck with gentle fingers. "You're gonna have some good bruises there."

"I thought you'd left me."

He started up the engine again and pulled back out onto the highway. "Yeah? Then I'd be out all the money you owe me for a day's work."

The lake home had resurrected emotions I didn't realize I had, and it was a long drive back to Minneapolis.

We headed west toward the Wisconsin–Minnesota border and were on I-35, just south of Duluth, when I asked, "When Meredith contacted you the first time, what did she want you to do?"

He checked the rearview mirror, then looked over at me. "Find out about her daughter."

"Find out what?"

He leaned his shoulder against the driver's door and switched on cruise control. "The girl came to her, claiming to be her daughter. I don't think Meredith doubted her, but she wasn't totally convinced, so she hired me to find out what I could."

"And what did you find?"

"Not a helluva lot. The girl had some arrests, trouble in school—typical teenage crap. I did a background check on the family—nice people. The dad had just gotten laid off from his job and they had some money woes, but who doesn't these days?" He must have remembered who he was talking to; he glanced over at me and shrugged.

"Anything else?"

"The girl was born in Illinois, and the adoption records were sealed. That's about it."

"When did she ask you about Joseph?"

He thought for a minute. "We were about a month into

it, and one day she called and gave me the info on your father. Don't know where she got it."

He looked at me sideways again. "Does that help?"

"I don't know."

"Lot of stuff to piece together." He shifted in his seat. "When was the last time you were at the lake home?"

I had to think. "It was before my father disappeared, obviously. Ruth's not an outdoorsy person. I don't think she ever went there, at least not that I can remember." I searched my memory. The details of that part of my life were sketchy at best. "I don't know that he took us up there after our mother died. Maybe too many memories for him. When I was about eight, I was looking at some family pictures and came across one of the lake home. I asked Ruth why we never went there. She said, 'It doesn't belong to us anymore.' I never even questioned that."

But, the part that disturbed me was where had that part of my life gone? Where were those memories hidden? And why? When Fred and I looked at the pictures of the cabin on Meredith's flash drive, why didn't my memory register what I was seeing?

We pulled up in front of Edman's office at ten after seven. He had his hand on the door handle of the car when he asked for about the twentieth time in the last four hours, "You okay, kid?"

I looked at him and shrugged. "You know..."

"Yeah, I know. Call if you need me."

I watched as he made his way to his office, unlocked the door, and went inside. I sat in the parking lot. It seemed that all roads led back to Dana. I didn't understand how, but she seemed to be the catalyst that started the chain reaction that got my sister murdered.

I thought of Lee Atwater, who'd known Meredith through high school and college. She also knew Father Mark and probably every other boy who could potentially have been Dana's father, and of course, she knew Tom. Lee was the one Meredith had turned to when she needed help.

I pulled out my phone and looked up the number for Dr. Lee Atwater's office. The odds of her being there were slim.

I dialed the office, and Lee was the one who answered.

"Lee, this is Liz McCallister. I didn't expect you to pick up, but I need to see you again."

There was the briefest hesitation before she said, "Sure. When?"

"Now?"

Again, that slight hesitation, then, "Okay. I have a break right now, before my last appointment tonight, if you can get here in the next half hour."

"I'll be there."

"Liz, what's this about?"

"I'm not sure. Meredith's daughter, I guess."

I headed toward Lee's office building in downtown Minneapolis, thinking of her connection with Meredith and still curious as to why, of all the psychologists in the Twin Cities metro area, my sister had chosen Lee. They had never been friends. In fact, there had been a time when Lee detested everything about Meredith, and I'm pretty sure that animosity ran much deeper than Meredith stealing Tom away from her. Meredith was everything Lee was not. Meredith was blonde and beautiful, and people were drawn to her. I think Lee had been jealous of that. Lee had worked her way through college; my sister had never had to worry about money.

I pulled into the near-empty lot by the building just as

Fred was coming out of the main entrance. He stood looking up and down the street, then Dana appeared behind him and tapped him on the arm.

They talked for almost five minutes before a car pulled up and Dana got inside. The next thing I knew, Fred was gone.

What the hell? I made my way inside and up to the ninth floor. The reception area was empty, and I passed through the outer office and knocked on Lee's door.

"Come on in," she called.

I pushed open the door. She was sitting at a round conference table in the corner, files and papers spread out in front of her.

She smiled when she saw me. "If you know anything about case notes or third-party billing, I'll hire you on the spot."

"Sorry, not my area of expertise." I stood in the doorway, not sure where to go with this. I'd thought I had it all planned out in my head, but seeing Fred and Dana together knocked me off-kilter.

"You okay?" she asked. She stood up and walked toward me. "Come in, Liz, and sit down."

I moved mechanically to a chair. "Was my cousin, Fred, just here to see you?"

She sat down in her chair behind the desk, I don't know it if was an automatic move or if she was trying to put some distance between us.

"Lee, was my cousin just here?"

"Liz, you know I can't talk about my clients."

"I'll take that as a yes. He was waiting in front of the building just now, and Meredith's daughter showed up. What an interesting coincidence."

She didn't say a word.

"Will you please tell me what the hell is going on?" I watched her face, wondering how much she knew.

She studied the top of her desk for a minute and ran her hand across it. "If anyone asks, I will deny that I told you anything," she said, then looked me in the eye. "Yes, Fred was just here to see me."

"As a client?"

"Yes. He started coming here in June. Meredith referred him."

"What? Are we getting a family discount or something?"

"I don't know why you're angry with me…"

"My sister was just murdered, remember? I'm angry with everybody right now. And all the people I know and love have these deep, dark secrets—lots of deep, dark secrets. Why the hell shouldn't I be angry?"

"Liz, take a breath."

"Don't tell me—"

She cut me off. "Take a breath and listen to me. I'm not the bad guy here. I want to help."

I took a breath. "So, help. Tell me what's going on. Tell me what I need to know."

She came around the desk and pulled a chair up close to mine. "I'll do what I can."

"I don't want to have to play twenty questions."

She smiled. "Whatever I can do, I will."

"Did you turn Meredith's files over to the police?"

"No. They need a court order. They'll be back, I'm sure."

"Have you met Dana?"

"Yes."

"I just saw Fred and Dana together. What's that all about?"

"When Fred came for his appointment tonight, he told

me that you'd met Dana. He wanted to know more about her, so I called, and she agreed to meet him here, downstairs, after his session."

"Do you know who Dana's father is?" I watched her eyes for any trace of knowledge, but I couldn't read her.

She shook her head, "No. I don't know who her father is."

"What about Mark Dutton?"

There was the faintest hint of a smile. "Father Mark?" She shrugged. "I guess anything's possible, but I highly doubt it."

"What brought Meredith to you? I didn't think you liked her after... Tom."

"That was a long time ago and I'd like to believe that I've grown up since then—that we'd both grown up since then. I don't know why Meredith came here, but I think it was because she knew me and wanted someone she could trust while she worked through all the feelings she had when Dana showed up in her life."

"Is that all she talked about?"

"No. That was just the beginning. She had a lot of guilt about Dana, but Meredith had other things in her life she needed to work through. We were just getting started, and then..."

Lee brushed her fingers across her cheek, then got up, and went to a filing cabinet, where she withdrew a manila file folder. She walked over and placed it in the middle of her desk. She looked at me, her eyebrows arched. "I have to go to the ladies' room. I'll be right back—make yourself at home."

She left the room, closing the door behind her. I reached for the folder and read Meredith's name on the tab. That little voice was back, asking, *Do you really want to see this?*

I opened it anyway. It had all started last March when Dana showed up in her life. Meredith was conflicted about her daughter's sudden appearance. Part of what she struggled with was never having resolved the shame surrounding her pregnancy. Ruth-induced shame, no doubt.

Lee had encouraged Meredith to build whatever relationship she could with the girl, hoping that would help her deal with her feelings, but Meredith seemed reluctant. It was weeks before she was even ready to try reaching out to her daughter. Something was holding her back.

Lee tried to get Meredith to revisit the pregnancy, but Meredith, clearly agitated according to the therapy notes, could never move beyond the shame.

Over several sessions and more billable hours, Lee encouraged Meredith to talk about her relationship with Dana's father, and was met with more resistance. When asked if she was still in contact with the father of her child, all she could say was that she felt betrayed. Understandable. I mean we're talking about a teenage boy who was just a kid himself and could offer no emotional support—or any support—to his desperate girlfriend.

I searched the file for his name, but he remained nameless, and I guess it didn't matter at this point.

Meredith expressed a lot of anger toward Ruth. Not surprising. Ruth would not be the one who could help my sister through the humiliation and fear of being a sixteen-year-old unwed mother. Martha or Rachel would have been there for her, I know, but Meredith's shame would never have allowed her to reach out to them. *Thanks, Ruth.* So, the solution had been to ship her terrified stepdaughter off to boarding school.

It was all about appearances.

Tears came to my eyes, thinking of Meredith alone, dealing with the biggest event in her life.

I skipped ahead. Meredith admitted to having searched Ruth's office at the house. I had to go back and reread that. It was a bold move for my sister. It sounded more like something I would have done. And I didn't understand what motivated her.

Ah. There it was. She was looking for Dana's birth and adoption records. She couldn't understand how her daughter, born in Illinois, had ended up in Bloomington, Minnesota. Which was a good question.

Ruth caught her going through the papers, and there was an ugly scene. Their final confrontation came in June and was the last time Meredith went to the house on Summit Avenue.

And that's what Martha had told me.

At her final appointment, before her death, Meredith talked about being in danger. Lee suggested they contact the police, but Meredith said no.

There was nothing more. I put the file back on the desk and reached for a tissue.

I wanted to go back. I wanted to go back in time and protect my sister from all the ugliness she'd had to face alone, just as she'd always protected me. But that wasn't an option. And I wasn't that person. And that made me sadder still.

Lee came back into the office and sat down behind her desk.

I looked at her. "I don't know any more now than I did when I came here."

She smiled. "You know that I'm on your side and I'm not trying to hide anything from you."

"I appreciate that."

"I have a client coming soon, but you can call me anytime. I'll help in any way I can, Liz. We'll get to the end of this, I promise."

SEVENTEEN

I SAT IN my car, wondering about Lee Atwater and how she, like Tom, had come back into our lives after so many years.

I headed back toward St. Paul but suddenly realized I didn't want to go home, so I swung onto the highway and headed east to Meredith's house on the lake. I don't know at what point I became aware of a blue minivan behind me, but I was pretty sure it had been on my tail since I'd left Minneapolis. Always two or three cars back, it had taken every exit I'd taken for the past twenty minutes. When I finally turned onto the road that led to Meredith's, the van disappeared, and I relaxed my grip on the steering wheel.

Dusk was settling over the lake as I pulled into the driveway and parked behind my sister's car. A brisk warm wind blew across the lawn. The crime scene tape was losing its grip on the wood frame as the week wore on. I slipped underneath it and let myself inside.

I waited, just inside the door, hoping to sense Meredith's presence there. The only comfort I had were the memories that still lingered in her beloved cottage.

"Whatever happens, please don't hate me." I could never hate you.

Her hidden journal and the flash drive under her box springs told me she knew something was coming, and she knew it was dangerous. But mostly it told me that she knew if anything happened to her that I would keep looking until I found the answers.

Meredith must have left more behind than I'd found. The flash drive had provided information about our father, but there was more. Something even the police hadn't found yet.

I started my search in the bedroom. Fifteen minutes later, I'd examined every possible hiding place. I went to the living room. It didn't seem likely that the police and I had missed anything; still, I looked under couch cushions and ran my hand under the coffee table and end tables and behind every picture hanging on the wall. Nothing.

I sat at Meredith's desk, imagining her sitting there paying bills, writing in her journal. Even though I'd been through it before, I examined everything on the gleaming wood surface: bank statements, car keys, a few family pictures. One of the pictures showed the two of us when we were small, our father holding a daughter in each arm, smiling at the camera. I picked up the framed photograph and looked closely at our faces—delighted children being held in the arms of their big, strong father—and wondered again why he'd left us. What had changed?

I started to replace the picture, then thought of one more hiding place, one last commentary my sister could have made on the lives we'd led. I slipped off the black velvet cover on the back, holding the picture in place. A small gold key was taped to the other side of it. I pulled the key away from the backing and held it in my hand. Where do you even start to find the lock where a key fits?

A gust of wind rattled the windows, and I jumped.

I looked around the room one more time, walked the perimeter, wondering what else I could have missed. Then

I slipped the key into my pocket and let myself out the front door.

Darkness had settled in. I moved toward my car. A dark figure ran out of the carport, wielding a bat high overhead. I turned. They swung. The blow landed hard against my right side. It felt like every bone splintered into a thousand pieces. I doubled over and fell to my knees, gasping for air, waiting for the excruciating pain to subside.

The figure, in a dark hoodie, stood over me, ready to strike again. It wasn't a baseball bat, I saw, but a large piece of firewood that was aimed at my head.

Instinctively, I raised my arm, trying to protect myself from the next assault. The wood came down on my fore-arm and glanced off the back of my skull, with a whole new level of pain. Warm liquid slithered down my scalp.

The firewood was poised again, but I rolled onto my back and aimed a kick right at the kneecap of the hooded figure, with enough force to knock them off balance. It bought me a little time. I rolled to the side and wiggled between my car and Meredith's.

I made it to the other side of the cars, but hoodie was right behind me. I'd just cleared the bumpers when I was grabbed by the hair, and my head snapped back.

I twisted. My long hair turned into a knot on the back of my head, and my ribs screamed with pain. On my knees, crouched between the cars, I turned to face the dark fig-ure and did a headbutt right into the diaphragm, the heel of my hand thrusting into the soft cartilage of a nose. A loud grunt escaped into the night, and the hand loosened its grip on my hair. I scooted backward like a crab, rolled over, and got to my feet, ready to take off for the woods. The pain in my side was like a searing iron.

I wasn't fast enough. One swift foot across my ankles sent me flying. I hit the ground, blood bursting from my lips. I didn't think I could feel any more pain, and luckily I didn't have to. I passed out.

Sometime later, I was jarred back into consciousness by the throbbing pain in my head, my ribs, my arm as I was dragged over bumpy ground on some kind of plastic tarp. The bright headlights of a car glared in my eyes until I thought my head would explode.

There were female voices, two of them.

"What the hell were you thinking? God, you almost killed her." Clearly angry. I recognized the voice but couldn't place it.

"I thought we wanted to get rid of her." The other voice, younger sounding, equally as angry, said.

"Scare her, not *kill* her."

"Well, I think she's scared now. Who *is* she anyway?" the younger one said.

The reply was terse: "Just someone trying to make trouble for Andy."

They pulled me around to the open doors on the side of a blue minivan. Fear suddenly trumped the pain. They *had* almost killed me, or at least the younger one had. No one knew where I was. I couldn't let them get me in that van.

Erratic breath spasmed out of my lungs in short bursts. I had to calm down, to think. My head thudded like a jackhammer, and blood trickled out of my skull—at least I hoped it was blood. I slowed my breathing and looked around without too much movement. I wanted them to think I was still unconscious. It was the only card I had to play, and I needed to use it to my advantage.

They stopped pulling me, which was a relief. The jolting motion over uneven ground had been excruciating.

"What do we do now?" the younger voice asked.

"Get her in the van," the other one said.

They were standing at the end of the tarp, down by my feet, breathing heavily. I kept my eyes half closed, hoping they couldn't see me in the dark. If I rolled hard to the left, maybe I could make it to the back of the van and to my feet—or maybe not. My ribs were on fire.

I took a painful breath in, ready to move, when a gun exploded in the night. Too close. My eyelids flew wide open. I expected to see one of them standing over me, a revolver pointed at my head.

They both screamed, their eyes scouring the darkness that surrounded us. It was the woman and her daughter from my father's cabin, but they had no weapons.

I heard another girl's voice. "Don't move." Dana? I wasn't sure. Everything in my head was muddled from the blow.

Dana stepped into the light, a gun in her hand. The shadows landing across her face from the interior light of the van gave her a menacing look.

"Put your hands up," she said.

They raised their arms. Scott moved in out of the darkness. At least I think it was Scott.

Dana waved the gun toward me. "Check on her," she said.

He moved to my side and pushed the hair back off my face. "You okay?" he whispered.

"My ribs," I said. "And my head."

"She's bleeding," he said to Dana over his shoulder. "We have to get her to a hospital."

"And you," Dana said to the mother-and-daughter hit-men, "are going to jail."

The woman took a step toward Dana. Dana pointed the gun at her.

"She attacked us," the woman said. "She went after my daughter. I had to protect her."

"Whatever," Dana said, in an I-don't-give-a-crap-voice.

The girl took a step forward. Dana didn't see her.

"Dana," I said from the ground.

She looked over at me. The girl moved in fast, did a high kick at Dana's hand, and the gun went flying. Mother and daughter ran, one to each side of the van, jumped in, gunned the engine, and took off, dirt and pebbles raining down on our heads.

"Scott, they're getting away!" Dana yelled.

"Let them go. We have to get Liz to a hospital."

"Where's your phone?" she asked.

"In my car." Words came out of my mouth, I hoped they made sense—to me they just sounded like gibberish. My head rolled into Scott's chest, and I could feel myself slipping again. I tried to hold on, but it was a losing battle.

The last thing I heard was Scott saying, "Hurry, Dane! Call nine-one-one."

I WOKE UP in the hospital, my head in more pain than the worst hangover in the world. Tom was sitting in a chair next to my bed, watching me. Fred was in a chair in the corner, his head nodding as if he'd fallen asleep.

"What time is it?" I asked Tom, my voice raspy.

"Two in the morning." He moved closer.

"Dana and Scott? Where are they?"

"I don't know. They weren't anywhere around when the paramedics arrived." He reached out and took my hand. "Did they do this to you?"

"No. Dana saved my life."

"Then who?"

It was such an effort to talk. "Two women. From Bayfield."

"What two women? How do you know they were from Bayfield?"

The nurse came in and checked the monitor by my bed. "She needs to rest," she said to Tom.

"I just need to ask her—"

"She needs to rest," she said in a voice that even the Bureau of Criminal Apprehension couldn't argue with. She bent over my bed. "What's your pain level on a scale from one to ten?"

"Twenty-seven."

She smiled and handed me a plastic thing hooked up to my IV. "You can give yourself a shot of pain meds whenever you need it. Just push the button."

I pushed the button. The room started to spin a little, and then it was lights out.

EIGHTEEN

WHEN I WOKE up later that morning a shaft of sunlight was struggling through the slit between the curtains. Fred was asleep in the corner, and Tom asleep in the chair next to my bed, his head resting on my hand.

I tried to move my hand, and he raised his head, creases from the blanket etched on his face.

"What time is it now?" I asked.

He looked at his watch. "Ten to eight."

"I want to go home."

"We'll see what the doctor says."

Fred opened his eyes and looked at us, then stood up and stretched. "I'm going to go find some coffee."

"Get me one too," Tom said.

"And me," I said.

Fred looked at me. "I'm not getting you anything that isn't medically authorized."

"I need coffee."

"Then get it from a nurse." He left the room.

Tom was watching me closely. "How do you feel?"

"Like I was hit by a semi. But better than last night."

"You want to tell me what happened?"

Just then the doctor came in. He was about forty, with dark hair and big, weird eyes. "You are a very lucky young woman," he said.

"I don't feel so lucky right now."

He looked at me with those strange eyes. "Your injuries could have been much worse. You could have ended up with a skull fracture or in a coma. You have a concussion, but it could have turned out differently."

He took out his penlight and shone it in my eyes, then made me look up and down and right and left. I was a little dizzy when he was done.

"Can I go home?" I asked him.

His face was all serious. "I'm going to release you, but you need to rest. Concussions are nothing to take lightly. Do you have someone to stay with you? I don't want you left alone for forty-eight hours."

Tom spoke before I could. "She'll have someone with her 'round the clock, Doctor."

Weird Eyes lifted my right arm and poked at it through the bandages. "Stitches come out in ten days. You're lucky it isn't broken."

I guess I was just damn lucky on every count.

"The nurse will be in with your discharge papers and care instructions soon. If you don't want to end up back in here, follow those directives carefully." Dr. Weird Eyes nodded at Tom and left the room.

"Help me get dressed," I said to Tom.

"What's your hurry? Why don't you wait for the nurse?"

"I want to be ready to go when the nurse gets here."

"Liz, just…"

"Help me get dressed or I'll do it myself."

He went to the closet and pulled out the clothes I'd been wearing the night before. My stomach cramped up when I saw how much blood I'd lost.

Tom looked at my blouse. "Maybe we can borrow some scrubs for you to wear home."

"No, I just want to go." I sat up very slowly, held my head in my hands for a few seconds while I caught my breath, then moved my legs over the side of the bed.

He walked over to the bed, took my arm, and helped me stand. I fell against his chest. "Are you sure you don't want to wait for the nurse?" he asked.

"No."

He sighed. "Okay. Take it slowly."

I stepped away from him and started to slip off the gown.

"Holy shit," he said when he looked at my side.

A cummerbund-like bandage wrapped around my torso. Deep purple bruises escaped the edges of the wrapping.

"Just help me," I said.

He looked at me and smiled. "I'm not sure I know how to do this. I've only *undressed* women. This will be a whole new experience for me."

Okay, it was funny. I started to laugh, but it hurt, so I stopped.

By the time Fred was back with two cups of coffee, I was dressed and sitting in the chair, waiting for the nurse to come and grant me dispensation to go home.

I SLEPT MOST of the day.

At four o'clock, Tom rubbed my shoulder. "You told me to wake you."

I rolled over onto my back. "You have to help me again."

"Tell me what to do."

"I have to take a shower and get dressed for the visitation. I don't think I can do it alone."

"You're really testing my willpower—all this nakedness and I have to behave myself."

"Well, you had your chance, and you turned me down, remember? Karma's a bitch."

His face got serious. "Liz, if you can't go to the visitation, it's okay. No one would judge you."

"I have to go. I have to do this for Meredith."

He knew he wasn't going to talk me out of it, so he helped me out of bed and into the bathroom, then into the shower. He leaned up against the vanity, watching. A few times I felt a little woozy and started to lose my balance, but he moved quickly to steady me before I fell.

The water stung my skin and scalp in all the raw places where the flesh had been torn. When I was finished, I was exhausted.

Back in the bedroom, I sat on the edge of the bed and gave him instructions to find the underwear and clothes I needed for the visitation. "What? No pantyhose?" he asked when he'd pulled my black bra and panties out of the drawer.

"It's too hot for pantyhose."

He helped me into a black sheath with capped sleeves and zipped it up the back. The mandarin collar hid some of the bruises on my neck from my trip to Bayfield.

"Fred will be here in about ten minutes," he said when I was dressed and sitting in the living room. "I need to go home and change. Will you be okay, or do you want me to stay?"

"I'm fine. I'll see you there."

He looked at me sitting on the couch. "We need to talk about last night. We've already waited this long, so it can wait now until after the visitation, but I need to know what happened out at Meredith's and who did this to you."

"Okay."

"And everything else you haven't told me."

I HELD ONTO Fred's arm as we made our way into the funeral home on Stillwater Boulevard. This was the hardest thing I'd ever done. How do you say goodbye to your only sister, to the one person in your life who'd always been there for you as your friend—your protector? How do you do that and then move on?

As crazy as the past several days had been, they'd been a distraction. Now, it was time, and I wasn't ready yet. I wanted to back up and get a running start. I wanted to prepare myself for the final goodbye.

Life would go on without Meredith, but it would never be the same. The most important person in my life was gone, and nothing could ever fill that void.

Ruth, David, Rachel, Martha, and John were lined up in the receiving area when we walked in. My appearance was, well, jaw-dropping, because their mouths actually gaped when they saw me.

"Didn't you tell them?" I whispered to Fred.

"No time," he whispered back.

Great. Now there would be endless questions. I didn't want to talk about me, I wanted this night to be all about Meredith.

Ruth moved forward. "Darling, what happened to you?" She reached out and gently touched my cheek.

"I had a little accident."

Rachel moved in beside her. "Are you okay?"

"Kind of sore, but okay."

"Should you even be here, Elizabeth?" Ruth asked.

Now, the old people were all huddled around me. John

put his hand on my back, a familiar touch of compassion, but when I looked in his eyes I wondered if he'd helped my father all those years ago. I wondered if he had been part of the betrayal that left my sister and me without a parent.

He looked into my eyes and must have seen the questions. He raised his eyebrows as if he didn't know what I was asking. And of course, he didn't.

Rachel was moving in for a hug, and I wasn't sure my bruised ribs would survive. I stepped back against Fred and my foot went down hard on his toes.

"Ouch!"

"Sorry."

And then people started coming to pay their respects to Meredith, and the questions would have to wait.

I held tightly to Fred's arm. "Don't leave me," I whispered.

He stayed with me as long as he could, but eventually got swept away in the wave of mourners. People from my office showed up, some of them I barely knew, and it touched me that they would come to show their support.

My boss, Jenny, took me aside. "Take as much time as you need, Liz, before you even think about coming back to work."

I hugged her before I got caught up in another wave of people.

Tom arrived and found me surrounded by Meredith's co-workers. He stepped in front of the women and kissed me on the cheek. "Elizabeth, I'm so sorry for your loss." There was a twinkle in his eye as he took my arm and pulled me away. "Could you help me find Ruth? I haven't seen her, and I'd like to offer my condolences."

I smiled at the women and stepped away. "Thank you," I said under my breath.

We walked out onto the patio and into the warm humid night.

"How're you holding up?" he asked.

"Physically or emotionally?"

"Both."

"Physically, I'm ready to drop. Emotionally…" there weren't even words to convey what I felt.

"I really should go say something to Ruth," he said, "and I'll hang around to take you home. You coming inside?"

"In a minute. I need some time alone."

He left me on the patio, and I sat down on a hard concrete bench by a fountain. Barb Forseman, Meredith's boss, came out through the French doors, sat down next to me, and took my hand in hers.

"What happened to you?" she asked.

"I had a little accident."

She looked like she didn't believe that, but let it go. "How are you doing?"

"Just going through the motions."

"You have no idea how much I'm going to miss your sister." Her eyes filled with tears. She took a tissue out of her pocket and wiped her eyes. "Oh, remember the day you came to the office and I told you about the man I'd seen Meredith with a few times?"

"Yes."

"He's here," she whispered. We were the only two on the patio, and I'm not sure who she thought would overhear us.

"Show me."

We walked over to the French doors. Barb scanned the crowd for the mysterious man.

"There he is. Over by the far wall, talking to Fred."

I was hoping there really was a mysterious man that was

going to lead us down the path to some answers. Instead, I saw Edman looking uncomfortable and out of place.

"I know him. He's not someone we need to worry about."

"Oh? Good," she said, but I think she was a little disappointed.

Barb went back inside, and I was sitting in front of the fountain again when someone placed a hand on my shoulder.

I looked up. Rachel was standing behind me. "I guess I can't let you out of my sight," she said as she sat down beside me. "Tell me what happened."

I thought for a minute. "If I do, this is just between you and me."

She raised her eyebrows, then nodded. "Okay. It's just between you and me. Unless you're in danger and the police need to be involved."

"They already are. You need to promise me, Rachel, that until I tell you otherwise, this is just between you and me."

"I promise."

It was harder than I realized to know how to say this to her. "My father is alive."

She said nothing. Maybe she thought I'd gone insane. Her eyes held mine for the longest time; then she shook her head.

"No, honey," she said. "No, he isn't."

"I've seen him, Rachel. He lives up in Bayfield at the old family cabin and goes by the name Andrew Zimmer. Somehow Meredith found him."

She looked out at the fountain. "How? Why? I don't understand."

"Neither do I. He started a new life, and he has a new

family. They showed up at Meredith's the other night and beat the crap out of me."

She stood and walked the perimeter of the fountain, her eyes on the ground, her feet shuffling slowly. When she was in front of me again, she looked up. "Does Ruth know?"

I shook my head. "Not yet. Please don't say anything to her. Don't say anything to anyone."

"Okay."

AT EIGHT O'CLOCK, I hit the wall, every drop of energy drained from my body—partly from the night before but mostly from the emotional exertion the visitation had drained from me.

Edman walked over and looked me up and down. "What the hell did you get yourself into now, kid?"

"I went out to Meredith's last night and got attacked by... the woman." I still didn't know what to call her. "And her daughter. They got in a couple of good swings with some firewood and were just about to load me into a van when Dana and Scott showed up."

He let out a low whistle. "And that's what happens when you mess with the status quo. Are you okay?"

"I'm in pretty rough shape right now."

"Tell me what you need me to do."

"Find them."

"They're probably long gone."

"You think?"

He nodded. "I'd bet on it. They'd be facing felony assault charges from the looks of what they did to you. They might be able to get off with a light sentence if they don't have any prior records, but if they're trying to protect your father, they won't want the sheriff sniffing around. I wonder if they know about his past?"

"I think the mother does. She knew who I was when she attacked me up in Bayfield. She knew that Meredith was my sister, and she said she knew where I lived. I don't think the girl knows anything. She might have just been along for a mother-daughter outing."

Edman snorted.

"What about Andrew Zimmer?" I asked. "Would he go into hiding with them?"

"He'd have a lot more to lose than they would if he got picked up—like his entire life. He's flown under the radar for a long time; he's not about to be outed now."

"Just find the bastard. I need to talk to him. He's not going to get away with this."

Tom came up behind me and nodded at Edman. "You two conspiring? Something I need to know about?"

"Just offering my condolences to the lady," Edman said and walked away.

"Don't even ask," I told Tom.

"Not here, not now, but we *will* talk about it later. You ready to go?"

The last of the visitors were leaving, and I made my way over to Ruth to say good night.

"I think you should spend the night at the house, Elizabeth. Then we can all go to the funeral tomorrow as a family."

"I want to sleep in my own bed tonight, Ruth. I'll meet you at the church in the morning." I hugged her quickly and turned away before she could say more.

John was blocking my path. "I haven't had a chance to talk to you all night."

I looked into his eyes, but no words came. John and Martha. They had always been there for Meredith and me, the one constant in our otherwise disjointed lives. They'd loved and nurtured us and held us when we cried. Nothing had changed, except now I knew he'd been with my father when he disappeared, and I didn't yet know what that meant to my life. How his actions might have contributed to the loss of my childhood.

I reached up and kissed him on the cheek, hoping that he really was the man I'd always thought him to be. "I'll see you in the morning," I said and left.

NINETEEN

Tom SAT IN the rocking chair in my bedroom while I went into the bathroom to get ready for bed.

"You don't have to stay," I said when I came out of the bathroom.

"You're not supposed to be alone for forty-eight hours."

"I'll be—"

"I promised the doctor I'd be here, and I'm a man of my word."

He slipped off his shoes, threw his tie on the foot of the bed, and lay down beside me, lying on his side, his head resting on his arm folded onto the pillow.

His lips were inches from my ear. "Okay, let's talk."

"I don't know where to start."

"Tell me what happened last night."

"I think I need to back up a few days. You know the files you got from Edman?"

"Yes."

"There were several pictures taken in Bayfield last spring." I paused, fighting back unexpected tears.

"And?"

"There were pictures of a cabin—a lake home—outside of Bayfield, that used to belong to my family."

"Okay. And?"

"There were several pictures of a man. He was—is—my father."

Tom sat up quickly and looked down at me. "I thought your father was dead."

"So did I. Somehow Meredith must have found out he wasn't and sent Edman up there to find him. Apparently, he faked his own death in that boating accident and has been living under the name Andrew Zimmer for twenty-some years."

Tom was looking at the wall behind my head, thinking. "Yeah, I remember the name from Edman's files. I'll check it out. Keep going."

"Isn't that earth-shattering enough for now?"

He looked me in the eye and shook his head. "No. Now that I've got you talking, I want to hear all of it."

So, I told him—all of it—about my trip to Bayfield with Edman, the bruises on my neck, being attacked the night before by my father's girlfriend and her daughter, Scott and Dana showing up and calling the paramedics.

What I didn't tell him about was my visit to Father Mark, the key I had in the pocket of my jeans that I'd found hidden in my sister's house, or the questions I had about John and his involvement with my father's disappearance.

And I couldn't bring myself to tell him all the feelings that rose to the surface—the hurt, the loss, the betrayal—knowing that my father, for whatever reason, had left us.

Tom got out of bed and slipped on his shoes. "Do you have names for these two women and an address for the cabin?"

"No, but Edman probably does. Give me my phone—his number is on it."

Tom handed over my phone and I looked up Maynard

Edman's cell phone number and gave it to him. "What are you going to do now?"

"Get the sheriff in Bayfield County to pick up those two women and your father."

He left the room, and I could hear him talking on his cell phone as he headed down the stairs.

I fell asleep before he came back upstairs, if he ever did. When I woke up the next morning, he was sitting in the rocking chair, watching me and looking very tired.

"Did you sleep at all?" I asked.

"Not much. I was on the phone most of the night. The two women—by the way, their names are Carly Turnquist and Brenda—are nowhere to be found."

"And my... Andrew Zimmer?"

"Gone."

That was frightening. If the mother-daughter team couldn't be found, then they could easily show up in my life unexpectedly again. And this time, little Brenda might finish what she'd started.

And if my father was gone—well, I needed to talk to him. I could tell myself I was looking for closure, but the truth is I wanted him to hear what I had to say. I didn't want explanations or excuses about why he'd left. What I needed was for him to know what he'd done to his daughters.

"You need help getting dressed?" Tom asked.

"I think I'm okay." I got out of bed and made my way to the bathroom. I was moving better than the day before, but it was still painful, and my reflection in the mirror was not a pretty one.

This was the day I'd been dreading. The funeral would be the final exclamation point on Meredith's life. Once the burial was over, she would be gone, and there was no turning back.

I stepped into the shower. The warm water ran down my back while hot tears trickled down my cheeks. It was more than the loss I was feeling, I felt like I'd let my sister down. I hadn't been there when she needed me. I hadn't been there to help her with the battles—whatever they were— that she'd been fighting alone. For whatever reason, she had shielded me from them, just like she'd tried to shield me from everything bad that had happened in our lives.

I let the sadness come, not pushing it away as I'd tried to do for the past week. Because underneath the sadness, something new was rising to the surface—the undeniable resolve that I wasn't done with any of this. I would bury my sister today, and I would keep going until I had the answers I needed, until someone paid for what they had taken from me.

Tom was still sitting in the rocking chair in the corner when I came out of the bathroom.

"How're you doing?" he asked.

I shrugged. "I just need to get through this."

He stood up and walked over to me. "You will," he said. "You'll do it for Meredith."

AT TEN THIRTY, we walked into St. Bartholomew's Church. This was the church where my parents had been married and where my father and Ruth had exchanged vows. This was where Meredith and I had been baptized and confirmed, and this was where I would say my final goodbye to my sister.

The family was already there. Tom squeezed my hand

and whispered in my ear, "It'll be okay." I don't know why, but those small insignificant words gave me comfort.

He settled into a pew toward the back of the sanctuary, and I walked down the center aisle to my family.

The open casket sat in front of the altar, and I looked at my sister for the last time, her delicate features composed and restful. I touched her cheek and put my hand on hers. I didn't want to let go.

Fred moved in behind me, his eyes red and puffy. His arm went around my shoulders, and I leaned into him.

"I don't think we should go to Bayfield today," he said in a low voice. "You're not strong enough for the trip yet, and I…"

"It's okay," I said softly. I hadn't told him yet that I'd already seen Joseph and that he and the women in his life were long gone.

"Maybe Monday, after you've had a few days to rest."

"We'll talk about it later."

Ruth came up next to me and touched my arm. "How are you holding up, darling?"

She looked so old and tired. I knew she was struggling with her own loss, but there were no tears. Impulsively, I reached out and hugged her, holding on tightly to the only mother I'd ever known. Her spine was ramrod straight, but she felt so thin. She patted my back, then stepped away.

People started filing into the church, and we took our seats off to the side—the family McCallister—old money, blood as blue as the ocean, and dysfunctional as hell.

David sat at the end of the pew, sobbing softly into his handkerchief. Ruth was beside him, and I sat next to her, with Rachel on my left and Fred on the other side of his mother. John and Martha sat behind us. I could hear Martha's sniffling and knew without looking that her husband had his arm around her. Rachel took my hand and held on tight.

Mourners made their way to the front of the church to view the coffin. Father Mark Dutton nodded to me as he went back to his seat. Barb Forseman and Lee Atwater looked over at us as they stood in front of the casket.

Fred's boyfriend, Dr. Charlie, stood solemnly for a minute, gazing at my sister. I glanced over at Fred and raised my eyebrows, indicating that Charlie should be sitting with the family. Fred shook his head. Okay, he hadn't told his mother yet about his new love.

Tom made his way to the front of the church and the casket. He looked down at Meredith for the longest time, and I wondered what was going through his head and if he'd ever really gotten over her.

And then Dana walked in, dressed in a black skirt and a black linen blouse, her blonde hair flowing down her back. Rachel poked my arm and looked at, me her eyes wide. I nodded, then looked at Ruth, who was staring at the girl.

Ruth and I had not yet had the discussion about Meredith's pregnancy. I tried to read her face as she watched the girl. The resemblance to my sister was unmistakable; she couldn't have looked more like Meredith if we had cloned her. Did Ruth know the girl had entered our lives after all these years? Was she surprised to see her?

Martha tapped me on the shoulder, and I turned around. She nodded her head toward the girl, her eyes unblinking.

"That's Meredith's daughter," I whispered.

She wrinkled her brow, not knowing what to make of this. I wondered if Martha had known why my sister was sent away to boarding school. Her face told me that she probably had not.

Scott held her hand as they paid their last respects. After a minute Scott and Dana took their seats.

I got up quietly and walked over to them. "Would you like to come and sit with the family?"

Scott made a move to stand up, but Dana shook her head and looked away. I started to turn aside, but Scott reached for my hand.

"That old dude sitting with you," he whispered. "He was at Meredith's the day before she died. They had a terrible argument."

"Which one?"

"The one sitting behind you."

I went back and sat down just as Father Palmer started the service.

The marble walls of the church did little to relieve the sweltering heat, and the mass seemed longer than usual. People in the pews fanned themselves with their bulletins.

When the service was over, we went downstairs to the social hall for a luncheon, doing a replay of the night before at the visitation. I was hoping Dana would be there to meet the family, but she and Scott had disappeared.

After the luncheon, we rode to the cemetery in limousines and said one last goodbye. And then it was over and Meredith was gone.

IT JUST SEEMED easier to go home with Ruth and David than try to talk my way out of it. And maybe it was my penance. I'd distanced myself from Ruth for much of the week, and she, as much as the rest of us, needed to feel like we were a real family.

After dinner, my stepparents went their separate ways. David holed up in his office, doing who knows what, and Ruth sat on the sun porch, listening to Brahms. By seven o'clock, I was ready to climb right out of my skin.

I stood in the doorway to the sun porch, watching Ruth, her eyes closed, but the look of serenity I'd seen the day I'd come to tell her about Meredith was gone. Now she just looked old and tired, and her skin had an ashen hue.

She finally opened her eyes and looked over at me. "Do you want to sit with me, Elizabeth?" she asked, but the invitation felt perfunctory, as if she'd rather be alone.

I walked in anyway and took the chair next to her, as I had a week ago. "Tell me about Meredith's pregnancy."

She closed her eyes, going back into her music.

"Ruth, tell me what happened."

When she didn't respond, I picked up the remote and turned off the CD player.

She turned to look at me. "That wasn't a very pleasant time in our lives, and it's best left alone."

"Well, Meredith's daughter is in the middle of our lives now, so I don't think we can pretend that she doesn't exist."

"She'll go away soon enough," she said, her voice flat. She reached up and brushed a strand of hair off her forehead.

"What the hell does that mean?" My tone rose, and I think it surprised her. We were not a family that yelled. Mostly, we gave each other disapproving looks and the silent treatment.

"It means that the young woman showed up because she wants something. If she doesn't get what she wants, she will go away."

This was a side of my stepmother I'd never seen before. "What is it you think she wants, Ruth?"

"Don't be naive, Elizabeth. The girl obviously wants money. Our name is well known in the metro area, and she is an opportunist. For all we know, she isn't even related to us."

"Or maybe she wants a family."

What came out of Ruth's mouth sounded like *humph*.

I thought this conversation was more disturbing than finding out Dana even existed. How could Ruth turn her back on the girl, even if all she wanted was money? Not a one of us had done a damn thing for the money we had. Why shouldn't Dana, by default, be as entitled as the rest of us?

I reached out and put my hand on Ruth's arm and once again felt a frailty that I hadn't known was there. I'd thought Ruth would outlive us all, but maybe not. Maybe the strain of the past week had taken more from her than I'd even realized.

"Ruth," I said again, "tell me about the pregnancy."

She looked me right in the eye. "No, Elizabeth, we won't discuss that—not now, not ever. That transgression was a private—very private—part of your sister's life. Out of respect for her, we will keep it private."

"Ruth—"

Oh God, I knew that look she gave me. And I knew nothing, absolutely nothing, would change her mind.

I handed her back the remote and left the room.

TWENTY

I FOUND MARTHA in the kitchen just as she was loading the last of the dishes in the dishwasher. When she turned around, she let out a startled yelp. "I didn't know you were there, baby."

"Sorry." I sat down at the table, and she came and sat across from me. "Martha, did you know that Meredith had been pregnant? That she'd had a child?"

She blinked back tears and shook her head.

"Why does that make you cry?"

She took a tissue from her pocket. "I don't know. I guess, I always wanted you girls to feel like you could confide in me. And then something like that happens, and…" She wiped at her eyes. "I feel like I let her down."

"You didn't let her down if you didn't even know." I reached out and rubbed her arm.

"But the point is, I *should* have known. I should have been paying better attention."

"Well, she and Ruth did a good job of hiding it, so you can't blame yourself."

"Was that what the year away at school was all about?"

"Yes."

She shook her head. "I should have been paying attention," she repeated.

We didn't talk for a few minutes. I guess both of us were

thinking about how we'd let Meredith down, how we hadn't been there when she'd needed us.

Finally, I said, "I need to borrow your car."

She looked at me. "I don't think you should be driving yet."

"Please, Martha, I need to get out of here for a while— I won't be gone long."

I could tell by her face there was a *no* coming, when John came up behind me and handed me a set of keys. "Take Ruth's," he said. "It hasn't been driven since I took it in for an oil change last week. Not good for a car to just sit."

"John," Martha said, but he just shrugged.

I took the keys and we looked at each other for a long time, something passing between us, but I wasn't sure what. I knew my eyes were filled with questions these days, and he wouldn't understand why. But part of me felt as if he was trying to answer those unspoken questions in his own quiet way. The problem was, I couldn't read the answers any more than he could read my questions.

"You want some company?" he asked.

I hesitated. "Okay."

Ruth's gray LeBaron was parked in the hot garage, the air heavy and suffocating. I slid into the driver's seat, and John bent his gangly frame into the passenger side of the car. We headed east, but neither of us talked for the longest time.

I looked at that sticker from the Express Lube where John had taken the car for an oil change eight days ago. "I thought you said the car hadn't been driven all week."

"Nope, hasn't been out of the garage."

"Then why are there sixty-five miles more on the odometer than there were when you took the car in?"

He leaned across the seat and looked at the odometer, then up at the sticker on the windshield. "I don't know. That's weird. I would have known if someone had taken the car."

"Must have been Ruth. David and Martha have their own cars."

We were making small talk, and it felt awkward. I'd never had to do that with John. All of a sudden, everything felt different between us.

I pulled over to the side of the road on a residential street, turned off the motor, and faced him. "I didn't know that you'd been with Joseph on his boat when it went down."

He leaned back in the leather seat. "I imagine there's a lot you didn't know."

"So, tell me."

"It was a long time ago, Elizabeth."

I didn't say anything.

He readjusted himself in the seat and ran a hand through his gray hair. "Your father had that big sailing trip planned, to hit all the Apostle Islands that spring, and he asked me to go with him."

He glanced over at me. Still I didn't say a word. "When he asked me to go, I was sort of flattered. But once we got on the boat, I saw that I was just the hired help. There was a lot to do, and the lake was rough so early in the season. Still too much ice to be out sailing." He stopped again.

"And Andrew Zimmer?"

"How did you know—well, I guess it doesn't matter. I was never sure where he came from. Your father went to the bar one night, and when I woke up the next morning, that Andrew guy was on the boat with us."

"You never knew who he was?"

"Not really. Just some drifter pothead who needed work. He seemed nice enough—just kind of useless."

"Did you get the feeling that they knew each other before that?"

He shrugged. "I don't really know."

"Go on."

John stared out the windshield, watching a mother putting her baby in a stroller. "Not much to tell. The water was rough, and we were fighting the wind constantly. Andy and I tried to tell your father that we should just give up and go home, but he wouldn't hear of it. And then…"

This pause was longer than the last one. I waited.

He looked down and closed his eyes. "I went down below that night, to try to get some sleep. The next thing I knew, your father was yelling for me to come up on deck. I went up the stairs and barely had my head above deck when something hit me on the back of the head, and I blacked out."

"So, you don't remember anything?"

He finally looked at me. "I came to at some point. The rain was in my eyes, and it was pitch-dark, but I saw the two of them—struggling, fighting, trying to help each other stay upright—I never knew, and I blacked out again."

Again the silence, and I waited. He took a deep breath. "When I woke up on the beach, the Coast Guard was already there. The boat was smashed against the rocks and Andy Zimmer was lying about twenty feet away—dead."

"And Joseph?"

"I never saw him again."

"You know he's alive, don't you?"

John nodded. "Meredith told me she'd found him and that he'd been living under Andy Zimmer's name."

"Do you know how she found out he was alive?"

The old John was suddenly back. He had that look in his eye like a reproving parent. "Elizabeth, Ruth was right when she said that this is a job for the police. Your sister pushed someone too far, and look what happened. I'd never forgive myself if something happened to you."

I looked him in the eye. "I'm not a child anymore, John. You don't have to protect me. And look at me…" I touched my face. "I am already in this thing and I'm not willing to quit until I know what happened to Meredith."

"And that's what the police—"

I put my hand on his shoulder. "The police will do whatever it is they do, but you know as well as I do that sometimes their hands are tied. Help me with this, John. Help me do this for Meredith."

He thought for a minute. "I don't know much, but I think Meredith found something at the house that started this whole thing going. Maybe she already knew something, but wherever she found her information, she and Ruth had a terrible fight."

"And you think it was connected to my father?"

"I'm almost certain of it."

"Did you go out to Meredith's the day before she died?"

He nodded.

"And you two fought?"

There were tears in his eyes as he nodded again.

"What did you fight about?"

"She wanted me to help her—I didn't understand what it was she wanted me to do, but it had something to do with your father. I told her to go to the police with whatever information she had, but she was totally unreasonable and wouldn't listen to me."

He took a deep breath. "I should have done more. If I had, maybe…"

I leaned over and kissed him on the cheek. "There's no way you could have known what was going to happen."

He put his face in his hands and started to cry.

I'D NEVER UNDERSTOOD what Ruth had against air conditioners—it's not like she couldn't afford them, but not one room in the house had one. My old bedroom felt like a blast furnace as I lay in the dark, trying to fall asleep.

With the funeral and all that had been going on, it was inevitable that I dreamed about Meredith again. It was the same dream I'd had the last time I was there, when I found my sister crying alone in the attic, but this time we changed the script, adlibbing a new dialogue into the familiar setting.

"What are you doing up here?" I asked, sitting down in front of her while she slid something behind her back.

"I'm just thinking," she told me. "You really shouldn't be here, Ellie."

The stream of sunlight that passed through the window made me feel warm and sleepy. Meredith was out of its path and silhouetted in veiled shadows.

"But, I'm bored," I said. "Let's play dress-up. Ruth has lots of old clothes up here."

"No, Ellie," she said, reaching out and touching me with cold fingers. "You shouldn't be in this house. You don't live here anymore."

"No!" I screamed, frightened more by the look on her face than the words she spoke. "I won't go away. You can't make me."

"You have to go, Ellie," she said, evil staring out at me from behind her eyes. "You don't live here anymore."

I started to cry and was still crying when I woke up, drenched in sweat. The harder I gasped for breath, the heavier the air became, until I thought I would drown in the humidity and my own tears.

I sat up and forced myself to slow my breathing, making every intake a conscious effort. My heart stopped racing, and the panic passed. But that dream, more than anything that had happened in the past week—or even in my entire life—made me feel alone in a world I couldn't control.

The odd thing was, my sister was nothing like that evil girl in the attic. No, the dream hadn't been about Meredith. I was missing something, and the Meredith in my dreams was trying to show me the way. I just wished she'd make the way a little more clear. I was lost.

The clock said two am. I got out of bed, slipped on a robe, and made my way through the darkened hallway and down the stairs. Ruth and David each had an office off the main hall on the left. I stepped into David's office and switched on a lamp in the corner. It was messy, with financial papers piled high on the desk and stacked on top of the filing cabinet. The walls were cluttered with pictures of David over the years, and all the kids he'd worked with through his volunteer activities. Interspersed with the pictures were citations, most of them for Volunteer of the Year. I couldn't imagine there would be anything here that I was looking for. This wouldn't be where Meredith found whatever it was that she'd discovered about our father.

Ruth's office was the next door down. I closed the door quietly behind me before I turned on the overhead light. This room was almost spartan compared to David's. A cherrywood desk and high-backed leather chair faced the doorway. There was a filing cabinet with a few plants on top that

Martha mothered regularly, and only one photograph on the desk, of my sister and me when we were probably twelve and seven. Two Andrew Wyeth paintings were on opposite walls, and a straight-backed chair sat in front of the desk.

I didn't even know what I was looking for, but I was sure whatever Meredith had found about our father was in this room. The filing cabinet quickly proved to be a dead end, filled with household accounts and utility bills; our family papers, including birth certificates; old report cards; and Ruth's appointment books, dating back at least two decades.

Nothing in the desk seemed to be what I was searching for. I wondered where Ruth would hide all her secrets. On one wall there was a built-in bookcase in dark mahogany wood. I walked over to it, running my hand along each shelf, jiggling the poetry and art books that Ruth kept there.

The panels behind the shelves seemed solid until I reached the middle one on the shelf about waist high. I pushed at it and felt some give, but nothing more moved. There had to be a latch somewhere, and I slid my hand under the shelf until I found a clasp and moved it to the side. The panel slid open. I wondered if it had always been there or if Ruth had had it installed. Not that it mattered much at this point.

I moved the books out of the way and bent down to look inside. There was a metal box, the kind people used to use to file cancelled checks, and underneath were four file folders. I took all of it out of the cubby hiding place, went back to Ruth's desk, and sat down.

None of what I found surprised me. Even Ruth's involvement in my father's disappearance only brought confirmation to what I had instinctively known. The metal box held the monthly receipts to cashier checks, going back twenty years—all made out to Andrew Zimmer. I wondered why she'd keep such incriminating evidence, unless it was her leverage against him—if she went down, she'd take him with her.

The top folder held the life insurance policy on my father, with Ruth as the beneficiary. Still no surprise. The correspondence between the two of them over the years tried to sound businesslike—amateurishly cryptic. My father, as Andrew Zimmer, requested additional funds for a *project* he was working on that would be mutually beneficial to both parties. I think the only one who would be fooled by their attempt to hide their true intent was maybe an eight-year-old, certainly not a cop or district attorney. It was so ridiculous it was almost embarrassing.

The final folder was where it started to get ugly—or as ugly as the two of them could get; they weren't very good at this. There was an email from Andrew to Ruth, telling her—and not very nicely—that he needed more money, leveraging the fact that he would report her for insurance fraud for cashing in his life insurance policy when she knew he was alive. Clearly, twenty years' worth of monthly payments to him would be proof enough.

So this is what Meredith had found—how she'd found Joseph—how she'd discovered that Ruth and Joseph must have planned this together. And this is how she'd worked out that neither our father nor our stepmother seemed to care that two children had lost yet another parent, or how that would affect our lives.

I hadn't been paying attention to anything but the papers in front of me and the thoughts chasing around in my head, so when the office door opened, it caught me by surprise, and my stomach dropped.

John stood there, barefoot, in his jeans and a T-shirt, his hair rumpled from sleep, an expression on his face that I'd never seen before.

He stepped inside and closed the door behind him. "What are you doing here?"

I didn't know whom I could trust anymore. It was obvious now that my entire childhood had been one big lie, and it seemed all the adults in my life had been in on the conspiracy. But I couldn't do this alone. I had to trust someone, and if I couldn't trust John, then things were worse than I ever could have imagined.

"I'm trying to find out what Meredith knew about Joseph."

He took a step toward me and set his jaw. "Elizabeth, are you trying to get yourself killed?"

It didn't sound like a threat, but the hairs on the back of my neck stood up. No. This was John and I had to believe in this man who had taken care of me and protected me since before I could remember.

"What I'm trying to do is find out what happened to my sister."

"How stupid are you? Leave this to the police. I'm not kidding. You are in way over your head."

"No. This is what I am doing for my sister. Are you going to help me or not? If you think you can stop me, you can't, so either help me or get out." I'd never spoken to John that way.

The look on his face told me he didn't know what to do. Finally, "What did you find?"

"There's a paper trail going back two decades, Ruth sending him monthly checks. A couple of months ago, Joseph upped the ante and wanted more money. There are emails back and forth between the two of them. Apparently, Ruth was in on this from the beginning and got my father's life insurance when he disappeared, so when Ruth refused to pay more money, he threatened to report her to the authorities for insurance fraud."

John sat down hard in the chair across from me. "They did this together? Why?"

"Money."

He shook his head, as if trying to clear it, trying to make sense of two people hell-bent on their own agendas.

"You didn't know?" I watched his face. He looked hurt.

"Of course, I didn't know. How could you ever think I'd be a part of such a thing?"

"Martha? Do you think she knew?"

The hurt morphed into anger. "What do you think of us that you'd ask such a question? Of course, she didn't—we didn't—know."

I bit my lip. "I'm sorry, John. I'm really sorry. I don't know who to trust anymore." A few tears slid down my cheeks.

"Don't. Don't cry." He softened. He didn't like tears. "It's just such a big, fucked-up mess."

There really wasn't much to add to that. It *was* a big fucked-up mess, but it didn't tell me what had happened to Meredith.

"What now?" John asked.

"I have to talk to Joseph."

He looked skeptical. "You know where to find him?"

"I found him once. He's been living at the old family cabin up by Bayfield."

"No way. All this time, he's been right there? I thought they sold that place after he disappeared. Are you sure?"

"I've seen him." I pointed to my arm. "This and my

concussion are compliments of his new wife, or girlfriend, and their daughter."

"This is too dangerous, Elizabeth. The authorities need to be involved."

How could I explain this and still garner whatever help he might be able to give me? "Well, they are, sort of. I told Tom Martens all about them. They've all gone into hiding, but Tom has the sheriff in Bayfield looking for them."

John knew me well enough to know a half-truth when he heard one. "So, the police are *sort of* involved. That tells me that you're about to do something stupid."

TWENTY-ONE

FRED PICKED ME up the next morning and dropped me off at my apartment. For once, Ruth didn't try to persuade me to stay. I think our talk about Meredith's pregnancy had made her realize that ugly secrets were coming out all over, and she'd rather not deal with them—or me.

I didn't want her to know yet what I'd found out about Joseph. It seemed only the beginning of a trail, and I wasn't sure where it would end.

We pulled up in front of my building. I closed the passenger door on the Jag. "Thanks."

Fred leaned across the seat. "You okay, Lizzie?"

"Yes."

I'm not sure he believed me, and I'm not sure I believed it myself. It would be the first day in over a week that held no direction for me. No agenda. It would just be me, with my thoughts of Meredith, trying to get through the next several hours.

"I'm spending the day with Rachel. You're welcome to join us," Fred said.

"Thanks. I'll be fine."

"Let me rephrase that: *Please* join us. Otherwise, it's just me and...her."

"Sorry. You're on your own, my friend. I did my penance last night."

He looked at me for the longest time. "Okay. Call me if you need to."

"I will."

I watched him drive away. He passed a blue Honda Pilot about half a block away, a woman sitting in the front seat. I turned toward my building, then turned back. The woman was Lee Atwater.

I walked down the block toward her SUV. She rolled down the window when she saw me approach, and smiled.

"Hey there," she said. "What are you doing here?"

"I live here." I pointed to my building.

She looked. "That's funny. A friend of mine from college lives here." She waved her hand at a small, traditional, brick apartment building on the other side of the street. "I stopped by for coffee and was just heading home."

"Who's the friend? Maybe I know her." I knew very few of my neighbors, and mostly just on sight—no names—but I knew a lot of Meredith's friends from college.

"Sorry. I should have said 'graduate school.' Her name is Melissa."

"No. I don't know her."

"Too damn hot out today."

"It's brutal." I started to turn away.

"Liz?"

I turned back.

"The funeral was lovely. A fitting tribute to Meredith. And I love the song 'The Rose.'"

The tears that were always there just beneath the surface came to my eyes. "Thank you, Lee. I'm so glad you came. It meant a lot to us. I know it would have meant a lot to Meredith."

I headed toward my building. She waved as she passed,

driving away. I was unlocking my door when someone called my name.

Tom had just parked across the street and made his way up the walk.

I unlocked the door and let us both inside. "What are you doing here?"

"It's my day off, so I thought I'd stop by and see how you're doing."

"What? No food?"

He smiled. "No food. Sorry."

I got us both something to drink, and we sat in the living room.

"Seriously? What are you doing here?"

"Checking on you. No ulterior motive. How are you?"

I watched his face. "I feel like I'm floundering."

"Anything I can do to help?"

I thought about it. "Just stay…for a while."

"I can do that."

Most of Sunday slipped away quietly. We streamed a few movies, talked about the old days, got caught up on the past fifteen years, and did everything we could to side-step references to my sister.

At six o'clock, Tom got up off the couch and stretched. "I should get home now."

I felt relaxed in his presence and didn't want him to leave, but more than that, I didn't want to be alone. Unfortunately, I only had one trick in my bag of tricks to make men stay and that hadn't been well received the last time I played that card.

I followed him to the door. He turned to say good night, and I leaned in close, kissing him hard and pressing my body up against his.

He returned the kiss, returned the embrace, then pulled away. "I have to go."

I reached to kiss him again, and he stepped away until his back was pressed against the door. "Not now, Liz."

I looked into his eyes. "*Not now* leaves the door open for a *when*."

"Let's find a killer first…and then see how we feel."

"I know how I'll feel."

"Maybe. Maybe not."

I didn't know what that meant. I didn't like the sound of it.

His gaze was intent. I thought it bordered on intimate, but I knew that was probably wishful thinking. Finally, he said, "Right now, I'm the white knight who's come to save you…to avenge your sister's death…to put your family back together again. But the truth is, Liz, I'm just a cop. Let's see if you feel the same way when you don't need me anymore."

"Tom—"

He kissed me on the cheek and went out the front door.

I knew that once Meredith's killer had been found, I'd still want two things: I'd still want Tom, and I'd still want a drink.

I went upstairs and took a shower, then grabbed the pair of jeans lying on the bedroom floor—they'd been there since I came home from the hospital the morning after the last time I'd been to Meredith's. I found a clean T-shirt and made my way downstairs again.

I stood in the kitchen for the longest time, wondering if my honeymoon with sobriety had finally come to an end. *One drink. Just one drink.*

I wanted to believe that I deserved it. I'd made it through one whole week. I'd buried my sister, gotten the crap beaten out of me by my father's new family, discovered that my childhood had been one lie after another. I wanted it. I deserved it. I needed it.

But somewhere inside, a very small voice said, *It won't change what's happened, and it could screw up whatever hopes I have for my future.* Whatever hopes I had of Tom being a part of my life. I could piss it all away with just one drink, because I knew that one drink wouldn't be one drink. It would be two or four—or whatever it took to fill the hole inside of me.

"It's a struggle, isn't it?" a voice said from behind me.

I turned to see Fred standing there. "Quit doing that! You scared the crap out of me."

"I knocked, but you didn't answer."

"Oh."

"What are you going to do about it?" he asked, nodding his head toward the cupboard over the kitchen sink.

I looked in his eyes and knew this time I would walk away. Maybe only this time, but it was a start.

"I'm going to have some coffee. You want some?"

He shook his head. "No. I'm good. You know you can call me whenever you need to, whenever you feel yourself weakening."

"I don't have to call you, Fred. You seem to just keep showing up."

He sat down at the kitchen table while I made a pot of coffee, then took a seat across from him.

"How was your day with Rachel?"

"Torturous."

"Did you tell her about Charlie?"

He shook his head. "Not yet."

"You have to, you know."

"I will."

We were both quiet.

"With Meredith gone, I feel like there's this big empty space in front of me now, and I don't know what to do to fill it up," he said. "What do we do now, Lizzie?"

"We keep going."

"Where?"

"I'm not sure. I have to go see Wainwright tomorrow and tell him what I know about Dana. And I need to find Joseph again. Edman said he's probably gone into hiding."

"You think Edman can find him?"

"I hope so." I bent forward, my elbows resting on the table, my head in my hands. Something poked into my right hipbone. I slid back, stuck my hand in my pocket, and pulled out the key I'd found at Meredith's, taped to the back of the picture on her desk.

"What's that?"

"A key I found at Meredith's the night I got beat up. She'd seemed to feel the need to hide it and taped it to the back of a picture."

Fred reached for it and turned it over in his hand. "I know this key."

"Really? You know *this* key? That's freaking amazing."

He rolled his eyes. "Very funny. I don't know *this* key, but it looks familiar."

"It's a key—they all look familiar."

He wasn't listening; he was looking at the key in his palm. Then he looked up at me. "It's the key to a safety deposit box."

"How do you know?"

"It looks like one Rachel has for her box at the bank."

"That seems too easy." But it was more than I'd come up with.

"What other kind of key would she hide?"

Good question. No one would need to hide a car key or a house key.

I reached for the key. "Let's assume you're right and Meredith has a safety deposit box somewhere. It will take months of probate to get to it. What do we do in the meantime?"

He smiled. "Do you know where she might have a safety deposit box?"

"I saw her bank statements in Tom's file the other day. She had accounts at three different places. So what? We still can't get to them."

"We can't. But Meredith can—or Meredith Junior."

"Dana?"

"Why not? She looks and sounds exactly like Meredith."

"Only sixteen years younger."

"Lots of makeup and a hat."

"What about a signature? Don't you have to sign for those things?"

"Where were her accounts?"

"U.S. Bank in St. Paul, a credit union in West St. Paul, and a local bank in Lake Elmo. Why?"

He thought for a minute. "U.S. Bank might be a problem—probably a more sophisticated security system. But if this key is for one of those smaller places, I think we could pull it off if Dana's willing to help."

"*If* Dana's willing to help."

He shrugged. "All we can do is ask."

"What if we go to all this trouble, risk getting arrested, and there's nothing there?"

"It's a chance we take. But if all she has in the box are

her passport and your mother's wedding ring, why would she hide the key? There's got to be something in there that she didn't want anyone to find."

THE NEXT MORNING, I headed to Wainwright's office, where I was greeted by the dour Ms. Norma Verhle. She made me wait in the bland reception area while she went to tell him I was there.

Wainwright stood and shook my hand when I entered his private suite. "Elizabeth, I didn't get a chance to pay my respects after the funeral. I had to leave for another engagement, but I wanted to let you know that it was a beautiful service."

"Thank you, Mr. Wainwright. I didn't realize you were there."

"I got there a little late and sat in the back. So, what I can I do for you this morning?"

"I told you the other day that Meredith had a child. I just wanted to update you on what I've found."

"Good, good," he said, nodding. "Go ahead."

"My sister had a daughter named Dana Beckwood. Dana is eighteen, and her adoptive parents live in Bloomington."

"I see." Wainwright steepled his fingers in front of his face. "I will need copies of her birth certificate and adoption records. And we may need to take this one step further..."

"What do you mean?"

"There seems to be some question as to whether Meredith was indeed Dana's biological mother. At some point, we may need DNA."

I didn't have a good feeling here. "What are you talking about?"

"Let's just say a family member has questioned Dana's

right to the trust, and we may need proof of her legal claim to the money."

I had this feeling of a pit in my stomach. "Which family member is questioning Dana's lineage?"

Wainwright looked at his steepled fingers, then back at me. "I'm not at liberty to say."

I closed my eyes, trying to figure out who would have done this. Fred? More money for him if Dana wasn't Meredith's heir? Ruth, who didn't want to acknowledge the girl in the first place? Who else was there?

I opened my eyes. Wainwright was staring at me. "I have no doubt that Dana is my niece, but we'll do whatever we have to do when the time comes. In the meantime, I will get you the documents you need. Now, to another matter…"

He waited.

"What if I have a half sister somewhere? What would be her claim to the trust?"

"*Do* you have a half sister somewhere?"

"It's quite possible that my father has another daughter."

He looked off into space. "I'll have to look into this, but after going over the trust last week, I believe the only persons legally entitled to the money are you, Frederick, your sister, and any legal spouses or progeny. Your grandparents were very specific in the wording of the document. The trust was put into place before your mother died and didn't leave room for the possibility of other children."

"Is that typical?"

His face was unreadable. "It's unusual, yes, but not unheard of, especially if there are issues in the family."

"What kind of issues?"

He hesitated. "Bad blood. I was under the impression

that your father's parents were not fond of your mother and disenchanted with their son."

And that was exactly what Rachel had told me. "Can't the trust be contested?"

"Of course, someone could try, but I doubt they would be successful. It was tightly constructed—for a reason."

"What about my father or Ruth? Couldn't they have used some of the money for raising us?"

He shook his head. "That wasn't an option. It appeared that your father tried at one point, but he didn't get very far."

"The other day you said that Meredith and I owned the family *properties*—plural. What were you referring to? Was there more than the house on Summit?"

"The family lake home outside of Bayfield."

"Ruth told me once that it didn't belong to us anymore."

"No. It's still part of the estate. Both properties now belong solely to you."

"I see." I stood to leave.

"The sooner you get me the documents about Meredith's daughter, the sooner we can move forward in settling the trust."

"I'll get you what you need."

I WAS RELUCTANT to share this information with Tom. I wasn't sure it was pertinent to his investigation, and more importantly, I needed to find my own answers. How could I ever put my own life back together again, or start a new one, if I closed my eyes to the reality of what my family had been— to what they had become?

I picked Fred up at ten, and we headed toward Meredith's to meet with Scott and Dana regarding our nefarious plans to gain access to my sister's safety deposit box. We were east of St. Paul when my phone rang.

"Want to take another jaunt up north?" Edman asked when I answered.

"You found him?"

"Yep. All of them. Do you know where Brimson is? North of Duluth?"

"Vaguely. What are they doing in Brimson?"

"Looks like they're holed up in some old hunting shack. The girl doesn't seem at all happy about her new accommodations."

"Are you there now?"

"Close by, but I don't think they're going anywhere any time soon."

"Tell me where to meet you."

Edman gave me directions to Black Woods Restaurant in Two Harbors, and I hung up.

"Edman found Joseph," I told Fred. "I'm going there now. Do you want me to take you home or drop you somewhere?"

He looked at me. "I'm going with you."

"You sure?"

"I'm sure."

We took a wide loop and ended up on I-35, heading north. It was the same route, in a different direction, that Edman and I had taken last week on our way back from Bayfield, when I'd seen my father for the first time since I was a child.

I was ready to see this thing through to the end. Even the beating I'd taken last week did nothing to deter my resolve. In some respects, I felt more in control of the situation than I had during the last go-round—almost as if there was nothing else that could surprise me.

I'd learned more about my family since my sister's death

than I'd ever known, and I was still standing. No matter what they did, no matter what I saw or learned, I would survive this. Maybe Ruth was right. Maybe when you've been kicked in the stomach so many times, you learn that you can take it and life goes on, and you truly do become stronger. I wondered if Meredith had gotten to that place.

We didn't talk much for almost an hour and a half, which was unusual for Fred and me, and I wondered what had changed between us. We hit Hinckley, Minnesota, the halfway point between the Twin Cities and Duluth, and I stopped for gas and a bathroom break.

When Fred came back from the restroom at the convenience store, I handed him the keys. "You drive."

"Okay."

In minutes, we were back on the freeway, heading north.

"I went to see Wainwright this morning," I told him.

He glanced over at me. "Uh-huh."

"I wanted to tell him about Dana."

"You told me last night that you were going to do that." He looked at me again and wrinkled his brow. "Does this story get any more interesting, or are you going to tell me now what you had for breakfast?"

"You're such a smart-ass."

"Yes, I think that's been established on numerous occasions. You don't talk to me for an hour and a half, and now I'm getting this. You want to tell me what your point is?"

I looked out the side window. Just as with John the other night, I didn't want to believe that Fred was playing for the other side. I needed to know that he was there for me, that he always would be, and now I was afraid to find out that maybe he wasn't.

I looked back at him, his strong, handsome profile, and

I wanted to go back to where we were before Meredith's death. I wanted to not have questions bouncing around in my head about the people I loved.

"Wainwright told me that someone in our family contacted him about Dana."

"What about her?"

"Someone is questioning whether or not she's really Meredith's daughter."

"Who?"

"He wouldn't tell me."

He looked at me again, and the light went on in his eyes. "Ah, I get it. You think that person is me. Right?"

"Is it?"

"I should be hurt, I guess, that you'd even think that."

"It would be more money for both of us."

There was a sign for a wayside rest, and Fred pulled the car into it and shut off the engine. "It wasn't me, Lizzie."

I couldn't look at him. He took my hand. "Look at me."

"No."

"Lizzie, I need you to look at me."

I turned toward him. "Is that the truth? No lies?"

"That is the absolute truth. No lies."

"Then who—"

"Shut up for a minute and listen to me. We'll find out who it is, but that isn't the issue right now. The issue is you and me: Where do we go from here?"

"I want us to always be like we were," I said. "I want to know that you'll always be my friend and my crazy cousin, and I can count on you for anything."

"And that's what I need from you."

"I know. It's just that the day Edman told me about Joseph's other family, and then I saw you outside Lee's office with Dana—I didn't know what to think. It felt like every-one was lying to me. That there was some huge conspiracy going on, and I was all alone."

"No conspiracy from this corner. If they've been lying to you, they've been lying to me too… Uh, wait a minute… what was that about Joseph's other family? You never told me about that. What the hell?"

"We haven't had a lot of time alone lately."

"Or you didn't trust me enough to tell me?"

I looked down at my hands, then back at him. "Yeah, that's part of it. I'm sorry."

He was quiet.

"Fred?"

"What?"

"I need you. I need to trust you again, and you need to trust me again. If we don't—if we let them win—then we have nothing. I want us to be like we were before."

"Me too."

"Okay, start driving, I have a lot to tell you."

BY THE TIME we pulled into the parking lot at Black Woods Restaurant in Two Harbors, Fred knew just about every-thing I did. I told him about my father's new family, my visit to Father Mark, Ruth's refusal to talk about Mere-dith's pregnancy, my ride the other night with John, and what I'd found in Ruth's office. The only thing I didn't—or couldn't—bring myself to tell him was how all this made me feel, how alone I felt so much of the time.

Edman was leaning up against his car, his arms folded across his chest, as we made our way across the blacktop. He nodded at Fred.

"How'd you find them up here?" I asked.

One side of Edman's mouth went up in what I assumed was a smile. "I have a lady friend at the bank in Bayfield—met her last spring when I was there looking for your father the first time. Get a few drinks in her, and she's a wealth of information."

The look on his face told me that she provided him with more than information.

"What could she possibly tell you that would have sent you to Brimson?"

"Nothing personal, honey, but your father's kind of a dumbass. He used his bank card at a convenience store not far from where they're staying."

"And the police aren't tracking that?"

"Not yet they aren't. She said she'd let me know when they get around to it." He did that crazy half smile again, and I tried to picture Edman flirting with the bank teller—or any woman. He wasn't a bad-looking guy—and definitely macho; it's just that he was, well, Edman.

We had lunch at the restaurant, then piled into Edman's car and headed for the hunting shack where my father and his family were hiding from the authorities.

It was half an hour's drive, and we were deep in the woods when Edman pulled the car off the road and turned off the engine.

"How far is the hunting shack from here?" I asked.

"About half a mile. What do you want to do now?"

"I want to talk to him, away from the women. I want him to meet us here."

"Okay." Edman gave me directions to the mile marker and fire road we were close to. "Anyone around here should be able to find it."

My stomach felt queasy. I got out of the car and walked

about twenty feet down the road away from Fred and Edman. I had in my contact list the cell phone numbers from the invoice I'd taken from the lake home in Bayfield. There were three numbers. It was going to be a little game of Russian roulette, trying to figure out which one was Joseph's, but I'd starred the main number from the bill when I entered it into my phone, and was hoping that it was his. I didn't want Carly Turnquist or her daughter, Brenda, to know how close I was to them. I didn't want them to get in the way of meeting with my father.

I pulled up the number and hit "Call," and then it was ringing. I thought it was going to go to voicemail, but then heard his voice. "Hello?"

My hand started to tremble, and I could feel the adrenaline running through my veins, igniting every cell in my body.

"Hello?" he said again.

I took a breath. "Joseph."

There was a pause. "You have the wrong number."

It took me by surprise, and I thought he was going to hang up. "Andy."

Another pause. His voice sounded wary. "Who is this?"

"It's Elizabeth, your daughter."

There was an even longer pause, and I was certain this time he'd hang up. Instead, he said, "What do you want?"

"Well, gee, Dad, that was all warm and friendly after twenty-two years."

"What is it you want with me, Liz?"

"We need to talk face-to-face."

"That's not an option. Tell me what you want."

"No, Dad, that's your only option, and here's how it's going to play out. I'm about half a mile from the hunting shack you now call home. You will come here, alone. If you're not here in fifteen minutes, then I will call the county sheriff, the state police, and the FBI. I'm sure all of them will have questions for you about insurance fraud and what really happened to Andrew Zimmer and your oldest daughter. I will tell them where Carly and Brenda Turnquist are, and I will file assault charges against both of them, with corroborating witness statements. If you choose to run, you won't get far, and your lovely fake life, as you know it, will come to a screeching halt. Do you understand?"

He hesitated again. "You wouldn't—"

"Yes. I would."

He exhaled deeply. "Where are you now?"

I told him and hung up, then looked at the time on my cell phone. I wasn't jerking him around; if he didn't show up in fifteen minutes, I would get every law enforcement agency in Northern Minnesota and Wisconsin on his ass.

TWENTY-TWO

THERE WAS NOTHING to do but pace, to walk off the adrenaline. As much as I'd thought I knew what I'd say to him when I saw him for the first time, I really didn't have a clue what would come out.

Edman and Fred got out of the car. Edman motioned for Fred to stay put, then walked over and stepped in front of me. I stopped mid-pace.

"Is he coming?"

I nodded.

"What do you need me to do?"

"Just be here—for backup—I guess. I don't know what to say to him."

"You'll figure it out, kid."

Fred joined us.

"Is he—"

"Yup," Edman said.

"You okay, Lizzie?" Fred asked.

My father pulled up just then and stepped out of the pickup, and my heart went into my throat. Fred took my hand, and Edman moved to my other side.

Joseph looked at me and nodded to the two men. "Nice to see you, Fred. You look a lot like your father."

Fred didn't respond. Joseph looked back at me. "I thought you wanted to meet alone."

"No," I said, "I wanted *you* to come alone."

"Okay, I'm here. What do you want?"

I didn't know where to start. "Meredith is dead."

He set his jaw and looked briefly down at his hiking boots, then back at me. "Yes, I heard. I'm sorry, Liz."

"That's it? That's all I get from you?"

"What do you want me to say?" He took a step forward, and Edman put out a hand to stop him. "What the hell?" He looked at Edman. "She's my daughter—what do you think I'm going to do to her?"

"Well, you don't have a very good track record as a loving father," Edman said, "so I'm not taking any chances."

"Elizabeth," Joseph said, "can we do this in private?"

I looked at Edman. "It's your call," he said.

I stepped away from the two men. "Okay," I said to Joseph, but then to Fred and Edman, "Don't go far."

Fred and Edman moved over to the car, planting their butts up against the trunk, arms folded across their chests. I almost smiled. My gay cousin and a washed-up PI were my protectors. But when I looked back at my father, I remembered there was nothing funny about this meeting.

"Okay," my father said, "what is it you want from me?"

"Answers."

"I might not have any you like."

"Why did you leave us? How could you run out on your own children? What was so terrible about your life that you would leave two young girls behind?"

He looked off over my shoulder. "It wasn't about you."

"You're kidding, right? It was all about us. You left us. Remember? You left us without a parent."

"You had Ruth. She's very responsible."

"And that's your solution? It's okay to run out on your

motherless children as long as you leave them with someone responsible?"

"You don't understand—"

"You're damn fucking right I don't understand." I took
a breath. We were spinning our wheels. "Tell me why."

He squinted his eyes as if trying to remember why he'd
had to leave his family. "Your mother and I went through
most of my inheritance. There wasn't much left after she
died. I could barely afford to keep the house."

"You could have sold it and gotten—oh, I don't know—
a *job*."

He made a disgusted look. "I wasn't cut out for that sort
of thing. That's when Ruth started coming around."

"Wait a minute. Ruth pursued you?"

"Does that shock you?" He seemed pleased.

"That doesn't sound like Ruth."

He forced a laugh. "Ruth does what she needs to do to
get whatever she wants at the time."

"So now you're saying derogatory things about the very
responsible woman you left your children with? How nice.
Don't forget, Dad, that Ruth was the one who raised us—
she was the one who was there for us when we needed a
parent."

His face turned to stone. Whatever connection we could
have made was gone. "And what did she get out of it? Ruth
does very little that doesn't benefit Ruth somehow in her
own warped way."

Anger boiled up inside of me. I took a quick step forward.
Out of the corner of my eye, I could see Edman, poised for
action. I looked over at him and shook my head, then turned
back to Joseph. "At least she was there, which is more than
I can say for you."

"All I'm saying is that Ruth gets what Ruth wants. Some people might think that an admirable quality. Ruth came sniffing around when I needed money. She had more than enough to bring to the game, especially after her mother 'died.'" He did air quotes around the word *died*, and a new realization welled up inside of me.

"What are you saying?"

He shrugged. "Didn't you ever wonder about the timing of our 'marriage'?" Again, with the air quotes.

I had no way to deal with this right now, and who even knew if his innuendoes were true. "Let's get back to you and why you ran out on your family."

There was a wall going up between us, brick by brick. I could feel it.

"I don't like where this is going," he said.

"I don't care. I hold all the cards, remember? So tell me what I need to know."

He set his jaw again. The charming man I remembered from so long ago seemed to have disappeared over the decades. "Ruth made herself available." He stopped and looked at me, and when I didn't respond, he kept going. "She had money, and I was broke. It was a marriage made in heaven. Her mother conveniently passed away in her sleep, and Ruth and I tied the knot."

"That doesn't tell me why you left."

"I'm getting to it. Ruth and I were legally married, and she brought her financial backing to our relationship, but that's about all we had. She wanted to be married and have a family; I needed to be able to survive. Simple as that."

It was pretty much what Rachel had told me, but it sounded disgusting coming from Joseph.

"After a while, Ruth's money started to run out and she was getting pretty pissed about that."

"So, you decided to fake the boating accident and Ruth could collect the insurance money?"

He smiled. "If you think it was all my idea, you're very wrong."

I didn't want to hear this. I didn't even want to know it. "It was Ruth's idea?"

He smiled again, and it was starting to creep me out. "You always were a smart girl, Liz. Ruth and I weren't happy, and the money was almost gone. You probably know better than anyone that Ruth is all about appearances."

"Meaning?"

"If we got divorced, we both lost. There wouldn't be any more money, and Ruth would be a divorced woman. But if I died—well, there was all that insurance money and Ruth would be the noble widow, raising her two stepdaughters after their father's tragic boating accident."

"How long did it take you to plan this?"

He thought about it. "We spent months putting things in order. It was probably the only time Ruth and I ever really connected."

Again, the secrets, the deception, the loss of my childhood and Meredith's—destroyed by the people who were supposed to love and protect us no matter what. How do you reconcile that on any level? No wonder I had trust issues.

I wanted to walk away then. I wanted to get in Edman's car and tell him to drive and keep going, but if I quit now, I might never have another chance. It took every ounce of determination I had to ask, "Did you kill Andrew Zimmer?"

I watched his face. "No."

I would never know if that was the truth. John was the

only potential witness, and he'd been unconscious, so Joseph could say whatever he wanted, and there would be no one to challenge him. The only thing my question established was that people knew—I knew—the possibility was there.

"And Meredith?"

That caught him off guard, and for the first time I saw genuine, uncontrolled anger in his eyes. "Good God! Are you asking me if I killed my own daughter?"

"Yes."

"I won't even answer that." He started to turn away.

"I'm not done here."

"Well, I am."

"That's not how it works, Joseph. You don't have a choice. I know all your dirty little secrets."

He stood with his back to me for a few seconds, then turned around again. "Are you going to call the cops?"

I thought about it. "No. Not yet anyway, but I need to know, what happened when she went to Bayfield? What did she want from you?"

Nothing in the past ten minutes prepared me for his response. Tears came to his eyes, and he looked down at the ground, blinking them back. When he raised his head, all the bravado was gone. He was just an aging playboy with nothing left to hide behind.

He shrugged and shook his head. "She was angry, just like you. She felt hurt and betrayed." He sighed. "I could deal with that. What I couldn't handle was that she was so very sad." His voice broke.

I would not cry. I *would not* cry. No matter where this took me, I would not cry in front of him. "What was she sad about?"

"That we were never really a family and I'd run out on you, that you grew up without real parents. She was sad that she couldn't trust me, that she'd lost her childhood because of me—that both of you did."

I blew air out of my lungs. "Did you ever think about us? Did you miss us at all?" My voice was so low I wasn't sure he heard me.

He looked at me for a long time, and then he nodded. That's all I got after twenty-two years—silence and the nod of his head.

I was done. I had nowhere left to go with him and started to turn toward Edman's car, when the Jeep Cherokee from the house in Bayfield flew down the road and skidded to a stop behind Joseph. Carly and Brenda jumped out, and Fred and Edman were by my side in seconds.

Carly was in my face before any of the men could intercept her. "You! I told you before to leave us alone. Haven't you caused enough trouble? Are you going to take him off to jail now? What good would that do anyone?"

Joseph reached for her arm, trying to pull her back, but she broke free. Edman tried to step in front of me, but I moved in toward her before he could block me.

"What have *I* done?" I screamed at her. "You and your daughter almost killed me, and for all I know you murdered my sister."

Carly's eyes got wide. "I didn't murder anyone."

"We are in hiding because of you," Brenda yelled.

I turned toward her. "You're in hiding because you attacked me."

Out of the corner of my eye, I saw Edman move away from the group and walk over to the Jeep. Fred stepped in next to me to take his place. Something was going on, and I tried to keep the shouting match going.

"*You're* the ones the cops are looking for, not Joseph," I yelled back at her.

Brenda stopped. "What? Who's Joseph?"

I pointed toward him. "My father."

She turned to look at him. "Joseph? What's she talking about?"

Joseph and Carly looked at each other. "We'll talk about it later," he finally said to Brenda. So, they hadn't told her Joseph's story.

Edman was back at his car. "Looks like you and your new family have a lot to talk about," I said to my father. "And for the record, the Bayfield Sheriff's Department is all over the lake home. You might want to stay put for a while."

"Who *is* she?" Brenda asked.

I walked up to Carly. "If you were trying to get me out of the way the other night, you should probably know that little Brenda is not eligible for the trust."

She turned to my father. "Andy, what's she talking about? What trust?"

So, Brenda didn't know about my father's former life, and Carly didn't know about the trust. The legacy of secrets had spread to encompass yet another family. I grabbed Fred's arm, and we started walking toward Edman. My father reached out and took my hand. When I turned, there were tears in his eyes again. "I am sorry, Elizabeth. You deserved better."

I turned back toward Edman and kept walking. I didn't want my father to see me cry. I didn't want him to think that I still cared.

We were halfway back to Two Harbors before anyone

spoke. Fred turned around in the front seat to face me. "You okay, Lizzie?"

I looked out the window. "I will be. At least now I know."

Edman glanced at me in the rearview mirror. "The status quo, kid. Ain't nothing to mess with if you don't have the guts for it."

I met his gaze in the mirror. "So I'm learning."

"You going to call the cops?" he asked.

I knew I should, but I wasn't ready for that yet. There were still too many missing pieces in the puzzle of what had happened to Meredith, and if everyone was in jail, I might not ever know. "Not yet."

He fished in the front pocket of his shirt and took out a slip of paper, handing it to me over his shoulder.

"What's this?"

"Just a little insurance," he said, his eyes back on the road. "I threw a disposable cell phone in the back of the Jeep. That's the number. You can track its location. If the girls ever get too close to you again, call the cops."

TWENTY-THREE

THE RIDE BACK to St. Paul on I-35 was getting old. I hated the hours that stretched before me and the emotions I had to deal with in the meantime. Fred drove and tried to keep things light, but I wasn't a very good audience, and he finally gave up.

A little after eight, we pulled up in front of his townhouse.

"What's next?" he asked.

I was tired—bone-tired—all I wanted to do was sleep. Seeing my father had been harder than I'd expected it to be.

"I guess we need to see Dana tomorrow and see if she's willing to help us get into that safety deposit box—wherever the hell it is."

He reached out and pushed the hair back off my face. "Are you okay, Lizzie?"

I took his hand and held on tight. "I will be. I really will be, but not right now. Right now, I just need to go home and lock my door and cry."

"Okay. I get it. Call me if you want to talk."

I checked my phone before I drove away. There were three missed calls, a voicemail from Tom, and a text from Rachel.

I called Tom, catching him at the office, and was greeted by a very tired investigator.

"Everything okay?" I asked when I heard his voice.

"Rough day. Got called in last night for a doozy of a case and have been going nonstop since then. How was your day?"

"Fred and I took a drive up the North Shore and had lunch in Two Harbors." All of which was true, I rationalized.

"Sounds nice. You home now?"

"Just dropped Fred off. I'm on my way."

"Sleep well. I'll talk to you tomorrow."

I made it home, undressed, put on a T-shirt and lay down on my bed. On the nightstand was the photo album I'd taken from Meredith's the day after her murder, the one I had tucked under my arm when Tom caught me coming out of her house that morning. I laid it on the bed, thumbing through the pages, feeling my heart break all over again every time I looked into her face.

I fell asleep hugging it to my chest, with the photo album open to the pictures of Meredith, Fred, and me at ValleyFair.

I PICKED FRED up at eight the next morning, and we headed out to Meredith's, hoping Dana would be there with Scott. I'd hesitated calling and telling her we were coming—she always seemed so skittish, and I didn't want to give her a chance to run again.

Fred knocked on the door to the guesthouse, and Scott opened it immediately.

"Is Dana here?" I asked Scott.

He moved to one side. "Yeah, come on in."

Scott had on a faded pair of jeans and a white T-shirt, but no shoes. Dana was sitting at the small kitchen table, wearing a long blue T-shirt that hit about mid-thigh, her legs bare, hair still tousled from the night before.

She looked at us, her expression unreadable.

Scott went to get us coffee, and I moved toward Dana. "We need your help," I said.

She looked suspicious. "What kind of help?"

"We need you to be Meredith for a little while."

The suspicion turned to curiosity. Fred sat down next to her and explained what we needed and what our plan was.

"Oh my God. I would so do that."

She was a little too eager to help, and I wondered why. "You do understand that we could all end up in jail if we get caught." I didn't know if that was true, but she needed to know the worst that could happen.

She shrugged and smiled. "No prob."

Scott was more cautious. "You sure, Dane?"

"I want to help," she said. "I've done enough to screw up people's lives. If I could do something to help, then I really want to try."

Scott turned to me. "Don't you have to sign for those things?"

Fred looked at him. "Yeah, I have a couple of things with Meredith's signature, and maybe Dana could practice on them."

She laughed. "My specialty. I knew my life of crime would pay off someday." She reached out her hand, and Fred gave her the papers. "Oh, this should be easy."

She grabbed a pen and some paper from the kitchen counter and got to work trying to duplicate Meredith's signature. Half an hour later, she handed me her practice sheet, pleased with her accomplishment. I have to say, she was good. I knew my sister's handwriting intimately, and even I would have sworn that the signatures I was looking at came from Meredith. Which made me wonder: Was this the first time Dana had copied my sister's signature?

"What now?" she asked.

"You and I need to go next door and find something of Meredith's for you to wear to the bank, and I'll help you with your makeup so you do it the same way she did."

An hour later, I walked back into Scott's cottage with a striking younger version of my sister trailing behind me.

"Holy shit," Fred said when he saw her.

I'd found Meredith's driver's license and a picture ID from work, so Dana had verification of her identity. And we decided to have her wear sunglasses and a baseball cap. The makeup helped to hide some of her youthfulness, but anything that drew attention away from her face was an added bonus.

Dana went back to the kitchen table and practiced the signature a few more times.

"Do you really think this is going to work?" Scott asked.

"It's the only chance we have," Fred said.

What he didn't say was that we could also be on a wild goose chase, risking jail time for a safety deposit box that had nothing of importance in it.

Now we had to decide where to start. Meredith's accounts were at U.S. Bank in St. Paul, a small credit union in West St. Paul not far from Edman's office, and a local bank in the town of Lake Elmo. U.S. Bank, as Fred had said, probably had more security measures in place, so we decided to leave them for last—hopefully, we wouldn't have to go that route at all. The bank in Lake Elmo was small and might even have known Meredith on sight if she was a regular, so that was a gamble.

We decided to start with the credit union, hoping no one there knew my sister, and if they did, they wouldn't connect her with the recent images of her on the news.

Fred drove, with me in the front seat and Scott and Dana in the back. Dana and Fred were psyched, like we were pulling off the biggest bank heist since John Dillinger. Scott was apprehensive as to where we might all end up spending the night if we got caught.

Fred pulled into the small parking lot off South Robert Street and turned off the ignition. Suddenly there was silence in the car when we realized this was it.

"What's our plan?" Dana asked.

I turned around in the seat to face her. "You and I will go in together. After you sign in, I'll go with you to the room where you'll open the box."

She seemed a little deflated that it sounded so mundane.

"What if this isn't the right place?" Scott asked. "Isn't it going to look suspicious that someone doesn't even know where their safety deposit box is?"

I looked at him. "This is a gamble no matter where we start."

There were only about six or seven other customers in the credit union. I followed Dana as she walked over to the desk of one of the personal bankers, a young man named Josh Carlson, according to his nameplate.

Dana flashed a smile. Good move. It got Josh's attention, and from the look on his face, I'm pretty sure he would have handed her the keys to the vault, had she asked.

"I need to get into my safety deposit box," she said, still smiling.

"Oh." He sounded disappointed. "You'll have to talk to Laura, over there at the last desk."

"Thanks." The smile never wavered; unfortunately, Josh's hopes had.

We walked over to Laura's desk in the far corner of the large open room. She was about fifty and matronly. Again, Dana turned on the charm.

"Hi. I need to get into my safety deposit box, but—well I can't believe I did this—but I can't remember the box number," she told Laura. "My boyfriend filed all our important papers *somewhere*, and I can't find them. He's out of town and I can't reach him right now."

Laura smiled back, some motherly instinct kicking in. "I'd be happy to help you. I need to see some ID, and you'll need to sign in."

Dana pulled out Meredith's driver's license. I wanted to walk away or pretend I didn't know her. I tried to keep my face expressionless, but my stomach was doing back flips. Drinking and sex were my forte—I wasn't meant for a life of crime.

Laura put her glasses on and read the name, then looked at Dana, who was still smiling her million-dollar smile. I was waiting for Laura to say, *"This isn't you."*

"Don't you just hate driver's license photos?" Dana asked and giggled.

"They're the worst," Laura agreed.

Oh fuck! I wanted to get this over with, but Dana was playing it to the hilt.

Laura took the license and typed the name into the computer. *This is it,* I thought. *The jig is up.* She furrowed her brow. I was sure Meredith didn't have a safety deposit box here, and Laura would soon be on the phone with security.

Then she smiled. "Oh yes, here it is. Box one-three-four-four-two. Do you have your key with you?" she asked as she turned and rifled through a small index card file box behind her.

I don't know if Laura heard the breath whoosh out of me.

Dana handed her the key, and Laura handed Dana a signature card. Dana didn't even bat an eye as she forged her mother's name and handed it back to Laura for comparison to the signature they had on file.

Then we were on our way, straight through the middle of the bank and down the wide central staircase to the basement and a locked room. We followed Laura into the room, which had safety deposit boxes covering three walls, where she used Dana's key and the bank key to open the box. She slid it out of its slot, carried it to the room next door, and placed it on a high table, then stepped out of the room.

"This is fun," Dana whispered when we were alone.

"Uh-huh. Don't get any ideas. Once we walk out of here, you're on the straight and narrow."

There wasn't even time to register what I was doing— going through Meredith's treasured things—as I opened the top of the box to look inside. Right on top was a manila envelope the size of copy paper. I took it and put it in my bag, along with Meredith's passport and birth certificate. There was a matching manila envelope under the first, with my name on it. I put it in my bag too, wondering why Meredith had marked it specifically for me.

At the bottom of the metal box were our mother's engagement and wedding rings and a small necklace case. Dana looked at the rings, then opened the case. There was an emerald and pearl necklace with matching earrings that had also belonged to my mother—exquisite, expensive jewelry, but not my taste. A little too gaudy for me, but I remembered my mother sitting at her dressing table, wearing them, looking stunning as she got ready to go out for the night.

Dana picked up one of the earrings and held it in her hand. "These are beautiful." She touched it gently as if it might dissolve before her eyes.

"Do you want them?" I asked.

She looked at me, her eyes wide and disbelieving. "Are you serious?"

"Yes. You should have them. They belonged to your grandmother, and I think Meredith would want you to have them."

Tears filled her eyes as she looked down at her hand. "I've never had anything like this." She put the sparkling earring back in its case. "No, you keep them."

I closed the case and handed it to her. "Dana, I want you to have them. Meredith was the oldest daughter and inherited them when our mother died. You are now the oldest daughter of the next generation, and they should be yours."

She moved so quickly I didn't see it coming—her arms went around my neck in a death-grip hug. "Thank you," she said into my shoulder, then stepped away and wiped her eyes with the back of her hand.

There was a stack of loose papers in the bottom of the box, secured with a paper clip. I put those in my bag. The box was empty and we closed it up. Dana carried it out to Laura, who locked it securely back in the wall with the others that held the secrets of other people's lives.

It wasn't until we were back in the car that I let the tension slide out of my neck and shoulders.

Fred looked at me. "Jackpot," I said, and he smiled.

We dropped Scott and Dana back at the lake. Dana leaned in through the passenger window and kissed me

on the cheek. "Thank you," she said. "Not just for the necklace and earrings, but for letting me help."

FRED AND I sat at my kitchen table. I took everything out of
my bag that I'd confiscated from Meredith's safety deposit
box, except for the envelope with my name on it.

"You think there's anything here?" he asked.

"We'll soon find out."

I put her passport and birth certificate to the side and removed the paper clip from the stack of papers, handing half
to Fred. Then I started looking through the ones I had in
my hand. Five slips of paper with only a name, address, and
phone number, and what I assumed were the date of birth for
these people—hardly worth storing in a safety deposit box.

"What have you got?" I asked Fred. We traded papers.
They were the same as mine, just different names, dates,
and numbers.

"What's that all about?" he asked.

"I don't know. It's weird."

"You know any of these people?" he asked.

"Some of the last names look familiar, but not really.
What about you?"

He shook his head, and went through each slip of paper
again, then handed them to me. "Notice anything similar
about them?"

I looked. "No. What do you see?"

"They're all female."

"So?"

He shrugged. "Just looking for a pattern, but that's all
I've got."

"I don't know why she'd lock these up at the bank. I
wonder if they were clients of hers."

"Why keep it in such an inconvenient place? She'd have all that information at work."

True. So, what was it about these names that was important to Meredith?

I went through the slips of paper again. "I know some Cochrans from church. Meredith went to school with Jane Cochran—she was Jane Goodhue back then—but I don't know an Amanda."

Fred took the paper from me. "Maybe their daughter? None of these girls are very old."

Fred reached for the unmarked manila envelope and started to undo the clasp, when Tom said from the doorway, "Do you know the penalty for tampering with police evidence?"

Fred looked at Tom, then at me, and put the envelope back down on the table. "Hi, Tom. I didn't hear you come in."

Tom looked at me. "I just made a trip to the credit union where your sister has an account, with a court order for all the contents of her safety deposit box. And guess what? It was empty." His look was dark. "Elizabeth, do you want to tell me what the hell is going on?"

"What makes you think I was involved?"

"Well, for starters, the security footage was pretty clear." He looked at the table, "Is that everything that was in the box?"

"There was some jewelry that belonged to my mother. I gave some of it to Dana."

He walked over to the table, scooped up the loose pieces of paper and the manila envelope Fred had just put down, along with Meredith's birth certificate and passport. "And this is all you have?" he asked, looking at me.

I nodded.

He stared at me for a long time, then turned and walked through the living room and out the front door.

Fred finally exhaled. "Is that really everything that was in the box, Lizzie?"

"Most of it."

"He's gonna be so pissed when he finds out you lied."

"Won't be the first time."

HALF AN HOUR LATER, Charlie pulled in next to the curb in front of my building in a big black GMC Envoy. Fred saw him from the living room window and left.

I watched as my cousin climbed into the passenger seat of the SUV and put his hand on the back of the Charlie's neck. Whatever they had going on between them, I hoped it would go on forever. I wanted Fred to be happy. I wanted *someone* to be happy, and Fred deserved it as much as anyone.

They were barely halfway down the block when I had an idea. I looked at the clock, grabbed my keys and purse, and stepped out into the heat.

Meredith and I had both attended St. Bartholomew's High School: nuns, uniforms, corporal punishment, and guilt—the whole nine yards. One of the drudgeries of parochial education was that we started school three weeks before our friends who went to public school. St. Bart's should just be getting out for the day. I had a hunch and was hoping it would pay off better than my past hunches that seemed to lead nowhere.

The stay-at-home moms queued up in their hybrids down the street for a block and a half. I went around the back, parked behind the school, and loped across the soccer field as the final bell rang. I made it to the front of the building just as a gaggle of adolescents burst through the door. It seemed like the stream of teenagers would never end.

Finally, I spotted a girl lagging behind the others, her backpack clutched to her chest, her head down, straight brown hair hiding her face. She walked down the steps and moved slowly toward the street.

"Amanda," I called when she was about fifteen feet away from me.

Her head snapped up, and she looked around.

I moved toward her, smiling. She looked so timid I didn't want to spook her.

Her body tensed as I moved closer. "Who are you?"

I stopped a few feet away, giving her a wide circle of personal space. "I'm Liz McCallister. I think you knew my sister, Meredith."

She didn't say a word. She was probably about fifteen, a potentially pretty girl with nice features and big blue eyes, but she was all closed in. Another moody teenager? Or a kid with serious psychological problems? I didn't know enough about children to even guess.

I took another step toward her. "You knew Meredith, didn't you?"

She nodded. "Sorry about what happened," she said and ducked her head again.

I took another step. "Thank you."

She glanced at me sideways, her eyes scanning the street. "What are you doing here? My mother's picking me up soon."

"I know your mother. She went to school with Meredith."

"I know."

I looked out at the street, watching for Jane Cochran to

drive up. I wanted a few minutes alone with Amanda before her mother appeared, and I had to talk fast. "The reason I'm here"—I moved closer so that I didn't have to talk above the commotion that surrounded us—"is that I found your name in some of Meredith's things."

There was a sharp intake of breath. "What did she say about me?"

"Nothing. Nothing at all. It was just your name, and I recognized it from church, and I wondered why she would have kept it in such a secret place."

The girl was scanning the street again, probably the first time in the history of the world that a teenager ever wanted her parents to show up. I saw a familiar car. David was behind the wheel, looking at me, his forehead scrunched, wondering what on earth I was doing at the high school. I waved and turned away. If he asked—if anyone asked—what would I say?

"Amanda?" I tried again.

"What?"

"Did you and Meredith ever get together to talk?"

"My mother should be here soon."

"I won't keep you when she shows up. It's just that—did you and Meredith ever get together to talk?"

"Sometimes."

"What did the two of you talk about."

"I don't know. Just stuff. There's my mother. I have to go."

She walked away faster than I thought she could move.

I watched her climb into the passenger seat of a mint-green minivan. Jane saw me and waved. I waved back. I didn't know Jane well—she was six years older than me—

but what I knew of her was grating. She was a favorite of the nuns, polite, diligent, serious, and obsequious.

They drove away, Amanda staring at the dashboard.

Well, that was a bust. I went home, walked into my living room, and saw Rachel's car pull into the spot where Charlie had waited for Fred.

I wasn't in the mood for company, but my car was sitting out front now, so Rachel would guess that I was probably home, and I couldn't think of a kind way to tell my aunt that now was not a good time. She knocked on my door.

"I was hoping you'd be home," she said as she moved past me in the front hall, brushing my cheek with a kiss. "It's so dang hot out there. I need something cold to drink."

She settled herself on the couch, and I went to get us both a couple of glasses of iced tea.

I handed one to her. She took a long sip. "This would be better if it had a little kick to it," she said.

"Lemon?"

She smiled. "That's not what I had in mind."

I hadn't even physically touched the bottle of vodka I had since the day Fred had asked me not to. I knew it was there, but I was afraid to get too close to it, as if it had a power stronger than my will. I ignored her inference. "What brings you by, Rachel?"

"Isn't seeing you enough?"

"I can't even remember the last time you were here. I'm surprised you remembered the address."

She smiled again. "Fair enough. I haven't stopped thinking about your father since you told me he was alive. I don't even know what I feel. After the shock wore off, I went through this whole denial thing, thinking you must be breaking under all the stress." She stopped and looked down at her glass, a look on her face I couldn't even read.

"And now?"

She shrugged. "It took a while to get past that denial. I moved into this empty place. I don't know how to describe it, almost like I couldn't even conjure up an emotion."

She paused again and I waited.

She took a breath. "I've been relieved, happy, sad, and now I think I'm just plain angry. I don't know how he could have done this to us. How he could have done this to you two girls. I want to punch him in the stomach. As hard as I can. But I want to see him too. I want to see him for myself. I want to know that he's okay. Does this make any sense? I know I'm rambling."

I moved over next to her on the couch. "It all makes sense. Your emotions, that is. Not what he did to us."

She took my hand. "Tell me how this all went down. How did Meredith find him? How did you?"

So I told her about Edman, that Meredith had sent him to Bayfield to find Joseph, about the day Edman and I went to the family lake home and saw my father. The hurt and anger I'd felt that day. And about the trip Fred and I had just made up north to Brimson.

"You talked to him?"

I nodded.

"What did he have to say for himself?"

"You were right when you said he married Ruth for her money, but when that started to run out, he needed another plan."

It took about two beats for her to get it. "Ruth knew. She was in on it."

"Yes."

"Are you sure?"

"I found the insurance policy in Ruth's office, along with correspondence between the two of them over the past twenty years, and Joseph confirmed it: they planned it together."

"Unbelievable. Part of me wants to see him suffer for what he did to all of us, but part of me keeps saying that I wasn't any better."

"What does that mean?"

She shrugged. "Who am I to judge? Your father did the unthinkable, leaving you girls, but was I any better as a parent just because I stayed? Fred needed a mother, and look what he got…me." A tear ran down her cheek.

I took her chin and turned her face so that she had to look at me. "But you did stay. You never abandoned him. You were there for every part of his childhood, and for whatever mistakes you made, you loved him."

She nodded but didn't look convinced.

"And look at him, Rachel. Fred's a great guy."

"Yes, he is, but he's having a hard time growing up, just like I did."

"Did you ever talk to him about it?"

"About what?"

"About why you're the way you are and all the things you wish you'd done differently?"

"I don't think that's a conversation Fred would want to have with me."

"Or maybe he would. Maybe it's what he needs to hear from you. If there's one thing we all should have learned from Meredith's death, it's that life is short, and the silence beyond the grave is deafening." My voice started to crack. "Our whole family is buried in secrets, Rachel. It's time to break the curse. If we don't say what we need to say to each other now, we may never get another chance."

She pulled me to her and held me tightly. "I know," she said into my hair. "I know."

Someone knocked at the door, and I reluctantly got up. Edman was standing on the front stoop, sweaty and tired looking.

I stepped to the side. "Come on in."

He moved into the living room, wiping his forehead with the back of his hand; then he noticed Rachel. "Sorry. I didn't know you had company."

"This is my aunt Rachel," I said. "Fred's mother. Rachel, this is Maynard Edman, the private investigator I told you about."

Rachel slipped on her cocktail-party smile, stood up, and crossed the few feet to Edman, holding out her hand. I wasn't sure if he was supposed to kiss her hand or shake it. He decided to shake it.

By the time I got back from the kitchen with a cold drink for Edman, there was a whole lot of uncomfortable flirting going on, middle-aged hormones pinging off the walls like a metro cell tower during rush hour. Well, I seemed to be the only one who was uncomfortable—they were both very at ease.

I interrupted Rachel mid-throaty laugh. "Was there something you needed to see me about?" I asked Edman.

He looked over at me. "What? Oh yeah. I got word this morning that your father was headed back to Bayfield."

"Why?"

"Don't know. He showed up at the lake home early this morning."

"Isn't that dangerous for him with the police on alert?"

I got the one-sided smile. "Well, I told you before, honey, your dad's kind of a dumbass and arrogant as hell. Besides, he's not the one who assaulted you, so technically he's not the one they're looking for. Although he's probably a person of interest in your sister's murder."

"So, Brenda and Carly weren't with him?"

"Nope. They're still in Brimson, but probably not for long. My guess is he's trying to get some things together for them to hit the road."

He watched me for a while. "What?" I asked.

"Just wanted to make sure you were okay and tell you to be very careful, not to do anything stupid. As of an hour ago, the two women were still in Brimson, but that doesn't mean they'll stay there."

"So, you think they might come after me again?"

"It's a possibility. I also wanted to give you this." He reached behind him into the waistband of his jeans and handed me a Glock 19. "You know how to shoot?"

I nodded.

"She's a great shot," Rachel said.

"I don't know if I want that," I told Edman. Even though I knew how to shoot very well, I didn't like the idea of concealed weapons.

"You'll want it, kid, if you get yourself into some kind of mess."

Reluctantly, I took the gun and put it in my bag.

"You might not ever have to use it," Edman said. "But it's a hell of a lot better to be prepared than to get backed into a corner with no way out. And sometimes it's a great equalizer."

Philosophy from Edman. That's what my life had become.

TWENTY-FOUR

RACHEL AND EDMAN left about the same time. I looked out the window to see Rachel make a U-turn on the narrow residential street and follow Edman past my house. It wouldn't surprise me if the heavy-duty flirting they'd started in my living room continued someplace else.

There seemed too many threads to this mystery about my sister, and I couldn't follow them all. I needed to talk it through with someone more detached than Fred or Edman, and the first person who came to mind was Lee.

I dialed her office and she picked up on the third ring.

"You're there late," I said.

"Some days I feel like I live here. What's up?"

"I need to see you. Can I swing by?"

A brief pause. I was getting used to the pauses that always followed my questions, but they made me feel like I was intruding. "Sure," she said, "I'm alone here, no clients tonight, just paperwork."

"Thanks." We hung up, and I headed for the door.

I took as many side streets as I could, to avoid rush-hour traffic on the freeway, and made it to her office in a little under forty minutes.

The reception area was vacant, and I pushed open the door to Lee's private office, where she was seated at her round table in the corner, a laptop and files spread out in front of her.

"I was just about to order dinner from the Chinese place in the lobby. You want something?"

"Sure. Pork egg foo young and a couple of egg rolls."

"You got it." She picked up her cell phone and called in the order. When she was finished, she looked at me. "So, what is it you need, Liz?"

I took a seat across from her at the round table. "It seems to me that everything that happened to Meredith in the past six or eight months was precipitated by Dana showing up."

Lee nodded. "I guess I never put it that succinctly, but now that you say it, I have to agree. That's when she started coming to see me."

"Okay, let's assume that's what started all this. Why? Why would Dana coming into her life send her into such turmoil? I get that she had the whole guilt-shame thing going on—whether it was Ruth or our Catholic upbringing, it doesn't matter—but she was a grown woman with a life of her own, and a trained social worker, so why would Dana throw her into a tailspin? It doesn't make sense to me."

Lee bit her lip and I couldn't tell if she was thinking or trying to hold something back. We sat in silence for several minutes. Finally, I couldn't take it any longer. "What?" I asked her.

"I don't know. I was just trying to piece together the sequence of events in my head."

"Tell me how you see it."

She spread her hands on the table. "Okay, Dana shows up. Meredith, for whatever reason is struggling with that part of her life. She starts coming to see me. I think we're starting to make some headway, but then Meredith wants to know more about Dana. That's when she went through Ruth's office at the house, looking for adoption papers or the birth certificate, and came across whatever she discovered about your father. That was when she really started to spiral out of control, when she found out that your father was still alive."

I looked at Lee. It had been shocking to find out that Joseph was alive, and like Rachel, I'd run the gamut of emotions, but why would that have had such an impact on Meredith? Our father was never really one we could count on, so why was the fact that he deceived us such a turning point? I asked Lee.

"I wish I knew what to tell you, Liz. You're looking to me for answers that I don't think I have."

I nodded. "Okay, so Meredith finds out that Joseph is alive and that Ruth had been supporting him all these years."

Lee held up her hand. "I didn't know that. When Meredith told me he was alive, I guess I never even thought about how he might be supporting himself."

"Ruth and Joseph planned it together for the insurance money."

"And Meredith knew this?"

"I'm pretty sure she did."

"Maybe that was another blow to her gut. Not only did your father run out on you, but the only parent you ever knew was a part of it. So how are you doing with all of this?" she asked, looking me in the eye.

"Maybe if I hadn't just lost my sister, the rest of this would be harder to deal with, but Meredith's death overshadows everything else right now."

The food came. Lee paid for it and moved files off the table so we could eat.

She was doing the chopsticks thing that I always find amusing and annoying.

One foot tucked underneath her on the chair, she speared into some chow mein. "So, Meredith knew about Ruth at some point. Go on."

"You probably know as much as I do. Meredith finds out about Joseph and Ruth and hires the private investigator who goes to Bayfield and finds our father, living there with a whole new family."

"And shortly after that, Meredith went to Bayfield and confronted your father. I wonder how that went?"

I didn't want to get into my conversation with Joseph. Maybe I wasn't as okay about everything as I wanted to believe. "The night Meredith went through Ruth's office they had a terrible fight, and Meredith never went back to the house."

"Understandable."

"The day before Meredith was killed, she called John out to her home and wanted him to help her with something that had to do with my father. John refused, and the two of them got into an argument." I looked at Lee.

"And what does all this tell you?"

"Not a damn thing."

We finished eating and Lee cleared the table, putting the leftovers in a mini fridge she had in the corner.

"Meredith never told you who Dana's father was?" I watched her face, and there was just the slightest tightening of her jaw.

"No, she never did."

"Who did you suspect?"

She shook her head. "I won't play that game. Any guess I'd make would be just that—a guess—and the repercussions if I guessed wrong could be very great."

"I wonder how Dana ended up in Minnesota when she was born in Illinois."

"I do know that," she said. "Meredith found out that Ruth and David knew Dana's adoptive parents somehow, and they arranged for Dana to be placed here."

I looked at her. That didn't sound like the Ruth I'd talked to the other night, but maybe David had been more forgiving of Meredith's indiscretion.

"So, what do you do now, Liz?" she asked.

"Keep going."

"Please be careful."

I stood up and moved toward the door, then turned to face her. "The first time I came here, you said that our biggest strengths can become our weaknesses if we're not careful."

She nodded.

"What was Meredith's greatest strength?"

She smiled. "You. You were her greatest strength. You were what kept her going. She loved you, Liz." Lee paused. "My guess is that very early on, the two of you must have instinctively known that the grown-ups in your life were unreliable, so you learned to rely on each other. Well, you relied on Meredith and she became your surrogate parent—your protector."

I met Lee's eyes. "And that became her greatest weakness?"

"I think it did." She tried to look kind, but it did nothing to soften the realization of what she was saying—that I was also Meredith's greatest liability.

I sat in my car in the parking lot for the longest time.

There was nothing cryptic in Lee's words tonight. Part of me felt as if I'd been the one who pulled the trigger on Meredith, which made me wonder if I had somehow played a role in her murder. None of that made sense, but emotions don't deal in logic—they have a life cycle all their own.

I put the car in gear and headed out to I didn't know where. I just drove, some primitive instinct trying to outrun all the demons that were chasing me.

I finally ended up at home about twenty minutes before Tom called. His voice sounded weary.

"You okay?" I asked.

"Exhausted."

"You still mad at me?"

"I should be. Maybe tomorrow. Right now, I don't have the energy for it."

"Did you find out anything from the stuff that was in Meredith's safety deposit box?"

"We're running down the names on those slips of paper that you had."

"And?"

"And I shouldn't be telling you this, but I'm too tired to care right now. We don't have any real leads. They were all girls who went to St. Bart's."

I wondered if Meredith had started some support group at the school, and Amanda was part of the group. "That's it?"

"That's it. We'll start interviewing them tomorrow, but I think it's a dead end."

"What was in the manila envelope?"

"You're taking advantage of a beaten man, you know."

"Uh-huh. So, the manila envelope?"

"Her will and a life insurance policy." He laughed. "All

your nefarious deeds for nothing. Things have finally quieted down around here, and I think I'm going to head for home. I'll call you tomorrow."

I SAT ON the couch, knowing something very important had been revealed to me in the past ten days, but I didn't have a clue what it was. The Meredith in my dreams had been talking to me—or more likely—the *me* in my dreams had been talking to me, but what was I saying? Did I know something that I didn't know I knew? Or was my subconscious simply trying to process the murder of my sister?

I grabbed my car keys and my bag and headed for the house on Summit Avenue.

Tuesday night, the house would be empty. David would drop Ruth off for bridge with the ladies, then head to his Church Council meeting. John and Martha had bowling league.

I pulled into the circular drive and sat staring at the house. For some reason, just like I usually referred to my father as Joseph, I usually called this place where I grew up "the house on Summit Avenue," or "Ruth's house." Never *home*. I'm sure Lee would have some deep psychological theory about that, but for me, it just didn't feel like home. I wondered if it ever had.

I unlocked the front door and stood in the foyer, as I had the day I'd come to tell Ruth about Meredith's murder. The ticking of the grandfather clock at the foot of the stairs filled the silence.

I didn't know what I was seeking here, whether it was clues or solace or some elusive refuge that I'd longed for most of my life. I wandered into Ruth's sun porch, touching the furniture, hoping I could feel a mother's love. I couldn't. It wasn't there. I don't think it ever had been.

I stood in the doorway to the kitchen, thinking how empty it felt without John and Martha, remembering sitting at that table decorating Christmas cookies and laughing. Feeling safe. Feeling loved. Had that even been real? I didn't know anymore.

The Meredith from my dreams—or my own psyche— led me up the stairs. I stopped by her bedroom door, my hand on the knob, but I couldn't move beyond that. I didn't want to see her empty room.

I headed for the attic and up the wooden stairs, pulling the strings to the overhead lights as I made my way to the corner room where my sister had found sanctuary, where the Meredith in my dreams seemed to live these days. I walked in and curled up on the mattress where she'd sat for so many hours in solitude.

"What's here?" I asked. "What did you find here?"

I lay there in the hot, dusty attic, waiting—waiting for her to tell me. Waiting for me to understand what she wanted me to know.

Twenty minutes later, I sat up and ran my hand over the stained mattress. Nothing had come to me and I felt a little foolish thinking that it would.

I went back down the stairs and into my old bedroom where nothing had changed in twenty years. Had there ever been any happiness in this house? The door that adjoined my room to Meredith's was ajar. I walked over, took a deep breath and this time I opened it.

Ruth must have been clearing things out, her way of dealing with the finality of death. The bed had been stripped. Meredith's possessions—her childhood—sitting in boxes on the floor and on the window seat. Tears ran down my cheeks. My sister's room was gone. My sister was gone. I walked over to the bed, curled up on the bare mattress, and cried.

The ache in my heart overwhelmed me, and I let the tears come. When I finished crying, when there was nothing left, I sat up and turned on the light on the nightstand, looking around the room for what I knew was the last time.

I caressed the mattress, where my sister had let me spend so many nights when I was scared, when she'd saved me from the monsters that came out of the dark. The mattress was old and soiled and there was a small dip in the side where Meredith used to sleep.

I needed to be here again. In this house. In this room. But I knew now, it was time to leave. Maybe forever. I knew I was letting go of this part of my life, and it made me sad.

In the front hall, I stood again, looking around in the darkness one last time, when all of a sudden, my dreams made sense. It wasn't Meredith talking to me in my dreams; it was me, telling me what I'd always known but could never articulate.

It was clear and it was frightening.

I stepped outside, locking the house behind me. Just then David pulled into the driveway, parking his car behind mine. I felt as if I couldn't breathe.

Ruth got out first, then David. I looked at them and moved toward my car. John's car turned off Summit Avenue and came to a stop behind David's. He and Martha got out.

I froze. I looked at them and didn't know what to do.

Ruth moved toward me, her face unreadable. "Elizabeth," she said, "was there something you needed?"

My eyes traveled from Ruth to David, to John and Martha. I shook my head and pulled on my car door. My hand was sweaty and slipped. My breath was jagged, and I wanted to cry. I wanted to run.

John walked over, put one hand on my back and with the other hand reached around in front of me and opened the car door.

I looked up at him. He bent in close to my ear and said, "Are you okay?"

"I have to go."

In my rearview mirror, I could see them all standing in the driveway, watching me as I turned left and sped down the street, past houses that were as familiar as my own skin. I made it to the Lutheran church two blocks away, drove into the middle of the parking lot, opened my door, leaned out, and threw up.

TWENTY-FIVE

THE CHURCH PARKING lot was deserted. I put my head against the steering wheel, trying to catch my breath. Trying to think. Fifteen minutes later, I fumbled in my bag for my cell phone and called Edman.

"I need a lawyer," I said when he answered.

There was silence. Finally, "You have a lawyer."

"I want you to find me a lawyer—the kind you use when you need to get things done."

"Tell me what you need."

I told him.

He let out a long breath. "Oh hell. You sure?"

"Yes."

"When?"

"As soon as possible."

"It might take a little while to set it up. I'll call you when we're ready to roll."

There was another burst of silence. "You still there?" I asked.

"Uh, yeah. Just thinking."

"About what?"

"You. Are you okay, kid?"

"I don't know."

I dropped my cell phone back in my bag and saw the envelope with my name on it from Meredith's safety deposit box, the one item I hadn't given to Tom.

I undid the metal clasp and pulled the few pages out of the envelope from an independent medical laboratory in Minneapolis. So, this was what Meredith had bequeathed to me, and now I was the one who had to do what she hadn't been able to.

Somehow, I made it home, but I don't remember how I got there. What I do remember is sitting in the kitchen until two in the morning, looking at the cabinet over the sink. At one point, I got up, walked over to the sink and opened the cabinet door. The bottle stared down at me. I didn't think I was strong enough for any of this. I didn't know if this new-found sobriety was even real. Maybe, it was an illusion, like everything else in my life.

Where was Fred when I needed him?

I finally went upstairs and crawled into bed. I needed to sleep, to be ready for what was to come.

I WAS UP early the next morning, checking my laptop—tracing the throw-away phone that Edman had tossed in the back of Carly's Jeep Cherokee, to see where she was today. What a surprise—she'd ended up in Bayfield.

By eight thirty I was on the road headed north. I needed to see Joseph one last time—I needed to see my father. With Carly now in Bayfield too, I was pretty sure he'd still be at the lake home, but I didn't call to find out. A surprise visit wouldn't give him the chance to run.

I made the four-hour drive in three and parked my car on the dirt logging road behind the house, where Edman had parked the day we visited up here. The path through the woods and the weeds was brittle with heat as I trudged to the hill overlooking the compound below.

Joseph's truck was parked in the driveway, Carly's Jeep sitting twenty feet away. My father came into view, carrying two large suitcases, and put them in the back of the truck, then headed into the house again. Moments later, he came out carrying a large box that also went into the truck; then back into the house.

I made my way down the side of the hill and was leaning up against the Ford Ranger when he made his way out of the house again, with two garbage bags, one in each hand.

He stopped halfway to the truck when he saw me. "What are you doing here?" he asked, looking around, maybe for Fred or Edman.

"Meredith told you, didn't she?"

He looked back at the house.

I took a step toward him. "Meredith told you," I said, louder this time.

He put the garbage bags down on the ground. "You shouldn't be here."

I moved forward and was right in his face. "Your daughter needed help, and you weren't even man enough to be there for her."

He set his jaw. "Yes, she told me, but what could I do at this point? It was all in the past. I couldn't go back and change anything. What could I do?"

I poked my finger into his chest. "You could have been a father. You could have been a man. For once in your life, you could have taken some responsibility for what you did."

He bent down and his face was inches from mine. "I. Didn't. Do. Anything."

The anger in his eyes scared me. No one knew I was

here. Not a soul knew where I was. I should have called Edman, but he never would have let me come here alone, and I needed to do this by myself.

"You ran out on your children," I yelled in his face. "You left us. When we needed a father, where the hell were you?"

"I am not going to go through this with you again, Liz. You need to leave now."

Carly came out of the house and took long strides toward us. "Andy, what's she doing here? You told me she wouldn't bother us again."

"She's just leaving," my father said.

I looked at Carly. "Do you know about this man you're living with? Do you know how he faked his own death and ran out on his children? Do you know what happened to his daughter because of him?"

She narrowed her eyes at me and jutted out her chin. "He told me everything. He had to get out of a loveless marriage, but he wanted to make it look like an accident, so there would be insurance money for you and your sister."

I laughed and looked at Joseph. "Really, Dad? That's the story you told her?" I turned to Carly. "The insurance money had nothing to do with his children. It was for him. All for him, so he could run away instead of taking responsibility for his family like a real man."

Carly started to say something, but I cut her off. "How will you feel, Carly, when he runs out on Brenda? When he runs out on yet another daughter?"

"She's not his daughter," Carly said. "And he would never run out on her—or us."

"Liz, you've said what you wanted to say, and now you need to leave." Joseph said.

I took a step forward, "You don't get this, do you? You're

the one who needs to leave. You need to get your useless ass off my land, or I'll have the sheriff out here in five minutes."

Carly's eyes went wide. "What's she talking about, Andy?"

He glared at me and shook his head. "Nothing."

"Andy?"

"Go back in the house," he said to her.

I pulled my cell phone out of my pocket and took a step toward Carly. "No," I said, "you leave now—right now— or I'm calling the sheriff."

"Andy?"

My father grabbed my upper arm. "What do you think you're doing?"

"The lake home belongs to me. Our grandparents left it to Meredith and me, and you've been living here rent-free for almost two decades. I'm telling you to leave. If I have to call in the authorities, I will."

He didn't know if I was bluffing or not. I wasn't. I had no feeling left for this man, and now I wanted him out of my life for good.

Carly looked me in the eye, and I think she knew how serious I was. "We still have stuff in the house."

"I don't care," I said. "You need to leave."

She looked at Joseph and back at me, then she took his arm. "Andy, let's just go." She started pulling him toward the cab of the truck. He stood his ground.

"My money is in the house," he said.

"Not my problem. You have two minutes to get out of my sight."

He was thinking, watching me. Carly moved toward the steps and called into the house, "Brenda, get out here. We need to leave now."

"I'm not ready," Brenda called back.

Carly looked at me and I held up my cell phone. "Brenda! Now! We're leaving."

Thirty seconds later, pouty little Brenda sulked out of the house. "What's she doing here?" she asked when she saw me.

"Go," I said.

Carly moved forward, grabbed her daughter's arm, and dragged her to the cab of the truck. "Get in," she said.

Brenda scowled at her mother and climbed into the front seat of the king cab. Carly got into the Jeep Cherokee, watching my father.

He hadn't taken his eyes off of me. "Is this your payback?" he asked. "Do you think this is going to change anything?"

"Go. Just get the hell out of here."

He held my gaze for half a minute, then got into the truck and took off, Carly following him down the driveway.

I think I'd been holding my breath. I felt lightheaded. I blew air out of my mouth, then looked at my phone and called Tom.

"Hey, you," he said when he answered.

"I know where my father is and his girlfriend and her daughter. I want you to have them picked up and I'm willing to press charges against the two women."

He moved into his cop persona. "Elizabeth, *how* do you know where your father is?"

"I'm in Bayfield. They just left our lake home, headed east. I want them arrested and if you're interested, I have proof that my father committed insurance fraud twenty-two years ago."

"What the hell are you doing in Bayfield?"

"Tom, I'm telling you where they are, and I want to press

charges for assault, but I don't have time for this. Are you going to call the sheriff up here or not?"

"Liz…"

"I have to go." I clicked off and felt all the adrenaline from the past twenty minutes shooting through my veins with nowhere now to go. I made my way up the stairs and into the house. I walked through every room, saying goodbye to the few good memories I had of my father. Out back there was a wooden shed twenty feet from the cellar door. Inside was a five-gallon red gas can, almost full. I took it back into the house and found a box of matches in a kitchen drawer.

Upstairs, in the master bedroom, I poured gas on the floor in a trail of amber liquid, out into the hall and down the stairs. I stopped in the living room and emptied the can, then pulled out my cell phone again and called 911 to report a fire at the old McCallister place. After I hung up, I lit a match and threw it into the gas. Flames jumped to life. I turned and walked out the back door and up the hill to my car.

I JUTTED EAST on highway 2 until I got to 53, then headed south through Wisconsin, flying along any stretch where I thought I could without getting stopped. Driving, as John would say, like a bat out of hell.

I shut off my cell phone and just drove, alone with my thoughts, which weren't the best company at the moment.

I made it to Lee's office building in Minneapolis shortly after four and pulled into the now familiar parking lot. On the ninth floor, I pushed open the door to the reception area of Lee's suite. The receptionist looked up at me and smiled. "May I help you?"

"I need to see Lee. Now," I said, walking toward her closed door.

The woman started to rise from her seat, but stopped, not knowing how to handle the situation. "You can't go in there," she said.

"Is she with a client?"

"Well, no." She had her hand on the phone, ready to call for security.

I moved over to her desk and put my hand on top of hers and said in a low voice. "Don't."

She blinked at me, her face turning red. "What?"

"Whoever you think you're going to call for help— don't." I turned and walked over to Lee's door and threw it open, the receptionist two feet behind me.

Lee was on the phone, looking out the window. When she heard the door bang open, she swung around in her chair. She looked at me. "I have to go now," she said into the receiver. She stood up and watched me move toward her desk.

"I'm sorry, Dr. Atwater," the receptionist said from the doorway. "I couldn't stop her."

Lee looked at me, then waved the woman away. "That's okay, Kathy," she said. "Could you please leave us alone? And close the door behind you."

Kathy backed out of the office, never taking her eyes off of me.

"What do you want, Liz?" Lee said, still standing behind her desk. She looked scared. That was good. I wanted her scared.

I stepped up to the desk directly across from her. "What did you do?" I asked. "What did you do to my sister?"

Lee wasn't used to not being in control. She stood up

straight, and I could see her trying to judge how much I already knew.

"Liz, why don't you sit down? I can see you're—"

My voice was low and deliberate. "Tell me what you did. Tell me how you set this whole thing up. Tell me or I will report you to the state licensing board for unethical behavior. And maybe HIPAA violations for when you all but handed me my sister's private medical file."

I understood now that money and the power it bought was my legacy. I didn't know if any of my threats would hold up in court, but I knew that I had the money—the power now—to bring anyone to their knees. Even if I was wrong, I could fight. I could hire lawyers from now until kingdom come, and break someone financially in the process. Break them with years of legal expenses that they couldn't afford.

It was an ugly realization, but I didn't care anymore. My sister was dead, and too many people had deserted her when she needed them the most.

Lee's eyes went wide, and she bit her lower lip. "Liz, please. Don't. I've worked too hard to get where I am. Please."

"Then tell me what I need to know. I don't want to play games or for you to give me cryptic, meaningless home-spun words of wisdom. Tell me everything."

She nodded and I think she was blinking back tears. Or maybe it was all for show. I didn't know and I didn't care.

"Okay," she said. "Can we sit down?"

I waved her into a chair in front of the desk. She walked around slowly, breathing deeply. Once she was seated, I sat down across from her.

"It started with Dana," she said.

I held up my hand. "I don't think that's true. It started in high school. Why don't you start there?"

She shot me a withering look and squared her shoulders. "All right, it started in high school."

"For twenty years you hated my sister."

She shook her head. "No, that's not true. I hated her back then. I was jealous of everything she had and everything she was. I was a kid from the wrong side of the tracks and only got into St. Bart's on an academic scholarship. My parents could never have afforded to send me there, and I worked my ass off to be able to stay."

"So, you hated Meredith because we had money."

"Would you quit saying *hated*?"

"What would you call it?"

"I was a plain, gawky kid with a chip on her shoulder. Maybe I thought I hated her at the time, but looking back, I know I was just jealous and insecure. Meredith was rich and smart and beautiful. Who wouldn't be jealous of her?"

Lee paused and looked at me. I said nothing. She looked down at her hands and took a breath.

"When I met Tom in ninth grade, I thought I was the luckiest girl at St. Bart's. I couldn't believe he asked me out. And I thought, finally, I could show them all that I was special." A tear slid down her cheek. She didn't bother to wipe it away. She looked up at me. "Until Meredith stole him away. If you think I hated her before, that was nothing compared to what I felt when she took Tom."

"And then they broke up, but you never got over it."

"Don't you see?" She reached for my hand, but I pulled back. She looked surprised, then annoyed. "Meredith was everything I wasn't, everything I could never be. No matter how many A's I got, or how many scholarships I won, I couldn't change where I came from."

"Nobody cared, Lee. You're the one who made a big deal out of that. Everyone else was just trying to maneuver their way through adolescence; they didn't have time to sit around and think about poor Lee Atwater."

The muscles in her jaw tightened. "It doesn't matter. When you're fourteen or fifteen years old, you think everyone is judging you. Then when I met up with Tom again in college, and Meredith took him away again, all those old feelings came back. I wanted to…"

"Murder her?"

She sighed. "Yes, at the time, that's what I felt. But I moved on. I made a life for myself. I became successful. I hadn't even thought about Meredith in years…until Dana showed up."

I raised my eyebrows. "Go on."

"Dana was having some issues, and her parents were concerned, so they sent her to me. She's a smart girl and we were making some progress. We talked about everything, even her feelings about being adopted. And then…"

She stopped again and looked at me. I wasn't going to help her. I knew what was coming, but I wasn't going to jump in. I watched her face. Finally she looked away.

"I'd been seeing Dana for a couple of months. One day she came here and told me she found her birth certificate and knew who her birth mother was. We talked about her feelings and what she wanted to do with that information, and then she told me her birth mother's name. Meredith McCallister."

Lee got up and walked over to the window. She stood there, her back toward me. "I did the math. I remembered

Meredith's year at boarding school, and I knew she left town just months after she'd been seeing Tom. It was like all those unresolved feelings came back and slapped me in the face. It felt like everything I'd worked for—everything I'd accomplished—was nothing. No matter what I did, I would never be Meredith McCallister. And the Tom Martens of the world would never love me like they loved her." She started to cry, her shoulders heaving, and put her face in her hands. I had no comfort for her because I knew what she'd done.

When she finally turned around, mascara was running down her cheeks. She reached for a box of tissues on the desk and dabbed at her eyes, then wiped her nose. "I'm sorry, Liz. I'm so very sorry."

"Tell me the rest."

She came around the desk and sat back down in her chair. All I saw was the mousy fourteen-year-old girl who'd gone to St. Bart's with my sister all those years ago.

She breathed in deeply. "The feelings came back, when I thought about Tom and Meredith. I was almost certain that Tom was Dana's father, but I needed to find out for sure."

"Why? Why would it even matter at this point?"

"Because I thought the two of them had betrayed me. That Tom had used me to get to Meredith, and Meredith had stolen him away from me—twice. It was crazy, I know, but I couldn't get past it."

"So, what did you do?"

"I googled Meredith, found out where she worked, and emailed her. Told her I'd been trying to keep in touch with people from the old days and maybe we could get together for coffee."

"Then what?"

"We met for coffee a few times. It was hard. She was more beautiful than before. I asked about Tom, but she said she hadn't seen him since college. I didn't believe her, and then when I found out she was lying—"

"Lying about what?"

"Tom. I saw them together last spring. I ran into them having coffee, and everything felt the same as it did all those years ago, and this thing just kept nagging me on. I knew it was wrong, but it was like I could never get past high school until I knew for sure."

"You set her up."

The tears started again. She nodded. "I had to. Once I knew about Dana, I was crazy—driven. I couldn't stop."

"So, what did you do?"

"I encouraged Dana to reach out to her birth mother, I told her that maybe some of the problems she was experiencing were because she'd never resolved the fact that she was adopted."

I closed my eyes. Meredith never even knew what was coming.

"I kept in touch with Meredith," Lee said, "and I kept pushing Dana to meet her. I needed to know."

I was getting tired of the story. I was getting tired of Lee. I wanted to beat the crap out of her because she was the one who'd set everything in motion. Meredith had been drowning, and no one could take their eyes off their own dysfunction long enough to throw her a life preserver.

"So, you pushed Dana to meet Meredith, and that sent Meredith into a tailspin," I said. "After all these years, she came face-to-face with the one thing in her life she couldn't deal with—her own shame. Very nice, Lee. And so damn professional of you." I stood up.

"I'm so sorry, Liz—really I am. I'll never forgive myself for what I did. You're right, it was totally unprofessional of me and it was wrong. I'm sorry."

"And Tom? Does he know that you pulled him into this thing too, with your *accidental* encounters?"

She looked down at her hands. "No, he doesn't know."

I turned toward the door.

"What are you going to do now?" she asked.

"Take down a murderer."

TWENTY-SIX

I LEFT LEE's office and drove around for an hour. It was my own kind of therapy, I guess. My cell phone was off, and I just drove like I was in my own little cocoon, safe from the world and all its ugliness. The only thing was, no matter how long or how far I drove, I couldn't get rid of the thoughts in my head. They just kept coming—bing—bang—*BOOM*!

It was after six when I pulled into a parking space across the street from my apartment. Tom was sitting on the steps, a beer next to him, leaning back against the front door.

I sat down next to him. "How long have you been here?"

"About an hour. Where have you been?"

"Driving."

"Wanna talk?"

"Uh-huh." I looked at him. "Were you in love with Lee Atwater?"

He squinted at me. "What? Where the hell did that come from?"

"Just tell me. Please."

"Okay. The answer is no. I was never in love with Lee."

"And you haven't seen her since college? Until now?"

"Pretty much. I ran into her a few times last spring. I think the first time, I was picking up my dry cleaning and she was there."

"That's it?"

He shrugged. "We ran into each other a few other places, twice when Meredith and I were having coffee. Why?"

"You must have liked her a lot. You dated in high school and again in college."

"What's this about, Liz?"

"I just need to know."

He nodded. "Okay. I met Lee in ninth grade. Some of my buddies went to St. Bart's, and I tagged along once to a dance. I was fourteen. You remember fourteen-year-old boys?" He looked at me and smiled. I was too tired to smile back.

"Well, whether you do or not," he continued, "they are a pile of walking hormones, wrapped up in a serious case of zits. And for all the bravado, most of us were pretty insecure at that age. So, when you go to a dance and a girl talks to you—a real live *girl*—you think you're in hog heaven."

He kept watching my face. I finally had to smile, thinking of a fourteen-year-old Tom Martens in hog heaven because a girl talked to him.

"So, you guys dated for a while?" I asked.

Tom laughed. "I don't know that you'd call it *dating*. My mom drove us to the movies a couple of times, we hung out after school once or twice a week. I kissed her twice and touched her breasts. I was quite a stud."

"Then you dumped her for Meredith?"

"Liz, what's this all about?"

I shrugged. "I don't know. I just need to understand."

"Understand what?"

"I don't even know."

He was quiet, then, "Okay. Lee and I hung out for a few months. I think she thought I was her boyfriend, and

I didn't even know enough at the time to understand what that meant. I met Meredith and thought she was beautiful. And kind. And smart. I know Lee thought that I dumped her for Meredith, but the truth is, Lee and I didn't really click on any level—assuming fourteen-year-old kids can click. I would have gotten tired of Lee eventually anyway. Meredith was there, and I didn't have a clue how to pursue a girl. Again, it was more about hanging out together."

"Were you in love with her?"

He closed his eyes and shook his head. "No. I was probably infatuated with her."

I leaned back against the door and looked at him. "Tell me about college, when you and Lee started dating again."

"Well, you just said it. Lee and I had a couple of classes together. She was familiar, we started talking and started going out."

"And you were engaged to her?"

He held up his hand. "No. We were never engaged."

"I thought that's what she told everyone."

"She did tell a few people that until I found out and put a stop to it."

"Did you sleep with her?"

"Liz, what are you fishing for here?"

"I don't know."

"I'm not sure you really want to know this."

"I do. I need to."

He was quiet.

I waited.

"Yes, we slept together a couple of times. She really wasn't my type, but she kind of threw herself at me, and I wasn't about to turn her down."

"Like I tried to do that first night?"

He actually thought about it. "Yeah, I guess."

Okay, now I'd gone too far. I didn't want to know that I was just someone passing through Tom's life like Lee had been.

He put his hand on mine. "What are you thinking?"

I couldn't speak. If I opened my mouth, I would cry, and I didn't want to do that right now. I tried to stand up, but he held me down.

"Tom…"

"Just listen. You asked me all these questions, now let me explain it to you. I never had anything going on with Lee, except sex, and that didn't last long. I was very attracted to your sister and cared about her very much. She was a good person. But Meredith had demons that I couldn't even begin to understand. As close as I thought we were, there was always something between us that kept us apart. Maybe I wasn't what she was looking for, but whatever we had turned into more of a friendship than anything else."

He looked me in the eyes. "The timing stinks for us right now, Liz, and I don't want to take advantage of you when you're so vulnerable. But the time I've spent with you these past ten days feels so different. I like being with you. I don't know where we'll end up, but when all this is over, I intend to find out. Okay?"

"Okay," I said. And then the tears came.

TOM MADE DINNER while I took a shower. When I walked into the kitchen, the table was set and he'd lit candles. There was a salad at each setting, and I slid into a chair across from him.

"This is nice," I said. "What's the main course?"

"Omelets."

His cell phone rang. "Martens," he said.

After a minute, he hung up and looked at me. "Your father and Carly and Brenda Turnquist are in custody in Bayfield County. They'll be transported here tomorrow morning. I hope you have proof about the insurance fraud on your father. Otherwise he'll walk. Right now, he's being held as an accessory."

"I have proof," I said.

He looked me in the eye. "By the way, there was a fire today at the McCallister lake home north of Bayfield."

WE DIDN'T TALK about the fire or my father for the rest of the night. Tom must have sensed how much I needed him right then because he didn't object when I asked him to stay with me. We went to bed at nine, and I fell asleep like I had the other night, listening to the sound of his breathing, and feeling safe just knowing he was there.

At seven thirty the next morning, he bent over me and brushed the hair off my face. "I have to get to the office. I'll call you later."

After he left, I jumped out of bed. It didn't take long to get dressed and put on some makeup. At eight o'clock, I made my first call to Barb Forseman, Meredith's boss.

"I need some information from you," I said.

Then I called Edman. "Are we on?"

"You sure this is how you want to play this?"

"Yes."

"Okay. I'll be waiting out front when you get here."

I parked behind Edman in front of Wainwright's office and climbed in the passenger seat of his car. There was a mousy little man in a suit two sizes too big for him sitting in the back seat. His glasses slid down the bridge of his nose, and he pushed them up with his index finger. His suit coat was unbuttoned, and I could see the shoulder holster hugging his frail body.

"This is Harry Belmont, Esquire," Edman said. "Harry, this is Liz McCallister."

I reached back and shook Harry's soft hand. "Are you a real lawyer?"

He looked offended. "Licensed in Minnesota and Wisconsin," he said, trying to puff out an underdeveloped chest.

"Did Edman tell you what I need you to do?"

"Yes, I drew up the papers last night. All we need is a signature."

I looked at Edman. "What happens now?"

"We wait. Your fancy lawyer and his secretary should be leaving any time now."

"How did you arrange that?"

He looked over at me and did that crazy half smile. "Don't even ask."

Fifteen minutes later, Wainwright and the sexless Ms. Norma Verhle came out of the office. Wainwright turned and locked the door behind him. They crossed the street and got into a gray BMW sedan. Wainwright drove as they took off, heading east.

"How long will they be gone?" I asked.

Edman opened his door. "I'd say at least a couple of hours before they realize they're on a wild goose chase. Let's get set up."

The three of us, looking like the oddest assortment of human beings on the planet, crossed the street. Edman took some small tools out of his pocket and started fiddling with the lock. I looked away. This was worse than getting into Meredith's safety deposit box at the bank. While I knew that was borderline larcenous, breaking into Wainwright's office was full-on, no-holds-barred illegal.

Seconds later, Edman opened the front door and ushered us inside, flipping on lights as he went from room to room.

"Do you think you should be doing that?" I whispered.

"We have to make it look like we're open for business."

"What if a real client walks in?"

He raised his eyebrows and cocked his head. "Then our new receptionist, Ms. Elizabeth McCallister, tells them that Mr. Wainwright is tied up for the day, and could she please make an appointment for them."

We set Harry Belmont up in Wainwright's private office and closed the door as he was laying out legal documents on the desk. I went out to Norma's workspace and started opening filing cabinets, looking for the file Harry would need. I found it and Edman delivered it to the mousy little man in the other room.

I opened another drawer and found the file regarding the trust that our grandparents had set up for Meredith, Fred, and me and fanned the pages. At the back were Wainwright's handwritten notes from the past couple of weeks and documentation of a phone call from Ruth, questioning Dana's connection to the family. Nothing surprised me anymore.

I put the file back and looked at Edman. "What time did you say?"

"Nine thirty."

It was 9:12. I had eighteen minutes to back out.

Edman was watching me. "I've told you before, kid, that you call all the shots. If you don't want to go through with this, we can leave now. No one will ever know we were here."

I looked at his big, craggy face and remembered what I'd felt the night I was sitting in that church parking lot and everything suddenly made sense to me—the terror, the anger, the sadness. "No. We follow the plan," I said.

"All the way to the end?"

I nodded. "All the way to the end."

Then he did a very un-Edman-like thing: he reached out and hugged me, pulling me into a bear hug with his big Popeye arms. When he let go, I looked up at him. "I need one more thing."

"What?"

"A cheap apartment in downtown St. Paul."

"How cheap?"

"Someplace even you wouldn't stay."

For the first time, I heard Edman laugh, a deep, guttural sound. "Harry can help us with that. He's quite the slumlord."

"I'll also need a couple of big strong guys to help move things."

"When?"

"Tonight."

"I'll make a call."

He left the room, and I sat down in the waiting area to, well, wait. I tried not to think about what was going to go down. And I tried even harder not to think about what Tom's reaction would be when he found out. I needed to do this, no matter what. I'd deal with the consequences later.

The antique wooden clock on the wall behind Norma's desk showed 9:27. I watched the minute hand move slowly, very slowly, to 9:28, then 9:29, and then the front door opened, and the sound of footsteps moved from the front hall to the entry to Norma's office.

We stared at each other for nearly half a minute.

"Elizabeth, what are you doing here?" David asked as he moved slowly into the room.

Edman came in from the copy room. David looked at him, then back at me.

"Elizabeth, what's going on here? Where's Norma? Where's Wainwright?" David had stopped several feet from where I sat. Edman moved in behind him, blocking any retreat.

"We have business to take care of, David." I sounded so calm. I sounded like I was in charge, and I knew what I was doing. But inside, tremors coursed through my muscles, making me feel like a jellyfish and I would collapse on the floor in a puddle of goo any second. What I wanted to do—more than anything, what I wanted to do—was to take Edman's Glock out of my bag and start shooting, right into David's heart. To keep shooting until there were no bullets left in the chamber. I reined that in. I needed to follow the plan. I couldn't help anyone unless we followed the plan.

David wrinkled his brow and tried to look perplexed, a thin film of sweat spreading across his forehead, but I think he knew. I think he'd figured it out the other night.

Edman locked the front door.

"Let's step into the office," I said.

David stalled. "I'm not going anywhere until you tell me what's going on."

Edman moved in close, towering over David. He bent down and spoke into David's ear. "The lady asked you to move into the office. Would you like to do as she asked, or do you need some help?"

David's eyes widened, and he walked into Wainwright's office.

Harry Belmont stood up from behind the desk. "Is this our, uh, client?"

Edman nodded.

"Have a seat, Mr. Alder."

David didn't move.

"Have a seat," Edman said, pushing him down into a black leather chair.

We all sat down, which was a relief. The jellyfish muscles in my legs couldn't hold me up much longer.

"Elizabeth, *what* is going on here?" David asked, but the bluster had gone out of his voice.

"I told you, David, that we have some business to take care of. Just shut up for a minute, and Mr. Belmont will tell you what you need to do."

"I don't know what's going on," David said, "but I don't like it. I'm leaving." He started to stand up, but Edman placed a large hand on his shoulder.

Harry Belmont had his papers all lined up, the edges parallel to the sides of the desk, very OCD. He picked up a document several pages thick, very legal looking. "Mr. Alder, I've taken the liberty to draw up a new will for you."

"I didn't ask for a new will," David said, and he glanced over at Edman, who smiled at him.

"I see," Harry said. "At any rate, this is your new will. Let me draw attention to the page specifying beneficiaries."

"I didn't ask for a new will," David repeated. No one was paying any attention to him.

"Any real property or financial holdings you have will be left to the Eastside Victims of Sexual Assault Agency located on Lexington Avenue, at..." Harry scanned the page. "Well, I'm sure you know the address."

"I didn't..." David started, but he didn't bother to finish.

"If you will just sign here, here, and here and initial here," Harry said, pointing to different pages as he handed David a pen.

David looked at me. "I'm not signing anything."

I glanced at Edman. He nodded. I took a breath. "David, you will sign this will. You will sign everything Mr. Belmont asks you to sign. You have no choice."

Some of his bravado was seeping back in. I could see it in his eyes. "And if I don't?"

"Oh, David," I said, "I don't think that would be very smart. You see, after all these years, you've finally been found out."

The color drained from his face. "I don't know what you're talking about."

"I think you do," I said. The jellyfish had been replaced by an electric eel. I wanted to hurt him. I wanted to kill him. "I know about you, David. I know that you molested my sister for years. That she got pregnant at fifteen because of you."

"You have no proof of that—"

"Actually, I do. Meredith had your DNA and her daughter's DNA tested, and guess what? It's a match. It's proof that you fathered a child with a fifteen-year-old girl."

His mouth hung open. He ran his tongue over his lips. Then he shook his head. "No. You don't have any proof—you're bluffing."

I lunged forward, grabbed his shirt collar, and held on tight. "Look," I said, "I'm not playing games here, and we don't have all day. You raped my sister for years, and you're going to pay for it. And all the young girls you've *mentored* over the years—what did you do to them?" My voice was getting louder. I tightened my hold on his shirt, his pudgy flesh bulging over the fabric. "So, you do as Mr. Belmont has asked you, and maybe, just maybe, I won't send the cops to the house today to find all the child porn on your computer."

It was a good bluff, because it got his attention.

He swallowed. "Okay."

I looked at Edman. "You can let go of him now," he said.

David's eyes darted around the room. "I'm not admitting to anything," he finally said, "but if I sign this, how do I know you won't go to the cops anyway?"

I shrugged. "You don't. It's a gamble either way. But I can guarantee you this: that if you don't sign those papers, I'll have the police here in ten minutes. I promise you."

He was breathing hard. "That doesn't mean that—"

"No, it doesn't. But either way, don't you think it would look better for you if you finally did the right thing?"

"I'm not admitting to anything," he said, then picked up the pen and signed and initialed all the appropriate places on his new will.

Harry Belmont looked pleased. "Very good." He moved the document to the side of the desk. "Now, moving on to financial matters."

"What financial matters?" David asked his voice hoarse.

"I have the portfolio with your financial holdings here. Mr. Wainwright keeps meticulous records. Kudos to him. Anyway, we are about to do some wire transfers."

"No," David said.

I looked at him and picked up my cell phone.

"Okay, how much?" he asked.

Harry Belmont did a little laugh. "Well, all of it, of course. Do you have the account number where the money will be going?" he asked me.

I handed him a slip of paper with the bank and routing numbers Barb had given me for the agency.

David looked at me and put his face in his hands.

"Just one call, David," I said. "One call, to the police and, oh, maybe another one to the St. Paul *Pioneer Press*."

He looked at me between splayed fingers. He was breathing hard. It took everything in me not to lift the big heavy bookend behind Wainwright's desk and smash in his disgusting face. *The plan,* I kept telling myself, *I have to follow the plan. I have to do this for Meredith.*

Harry was talking again. "As with your will, we'll be transferring funds today to the Eastside Victims of Sexual Assault Agency on Lexington Avenue." He started thumbing through pages. "Well, I'm sure you know the address. Looks like you'll be making a sizable donation." Harry Belmont smiled at David, and it was then I realized Harry Belmont was a little crazy. "I'll just need your PINs for your accounts, and we'll be on our way."

Belmont booted up Wainwright's computer and opened up the webpage for David's bank. Edman had everything under control, so I got up and walked out of the room. I made it to the powder room off the front entry hall, closed the door behind me, and slid to the floor. I lay down and pressed my face against the cold tile, wondering how long I could stay there—wondering what Norma and Wainwright would do when they found me there.

Minutes later, someone knocked on the door. It was Edman. "You okay, kid?"

"Yes."

"Then open the door."

I reached up and turned the knob, releasing the push-in lock. Edman stepped over me. I didn't move.

He closed the door behind him, walked the few feet to the toilet, put the lid down, then sat down on it—a picture of Edman I will never forget. "We don't have to do this, you know."

My cheek was pressed against the tile; it felt so good. "I know."

He was quiet for a minute. "Tell me what you want to do."

I opened my mouth, but he put up his hand. "Sit up and tell me what you want to do."

I sat up and looked at him sitting on the toilet. "I want to finish this. I just don't know if I can."

He held my gaze for the longest time. "You want to know what I think?"

"Yes."

"This is revenge. This is butt-ugly, down-and-dirty revenge."

"Your point?"

"My point is that you and I both know we can call the cops right now, and David, with all his money and all his resources can fight this in court till the day he dies and never once be punished for what he did."

"Go on."

"You—we—are stripping away everything he has, everything that's important to him, so when you finally do call the cops, he won't have more money than God to pay for some high-priced, fancy-assed lawyers."

"That's part of what I was hoping for."

"And the other part?"

"That all the girls who are being abused like Meredith was will have a place to go when they need help."

He raised his eyebrows. "Well, that seems like an important thing to do. So, do we keep going?"

"I want to. I just don't know how much more I can take."

"I think you can take more than you realize. And every time you doubt yourself, every time you want to quit—you think about your sister and what he did to her."

I reached out my hand. "Help me up."

TWENTY-SEVEN

DAVID WAS SITTING in a chair in the waiting area, Belmont seated across from him, his briefcase at his feet, his gun in his lap, cleaning his fingernails with a long, sharp letter opener.

Harry looked at Edman. "We'd better get going, Maynard. I want to get all this in motion as soon as possible. It's going to take at least twenty-four hours for the wire transfers to go through, but I need to drop these authorizations off at the bank. And I want to show you the apartment I have available over the Old German Bakery. I think it will be just what you're looking for. And it will be a nice place to keep our client here until the money changes accounts. Unfortunately, it won't be, uh, free until this evening. Someone is being displaced today."

So, Harry the slumlord was evicting a tenant. Nice.

Edman looked at David. "What do we do with him?"

"How long will you be?" I asked.

"Not long," Harry said. "We can be back here within an hour."

I looked at the time. What if Wainwright showed up before Edman came back? This was a part of the plan I hadn't anticipated. We'd gotten David to Wainwright's office and taken care of the legal matters, but I hadn't realized that we would have to hold him someplace until the money changed accounts.

Edman was thinking. "We can't keep him here. Give me your car keys," he said to me.

I pulled them out of my pocket and handed them to him. "What are you going to do?"

"There's an alley behind the building, I'll pull your car around and we can get him in there. You'll have to take him someplace until I get back. Will you be okay?"

I nodded. "I'll take him to Meredith's."

"And you'll be okay until I get there?" Edman asked me again.

David was a paunchy, out-of-shape, seventy-year-old man. I wasn't afraid of him. His specialty was preying on vulnerable young girls, not adults who could take care of themselves. "I'll be okay. Just hurry. I don't want any hiccups here. We need to get this done."

It was the first time I'd seen Edman vacillate. I patted my bag. "I have the present you gave me the other day."

"We could take him with us," Edman said.

I shook my head. "That's too risky. If he created a commotion in public, we would never get the money where it needs to go."

Harry was starting to get antsy. "We really need to get moving on this. And we need to get out of here before Wainwright gets back."

That did it. If the money wasn't transferred, if the legal papers weren't filed, if David had a chance to talk to Wainwright, this whole thing could fall apart.

Edman nodded. "Okay, let's go."

He pulled my car around behind the building, escorted David out, and opened the driver's door. David got in and started to buckle the seat belt.

"Buckle it behind you," Edman said.

David looked up at him. "What?"

"Buckle it behind you," he repeated.

"Why?"

"So, you don't think driving off the road or causing an accident will save you."

David tried to turn around in the seat to buckle the seat belt, but his girth kept getting in his way. Edman yanked him out of the car, leaned in and buckled the seat belt, then pushed him back into the driver's seat. I got into the passenger side.

Edman looked across at me. "Don't take your eyes off him for a second."

"I won't."

"I'll be out at Meredith's as soon as I can." He turned to leave, then turned back to the car. "Just one more thing." He opened the driver's door again, pulled David to his feet and hit him hard in the stomach, a whoosh of air coming out of David's mouth as he doubled over.

Edman pushed him back in the car, leaned in, and whispered loudly in David's ear. "For Meredith," he said, then slammed the door behind him.

David was still trying to recover his breath when Edman and Harry left. I took the Glock out of my bag and pointed it at his midsection. I thought about shooting him in the head, rolling him out into the alley and just driving away. Who would ever know what happened? Maybe when they traced the paper trail of the new will and the wire transfers, someone would figure it out, but could they ever tie it to me?

But even more than watching David die, I wanted him to suffer. A bullet to the head would be too quick. Meredith had endured years of abuse. David needed to suffer too.

Sweat was pouring down David's face as we pulled out

of the alley and into traffic. Two blocks later, we stopped for a red light. I saw him scanning the intersection, looking for something or someone that could help him. I pushed the gun harder into his flesh.

The light changed, and we drove through the intersection, passing John headed the other direction. He saw my car, started to wave, then saw David in the driver's seat. When we were almost parallel, I looked over at him and smiled, trying to make this look like a family outing, hoping John didn't suspect what might be going on or that I had a gun pointed at David's stomach.

The drive to Meredith's seemed to take longer than usual. When we pulled into her driveway, Scott's car was nowhere to be seen. That was a good thing. I didn't want Scott and Dana involved in any of this, and I didn't want to have to explain to Dana the circumstances of her conception. With all the ugly secrets our family had, this was one I was determined to take to the grave. The girl had enough things in her life to deal with; she didn't need to know about David.

David parked behind Meredith's car at the edge of the carport and turned off the engine.

"Give me the keys," I said. He handed them over. "Now get out."

David wasn't a physical threat. He couldn't outrun me. We exited the car at the same time, and I walked around behind him, the gun poking into his back. "Let's go inside."

I unlocked the front door and motioned him in with the Glock in my hand. We moved into the living room. The drapes to the patio were open. Even though Meredith owned over two hundred feet of lake frontage, sometimes her neighbors walked by as they made their way around the lake. I closed the drapes and pointed to a club chair for David to sit and sat down across from him in a matching royal-blue chair.

As with everything else these days, I didn't know the protocol for holding someone at gunpoint. I hoped Edman would hurry.

"What are you going to do to me, Elizabeth?"

"I don't know yet. But I do know that at this time tomorrow, the Eastside Victims of Sexual Assault Agency will have a butt load of money."

"You won't get away with this."

"Why is that, David?"

"Because it's coercion. It's illegal."

I pointed to Meredith's landline, sitting on her desk. "Feel free to call the cops. And please don't be shy about the fact that you're a pervert, a child molester, and a rapist. I think that might get their attention more than the papers that have been delivered to the bank with your legal signature on them."

He opened his mouth to say something, but stopped.

We sat in silence for a while. Finally, he said. "I need something to drink."

"Maybe later."

A full twenty minutes passed with neither of us talking. I looked at him. "How could you have done that to her?"

He raised his eyebrows. "You'll never understand."

"Your perversion? You're right—I will never understand that."

God, I wanted to hurt him. I was hoping Edman would show up before I did something I'd regret. It was after noon, and I still hadn't heard from Edman. I turned on the TV and stepped into the kitchen, where I could watch David through the open counter area. I guess we had to eat, so I made sandwiches and got some Diet Coke out of the refrigerator, and took them into the living room.

An hour later, still no word from Edman. I was starting to get worried—and bored.

"I have to use the bathroom," David said.

And another thing I hadn't anticipated. I walked behind him down the hallway to the bathroom. There was a small window on the outside wall, but too high and too small for David to make an escape.

"Leave the door open," I said and moved to the side of the doorway so I wouldn't have to see anything I really didn't want to see.

I could hear my phone ringing in the living room. I hoped it was Edman, telling me he was on his way.

The toilet flushed and I heard the water running in the sink, then David walked back into the hallway. We headed back to the living room. My phone was ringing again. I motioned David back into his chair and grabbed the phone. It was Fred.

"Where are you?" he asked.

"Out running errands. Kind of busy right now."

"Swing by and pick me up. I'll go with you."

"Uh, no. That's not a good idea."

"You sound funny. Where *are* you?"

"Gotta run, Fred. I'll call you later."

I could hear him start to say something as I clicked off.

I hung up and my phone rang immediately again. This time it was Lee.

"Liz," she said, "I've been thinking about our conversation ever since you left yesterday. We need to talk. Can you come by my office?"

"Lee, there's nothing left to say."

"I can meet you somewhere." She wasn't going to give up.

"Lee, there is really nothing more for us to talk about."

Her voice got quiet. "I'm worried about you. If you've figured everything out, you could be in real danger. Look what happened to your sister."

"I have everything under control. I have to go." I hung up on her.

The afternoon slid away and still no word from Edman. Four o'clock—where the hell was he? I pulled up his number and hit "Dial."

"Where are you?" I asked when he answered. I could hear cars honking, people yelling.

"We got held up at the bank and the broker's office. Now we're stuck on I-35. There's been an accident—a pile-up—and traffic is backed up for about a mile."

"Are you hurt?"

"No. We just got into the tail end of this thing. I don't know when the hell we're going to get out. Are you okay?"

"Yes. I guess. I just don't know what to do with him."

"Tie him up if you have to. I'll be there as soon as I can. Call me if something happens."

I didn't know what that meant. "Okay."

Crap! I didn't want to do this alone. I wanted Edman here.

I put my phone down. David was watching me. He started to get up out of his chair.

I stood up. "Where do you think you're going?"

"Home. I'm calling Ruth and I'm putting an end to this ridiculous charade. If you stop this now, I won't tell anyone. We'll just chalk it up to poor judgment on your part."

I pointed the gun at him. "Sit down."

He looked at the gun. "Are you going to shoot me?"

"If I have to. Sit down."

"I don't think you would," he said, his face flushed; sweat ran down his cheeks.

"Sit down."

He looked as if he was going to sit, then arched his back and clutched at his chest, groaning and gasping for air. Seconds ticked by as I watched him struggle, part of me relieved that maybe a heart attack would take him and end this nightmare.

Eyes bulging, he stumbled forward. One step. Two steps. I watched. And then he made his move and threw his entire body weight at me. The impact of his pudgy torso knocked me backward, and the gun fell from my hand. I hit a chair, then the floor, hard, on my back. He was on top of me, pinning me beneath him.

The gun slid under the coffee table, inches from my fingertips. David saw me looking for it. He sat up, straddling my midsection, punched me in the jaw with a force that surprised me, and grabbed at the gun.

I tried to turn, but he had more leverage and he was faster. He shoved the gun in my face. "Looks like the tables have turned," he said, breathing hard.

Looking into the barrel of a gun, inches from your head, held by a psychopath is beyond any terror I'd ever known. David's hand was shaking, and his eyes were wild.

"What are you going to do now?" I asked him.

He raised his eyebrows. "I should shoot you."

"Then go ahead."

"No one would ever suspect me. This is Edman's gun—he'd have a lot of explaining to do."

"Edman would tell the police that you're a child molester and a rapist."

"Shut up!" He shoved the gun under my chin. One shot, straight up, into my brain. That's all it would take.

His eyes met mine, and I wanted so badly to look away. I didn't want to stare into the soul of this pervert. I didn't even want to see his face. But I didn't look away. I wouldn't show fear.

"She was special, you know," he said.

The sound of a rabid animal came out of my throat as I pushed the gun away from my chin and clawed at his eyes. He brought the butt of the gun in hard against my cheekbone. It was enough to stun me, I felt the flesh tear, and in a matter of seconds my eye swelled shut.

I pushed against him. "Get off of me."

He looked down at me, and finally he slid to the side, his back up against the couch. Then he pushed himself up and was standing over me, the gun pointed at my head.

"Stand up," he said.

If he had just been a little bit closer, I could have kicked him in the knee or the crotch, but he kept a safe distance away.

I stood up, blood running down my cheek. "What are you going to do?"

He grabbed my upper arm, digging his fingers deep into the muscle. I tried to pull away, but he was much stronger than I'd realized. He pushed me onto the couch and pointed the gun at my head.

"Don't move," he said and backed into the chair where he'd spent the better part of the day. He took his cell phone out of his pocket, looking for a number, glancing up at me every other second. I figured he really was going to call Ruth, and everything we'd just done would fall apart.

I kept my eyes on the gun.

He was quiet for a very long time. He was breathing so heavily I was hoping his heart was giving out. "I'm going to call my bank and put a stop to the wire transfers, and then I'm going to contact Wainwright and rewrite my will."

"I don't think you want to do that, David."

"Why not? You can't just coerce people into giving away their money and their assets against their will."

If I'd had the Glock in my hands at that moment, he'd be dead. "And you can't force yourself sexually on girls against their will, and that's what you've been doing for decades. So, if we're going to play this game, David, remember, you're not blameless."

Just when I thought he couldn't surprise me anymore, he did. He was out of his chair and in front of me so fast I didn't even have time to flinch, the butt of the gun came down against my cheek again. The impact wasn't as hard as the first time—maybe he was losing steam—but my face was already raw, and I groaned when he hit me. I started to fall but caught myself.

He *would not* win. "David, whatever happens here, whether you kill me or not, you will pay for what you did. Do you understand that? Do you understand that you violated children? That you subjected them to the most horrific thing a child can endure? You took away their innocence."

His breathing got heavier. He looked down at his cell phone, hit "Dial" with this thumb and put the phone on speaker.

"This is David Alder," he said when he finally got

through to a real person at the bank. "I need to talk to Pat Dowling right away."

"I'm sorry, Mr. Alder," the female voice said, "Mr. Dowling has left for the day. Would you like his voicemail?"

"No," David yelled into the phone, "I need to talk to someone in the Finance Department right away. It's an emergency! I've been the victim of fraud."

"I could transfer you to our Fraud Department in Chicago."

"No! Dammit! Don't you understand? This is an emergency. I don't have time for call centers or paperwork. Give me Dowling's assistant, Grace-somebody."

"Grace Redding."

"Whatever—just put me through." His face was turning red, and he was sweating again.

I could hear the phone ringing, and then it went to voicemail.

"Dammit!" he yelled. He left a message for Grace Redding to call him back ASAP, then clicked off.

"Get up," he said, motioning me off the couch with the gun.

"Why?"

"Just *get up*. We need to get to the bank."

"We won't make it in time," I told him, not moving off the couch. "It's after four. It's a half-hour drive back into town, and once we get there, we'll be stuck in rush-hour traffic."

He started pacing.

"We're going to take a little ride," he finally said.

"I'm not going anywhere with you."

"Oh, I think you are." He watched my face. "There are others. You know that, Elizabeth. Your sister was special, but she wasn't unique. If you don't come with me, if I have to kill you here, you will never be able to help them." His voice had taken on a singsong quality that was really creepy.

I thought of Amanda Cochran, and I knew now for sure that she was one of the others. The girl needed help. I couldn't help her if I was dead. And I really didn't want to be dead yet. If I could play this out just a little while longer, Edman would come, or David would trip himself up. Or if I was really lucky, he would have a real heart attack.

He pulled me to my feet and propelled me toward the door, his fingers imbedded in my arm, the gun pushed up against my ribs. Then he looked back around the room, probably wondering if there was anything there that would incriminate him.

"This is what we're going to do," he said into my ear. I could feel his hot breath on my face. "When we get to the car, you'll get into the driver's seat, and I'll be in the back seat right behind you. If you call for help, I will shoot. Please don't think I won't, because at this point, I really have nothing to lose. Before anyone could ever stop me, I could be gone and everyone you love—*everyone* you love—would be dead within the hour. Fred, Rachel, Ruth—that girl, Dana—all dead because you refused to do what you were told."

I looked at him. His eyes were wild. I knew he meant what he said, but I wondered if he could pull it off. It didn't matter if he got them all before he was stopped. If he only killed one of them, that was unthinkable.

I nodded.

We walked to the carport, a disheveled, out-of-shape older man with a young woman at his side whose eye was swollen shut and with blood running down her face. Would anyone even notice us?

When we got to the car, he pulled open the driver's door and pushed me inside, then got quickly in behind me.

"David, think about what you're doing. Whatever you've done over the years, whatever you have to pay for—you're just making it worse."

"Shut up."

"Kidnapping, murder, those will send you to prison for sure. The other stuff…" it was so damn hard to downplay the horror he'd inflicted on all those girls, but I was stalling for time. I was stalling for Edman. "Maybe a good lawyer could get you into treatment. Maybe there wouldn't be any jail time. But that's not going to happen if you don't stop now."

"Shut up."

I shut up. Every second that passed was a second closer to Edman's arrival.

Finally, he said, "Let's go."

"Where?"

"Just start driving—I'll tell you where."

"No."

He pushed the gun harder into the back of my head. "What do you mean *no*?"

"You're going to shoot me. One way or another I'm dead. Do it now. I don't want to play your games." I sounded brave. I wasn't, but I'd resigned myself to the fact that this wasn't going to turn out well. Why should I help him get away? Besides, child molesters are cowards, preying on the vulnerable. I was also banking on the fact that he really didn't have the guts to shoot me.

I think he was considering it. I braced myself for what would come.

"I saw you the other day at the school, talking to Amanda."

I looked at him in the rearview mirror. "You wouldn't."

"She will be the first one I shoot, after you, that is."

I turned the key in the ignition and backed out of Meredith's driveway. David slid the gun down between the seats, poking it into my ribs.

"Drive to St. Bart's," he said from the back seat.

"Why? School's already out. No one is there."

The gun poked harder into my ribs. "Just do it. Amanda should be getting out of choir practice soon."

"Please, David, I'll do anything you want me to do. But please, let's not go there."

"Drive by the school."

It was after five when we pulled up in front of the school. There were only a handful of kids milling around on the grounds, kids in familiar uniforms, sitting together in small clumps, talking, laughing—just being teenagers.

I spotted Amanda Cochran with another girl, standing next to the chain link fence that surrounded the school grounds. Whatever their conversation, it seemed so much more serious than the other girls'. She looked up and saw David's face and froze. She saw me and our eyes locked. I wanted her to run. I wanted her to find a safe place to hide, but I didn't know how to tell her that. We just watched each other. If I yelled across the street, would David start shooting wildly? How many children would be killed in his random fire?

David finally spotted her. "There she is," he said.

"Please, David, let's just go. Leave that girl out of this.

Please. Why are you even doing this? You have me. You don't need her too."

"She's my insurance. I can't stop the wire transfers until tomorrow. We'll stay at Meredith's tonight, but just to make sure you don't get any ideas, Amanda is my trump card. Now get out of the car."

"No."

"Get out of the car."

I opened the driver's door and slid out as he fumbled his way out of the back seat. I'd hoped Amanda would have gone for help. When I looked up at the fence, she was still there, frozen in place, watching us. Her friend had disappeared, and she was all alone.

We walked to the fence. Amanda saw my swollen eye, and her face went white. David moved his hand just enough so she could see the gun.

"Hello, Amanda," he said. "Just getting out of choir practice?"

She didn't say a word. She looked at him and then at me. I was trying to calculate how much time I could buy for her to get away. If I could back into David with enough force, knock him off balance, maybe there would be time for her to run. Almost as if he could read my mind, he took a step back.

"Let's go for a ride, Amanda," he said in that creepy singsong voice.

"My mother will be here soon." She kept her eyes on me, hoping I could tell her what to do.

"Get in the car, Amanda." His voice was harsh now.

"No," I said. "Run."

She hesitated too long. He pointed the gun at her. "Get. In. The. Car."

She walked through the opening in the fence toward my car. I wanted to cry. I couldn't save her. He opened the driver's door, and she got in and slid across the front seat, maneuvering her legs over the console. I got in next, and David took his place in the back seat.

"Go," he told me.

I started the car and pulled into the driving lane. If I thought the drive to Meredith's with David as my hostage was long, this ride was interminable. No one spoke. I kept glancing over at Amanda, willing her some courage, but she kept her eyes on her hands folded in her lap.

Traffic in town was heavy at that hour. We came to a stop at a red light, and I scanned the intersection, looking for anything to change our dynamic. David noticed me looking, and the gun went harder into my ribcage. The light changed and we were moving again. John's truck passed us, headed the opposite direction. I hoped like hell that he saw us and this time he'd know that something was amiss. But what were the odds, with all the cars moving forward in a giant metal mass, that he'd notice mine for the second time in one day?

Finally, we reached the lake. Scott's car was still nowhere in sight, and no Edman. My heart sank. David ushered us around the back of the house toward the boathouse. "Where's your phone?" he asked me.

"In my pocket."

"Take it out and throw it in the lake."

I did as I was told. He gestured toward the boathouse with his gun. "In there."

Amanda went in first and I followed her. Except for the light that seeped in through the cracks in the sides from the rotting wood, the boathouse was losing daylight quickly.

David pushed the gun into my ribs again. "Over there," he said.

On the far wall, where part of the structure overhung the water, was a wooden bench. Amanda and I stepped gingerly over the wooden planks and sat down on the bench. There were coils of rope on the floor. David kicked them toward me. "Tie her up," he said to me, "hands behind her back."

Amanda turned her back to me, and I started tying her up.

"Make it tight," David said.

I pulled the rope tight and Amanda flinched. "Sorry," I said and patted her arm.

David checked the ropes on Amanda's wrists. "Now you." He motioned for me to turn around and pulled the rope so tight, it cut into my flesh. "Now sit."

I sat next to Amanda, and he tied my left ankle to her right and looped the rope around one of the legs of the bench. She was trembling, and I wanted to reassure her, but what could I say that would make any of it better?

David pulled at the rope around our ankles, to make sure it was secure, then stood up, red-faced and wheezing. "I'm going to be right outside," he said. "No talking, no yelling, or I'll be back and one of you gets shot."

Amanda whimpered and leaned into me. I waited until David was outside. "We'll be okay," I whispered. "A friend of mine is coming."

She looked at me and shook her head, then nodded toward the door.

I could hear David's heavy breathing move farther and farther away. Then the door to the house slammed shut. I really hadn't thought he'd spend the night outside the boathouse.

"He's in the house," I whispered.

She bent over and whispered in my ear. "Are you sure?"

I nodded. "I'm so sorry about this, Amanda. I'm sorry for all of it, and I'm sorry for what David did to you."

Her eyes filled with tears. "He didn't do—you know. I mean, he sort of, you know, touched me. But…"

The light in the boathouse was fading fast, I could still see her eyes when she looked at me. "You're sure? You can tell me, you don't have to be embarrassed. He did things to a lot of girls—even Meredith."

Tears slid down her cheeks. "Really?"

"Uh-huh."

She put her head down. "He really didn't do, you know, *that* to me. But he did to a friend of mine."

God, I wanted to kill that bastard! But first I had to get us out of here.

"I think Meredith knew," she whispered in the dark. "She started this group, and she was trying to talk to us about stuff like that and how we should, you know, tell someone."

"Did you ever tell anyone?"

She whimpered. "No. He said he'd hurt my family. Maybe kill them or make my dad lose his job. I didn't know what to do." She started to cry.

I let her cry for a while. When she finally wound down, I said, "I need you to listen to me, Amanda, and I need for you to try to be brave."

She looked up at me. "Okay."

"A friend of mine is coming, but we can't wait. We need to try to get out of this. Are you with me?"

"Okay," she said again, but her voice was trembling. I knew we had to move quickly or I'd lose her.

I looked around the boathouse for something—any-thing—that would help. "Any ideas?" I asked.

"Maybe we could, you know, try to untie each other's hands."

"Good plan." It was hard to do with one foot tied to the other and both our ankles secured to the bench. After a couple of minutes, we were able to maneuver our free legs over the back of the bench, so that we were sitting back to back.

Still, it was a challenge, not being able to see what we were doing, both of us fumbling with the rope and our hands getting in the way of one another.

"We need to do this differently," I told her. "Let me untie you first, and then you can untie me."

It was easier with only two hands moving than it was with four. I tried to recall how I'd tightened and threaded the rope around her wrists, then tried to do it in reverse. Five minutes passed, and I finally felt the knot loosen. I kept going until the rope fell away.

Amanda swung her free leg over the front of the bench.

"Untie our feet," I said.

She bent over, struggling with the knots that David had tightened so securely.

"Wow," she said, "this is really tight." She rubbed her fingers on her skirt and started the process all over again.

She was breathing hard, all bent over, while I listened for David. I really needed to get her out of here.

"I got it," she said, and I felt the rope loosen around my ankle.

"Turn around," she said, "I'll untie you."

I turned my back to her, but I could tell she was strug-gling again with the knots. She'd just loosened them enough that blood was starting to flow back into my fingers, when I heard the door slam at the house.

"You have to go now, Amanda," I said. "David's coming and I don't want you here."

"No. I can't leave you."

"Listen to me," I whispered in the dark. "You need to get out of here, and we don't have much time. Do you have a cell phone?"

She shook her head. "My mom won't let me have one."

"Okay, listen. Go out through the door behind us. There's a walkway over the water around the boathouse. When you get out the door, turn to the left, away from the house. You can jump onto the beach once you get to that side of the building, then circle around the house and head for the road. Don't stop until you find another house and have them call the police."

"I'm afraid."

"Then this is where you need to be brave. David's an old man. You can outrun him, but you have to go now, before he gets here."

Even in the dark, I could see the terror in her eyes. Then she took a deep breath, stood up, and slipped out the door for the boat launch. Minutes later, David came into the boathouse, carrying a battery-operated lantern in one hand, the gun in his other.

"Where is she?" he shouted at me.

"Long gone," I said.

He moved quickly across the planks and backhanded me across the face with his gun hand. The taste of blood filled my mouth.

David noticed the open boat launch door and walked over to it with his lantern, then stepped out onto the planks.

I wriggled a hand out of the rope, but kept both hands behind my back.

He stepped back into the boathouse and pointed the gun at my head. Now all I could hope for was that Amanda had run like hell, and Edman was on his way.

TWENTY-EIGHT

HE MOVED IN front of me, waving the gun in my face. "Where is she? When did she leave?"

"It doesn't matter, David. She's gone for help. This is over now." My voice was calm, trying to placate a wild man who had nothing left to lose.

He paced back and forth. I slipped my other hand free, careful not to let the heavy rope fall to the floor with a thud.

He bent down and reached for the rope that had tied my ankle to Amanda's, looping it around the bench and my leg, pulling it tight. I thought about trying to overpower him, kicking him in the head, but realized my chances would be better once he left. If he was tying me to the bench, he wasn't planning on shooting me—yet.

He stood and walked toward the door.

"What are you going to do with me?" I asked.

"We're leaving. I need to get some things together."

"Where are we going?"

"I don't know yet."

Something moved outside, the sound of footsteps on gravel—we both heard it. David looked at me, motioned for me to be quiet, then pointed the gun at me just to be sure I understood what would happen if I called for help.

He opened the door and stepped quietly outside, leaving me again in darkness. My mind started to reel. What if it was Amanda, coming back for me? Or Scott or Dana? The last thing I wanted was for any of them to get hurt—or worse. David was crazy.

I could hear him outside, moving closer to the house. My hands wiggled out of the rope and I bent over to untie my ankle again when the door to the boat launch opened. Tom came in, putting a finger to his lips, as if I had to be told not to make a sound.

"You okay?" he whispered, kneeling in front of me.

"Yes. What are you doing here?"

"Edman called me. He was out here earlier, and you were gone. He told me that you were with David and you were in trouble."

"Where's Edman now?"

"I don't know. Fred's around here somewhere, I think in the house."

Tom put his gun down, took a knife out of his pocket, and started sawing through the rope. I didn't hear David come in. I looked up to see him standing in the doorway, holding a wooden oar over his shoulder like a baseball bat. Two quick steps and he swung hard at Tom's back, landing a blow between his shoulder blades. Tom fell into my knees with a grunt, and David stepped back, ready to strike again.

Tom reached for his gun. David hit him again, this time in the back of the head. Tom fell against the floorboards.

David raised the oar again.

I looked down at Tom, unconscious at my feet, blood pooling on the floor around his head. "Don't," I shouted. David stopped and looked at me.

"What are you going to do, David? Kill us all like you killed my sister?" My voice shook more from anger than fear.

"What are you talking about?" his voice was hoarse. "I

didn't kill Meredith. I would never have hurt her. I loved her. She was such a beautiful child…"

The sound that came out of my throat was anything but human. The rope that had tied my hands dropped to the floor, I pulled my ankle free, stood, and bent into a tackle, hitting him hard in the gut with my right shoulder. He landed on his back. His head hit the floor with a loud whack. I crawled on top of him, pounding his chest with a strength I didn't know I had. Sweat ran down my face, into my eyes. I kept punching.

An arm went around my waist and pulled me off. I fought the arm. It tightened its hold. "Stop now, Lizzie," Fred said. I flailed against him. The pressure from his arm grew stronger, until I thought I couldn't breathe. "Stop. It's over. It's okay."

The anger, the hatred that I felt slipped out of me. I felt like a ragdoll in Fred's arms. If he let go, I'd fall to the floor next to Tom.

"It's okay," he said again.

I leaned my head back into his shoulder, tried to catch my breath. Then I pulled away from him and knelt down next to Tom, searching for a pulse, listening to his breathing. Fred knelt next to me. He pulled some tissues out of his pocket and pressed them against the back of Tom's head, where the blood was running out.

"Hold this," Fred said, putting my hand on the tissues. "Keep some pressure on it. I'm going to call for an ambulance." He reached in his pocket for his cell phone.

Neither of us noticed David until he was standing over us, his gun pointed at Fred.

"Put the phone down," David said to Fred.

Fred placed his phone on the floor. Tom's gun was six

inches from my hand, I reached for it slowly. There was a shot, the bullet splintered the wood, halfway between my fingers and Tom's gun.

"Get up," David said.

We both stood. He aimed the gun at Fred's head. "Kick that gun and your cell phone out into the lake."

Fred maneuvered the gun and cell phone with his foot toward the door of the boat launch and poised to kick them both out the door into the water when the door on the other side of the boathouse flew open, banging against the wall. Edman moved in, a gun pointed at David's back.

David swung around, aiming the Glock at Edman's chest. He smiled. "Looks like we have a Mexican stand-off here."

When had this become a game?

"Drop the gun," Edman said. "I don't want to shoot you, but I will if I have to."

"I could put a bullet in your heart before you could even pull the trigger. I'm an expert marksman," David said.

Edman lowered his gun eight inches and pulled the trigger. A bullet hit the floor right in front of the toes on David's left foot. "So am I," he said. "Drop the gun."

Fred bent down and picked up Tom's service revolver and pointed it at David. "And, so am I." Another bullet whizzed through the air, landing an inch behind the heel of David's left foot.

Everyone stood their ground.

Finally, David lowered his gun to his side. "Okay," he said. He did a clumsy half squat, placing the gun on the floor next to him, then stood back up, putting his hands over his head.

Edman took a step toward David. Then a shot came from

the doorway of the boathouse, past Edman's right bicep and straight into David's chest. David's eyes flew open, and he grabbed his chest and slumped to the ground.

Edman swung around pointing his weapon toward the door.

John stood in the doorway, his revolver still aimed at David. Tears ran down his face, and then he started to sob—gut-wrenching cries that shook his entire body. He fell to his knees. No one moved.

It felt as if time had stopped. The air stilled. The water lapping at the boathouse ceased. It took a beat to register what had just happened.

John was moaning. "I heard…" he said. "I heard what he did to her. Oh God!"

And still no one moved.

For the second time in one day, I saw Edman unsure of what to do. Finally, he bent down next to John, removed the gun from his hand, and patted his shoulder. Then he moved over to David, feeling for a pulse.

John's cries subsided. He sat up and looked at me. "I'm so sorry, Liz. I'm so sorry. I don't care if I spend the rest of my life in prison. It's what I deserve. I should have known what he was doing. I should have protected her."

Edman stood up. "No, that's not going to happen."

Fred looked at Edman. "What are you saying?"

"Who are we kidding? John did what we all wanted to do. He's not going to jail for that. Give me a hand here."

Edman and Fred squatted next to the body. "Help me sit him up."

It wasn't easy to get David's pudgy body upright. Edman took a handkerchief out of his pocket and used it to pick up the Glock. Not touching the gun with his hand, he placed it in David's hand, wrapping his fingers around the handle, threading his index finger around the trigger.

"Hold his arm steady," he said to Fred, pointing it at the wall, where John had been. Edman put his finger over David's trigger finger and squeezed. Another shot in the small boathouse, hitting the wall almost shoulder height.

"Not perfect, but I think it'll do," Edman said. "David has gun residue on his hands, and we know that John had to shoot him in self-defense."

Edman looked at John. "And you have three eyewitnesses."

John stood. His legs wobbled, but he caught himself against the wall.

I looked at Edman. "We need to go, and Tom needs to get to a hospital."

He nodded. "Okay. Fred, call the cops and the paramedics."

I told Fred to tell the cops to be on the lookout for Amanda, then bent down and stroked Tom's hair.

He opened his eyes and I kissed him. "The paramedics will be here soon. I have to leave. Fred will be here with you."

He reached for my hand, but there was so little strength in his grasp. "Don't go."

I kissed him again. "I have to."

WE TOOK EDMAN'S CAR. Some kind of numbness had settled over me. I was on autopilot, which was maybe a good thing: there wasn't much more I could process.

Edman had been talking into his cell. He hung up and put it on the console.

"Are they coming?" I asked.

"They'll be there when we get there."

I looked out the window.

"Hell of a day," he said.

"Yeah."

"Want to quit?"

"Nope."

We rode in silence for about five minutes. "Where were you all day?" I asked.

"I told you, we got caught up at the bank. Harry had to do some fancy footwork to get everything processed, but he did. Then there was that pile-up on the freeway. By the time I made it out to your sister's, you were gone—scared the shit out of me. I hung around for a while, then called Tom and Fred. I drove around looking for you and then ended up back at the lake."

I looked at Edman. "David said he didn't kill Meredith."

"Do you believe him?"

"I don't know."

A panel truck and three pickups were parked in the street in front of Ruth's house when we pulled into the circular drive. Five men leaned up against the vehicles, and they were huge. Tattoos fought for space against the massive muscles that ran up and down their arms and across their chests.

One of the men broke away from the group when we got out of the car. He had a braid halfway down his back and was wearing sunglasses in the waning light. He walked over to Edman and shook his hand.

"Hey, bro, we weren't sure this was the place," he said.

"This is it," Edman said. He introduced me to the man, whose name was Lester. I smiled when I heard that. I'd been expecting Mad Dog or the Pulverizer or something equally intimidating. Lester slid his sunglasses down his nose and looked at me over the top. I stopped smiling.

"What now?" Edman asked me.

"I need to do this alone. Wait outside."

I think he was going to protest, but he did as I asked. He and Lester planted themselves up against Edman's car. "I'll be here when you need me," he said.

I opened the front door and stood listening. Listening for anything that would remind me of home. But it wasn't there, and I knew in that moment that I could wait for the rest of my life, but it would never be there again.

Ruth was sitting in her chair on the sun porch, but there was no music tonight. Her hands were folded in her lap. In the fading light, I could only make out the silhouette of her face, her features just a shadowy blur.

"What is it you want, Elizabeth?" she asked.

I took the chair next to hers. "I need to finish what I started."

"And what is that?"

"I need to find justice for my sister and for all the people who weren't there for her when she needed them."

"That sounds so noble, but you have no idea the sacrifices that were made for you and your sister."

I looked out the window over Ruth's shoulder, trying not to cry. If David or Joseph—or anyone—had said those words to me, I would have lunged at them in rage. But with Ruth, it only made me sad. Sad at the lie, sad that maybe she believed the lie, but mostly sad that the lies never seemed to stop. They were the cancer that ate at our family.

"There were no sacrifices made for me or my sister, Ruth. You can tell yourself that if you need to, but you know it's not true. My sister and I were the ones who were sacrificed. Our entire childhood was a sacrifice, stolen by you and Joseph and David, so you could all live out your sick delusions at the expense of two innocent children."

"So very dramatic, darling." Her hands moved in her lap.

We sat in the darkening silence. Finally, I looked at her. "You knew didn't you, Ruth?"

"Knew what?"

"You knew what David was doing. You knew from the beginning, and you never tried to stop it."

She squared her shoulders. "I don't know what you're talking about."

"And on it goes," I said. "He molested my sister until I left home. Meredith was the one who made you send me to boarding school in Boston that year, and she was the one who talked me into moving into the dorm when I started college. She didn't want me alone in this house with that monster, and she couldn't leave until I did."

Her voice was cold. "You are a liar."

"You knew. How could you allow that to happen to any child, but especially to one who looked to you as her mother?"

"Meredith had choices."

"What the hell does that mean? Are you blaming this on *her*?" My voice was getting louder. "She was a victim. She was a *child*!"

"She could have stopped at any time."

I leapt out of my chair and slapped her hard across her face. I wanted to hit her again. I wanted to hit her until I had no strength left inside me. I pulled back my arm to slap her again and felt the cold steel of a gun barrel poking into my stomach. I backed away.

"Don't ever strike me again, Elizabeth." There was nothing of the woman I'd known in that voice.

"Good God, Ruth! What kind of monster *are* you? You're no better than David—maybe you're worse. You prostituted your own stepdaughter. For what? To live in the McCallister home? To be married to a child molester? To have all your friends think that your life was so much better than theirs? I have news for you, Ruth. It's gone now. It's all gone."

There was a Tiffany lamp on the table next to her chair. She turned it on, and I saw the gun in her hand and knew she'd been waiting for me.

"Did you murder my sister?" I screamed at her.

"Don't be ridiculous. Of course, I didn't. I tried to stop her, but I certainly didn't murder her. Meredith was out of control once that girl came into her life."

"You mean her daughter? The one she conceived when your husband raped her?"

Her eyes were like ice. "I tried to stop her."

"You drove out to her house the night she was killed. John and I saw it on the odometer."

"I went out there to try to talk some sense into her, but she wouldn't listen to reason. After she found out about your father, she was possessed."

All the convoluted logic, all the twists and turns that Ruth and David and Joseph used to justify what they'd done—it hurt my head; it made me feel like I was the one who was crazy.

I bent over and my face was inches from hers. "What was she going to do, Ruth? Reveal a pervert? A child molester? Have him arrested for what he'd done? Is that what you were trying to talk her out of?"

"No matter what his faults, David provided for this family for years."

I slapped her hard, and again I felt the gun against my stomach.

I backed away. "Do whatever you want to, Ruth, but you have nothing left. It's all gone. David is dead. His will has been changed, and his money has been transferred to other accounts. It's all gone. You're just an old woman with nothing left in your life and no one left who cares about you."

For the first time since I'd walked into the room, her face showed a genuine, human emotion—terror. "What are you talking about? Where's David? What happened?"

"He's dead. He's been shot. And all his money—gone."

"No. You're lying." She reached for her phone on the table. Her hand shook as she tried to pull up David's number.

"If you're going to call him, he won't answer. He can't. He's dead."

She dropped the phone and pointed the gun at me. "Stop saying that!"

There was a noise behind me. I turned to see Edman standing in the doorway, a gun pointed at Ruth. She saw him too.

I looked back at Ruth. "It's over now." I reached over and took the gun out of her hand. "All the papers in your office, all your correspondence to Joseph over the years, I'm going to give to the police. You and my father will probably spend some time in jail for insurance fraud."

She smiled up at me. "Don't be naive, Elizabeth, the papers have all been destroyed. I'm not stupid, darling. Besides, your father called me yesterday to tell me what you'd done."

She took a deep breath. "I'm sorry to hear about David, but we will get through this too. Once the funeral is over, we will settle back into the routine of being a family. You'll see—we'll get to a better place."

Maybe if you've lived so long with the lies, the delusions, they become your reality. But at what point do you turn? At what point do you tell yourself that it's okay to live the lie? At what point does the lie become *you* or you become the lie? Again, the insanity of it all hurt my head. With everything in me, I didn't want to become what these people had become. I didn't want to sacrifice the ones I loved in order to maintain my own delusions.

I handed the gun to Edman. He gave me his Edman look, which told me it would all be okay—that one way or another, I had the power to make this right. Then he turned and left me alone with my stepmother.

I looked down at my hands, then up into her face. I wanted, if only for a second, to feel what it was like to have a mother, but whatever she'd been to me over the years was gone. It had been gone since that moment she'd known what was happening to my sister, all those years ago, and chosen to remain silent.

"Ruth, I have men outside who will be moving you out of the house tonight."

She looked at me as if I'd crossed that line into insanity along with the rest of them.

"No," she said, "I'm not going anywhere. This is my home."

"Actually, Ruth, it's *my* home. It was mine and Meredith's, and now it's all mine. The men will move all of your clothes and personal belongings from your bedroom to an apartment in downtown St. Paul. After that you're on your own."

That look of disapproval was on her face. "No, Elizabeth, that isn't going to happen. You can't force me out of here if I refuse to go."

"I'm hoping it won't come to that, but if I have to, I will call the police and have you forcibly removed from the property."

She stared at me. "I still have David's money…"

"You weren't listening. It's gone. It has been transferred to the Eastside Victims of Sexual Assault Agency so that all the innocent victims who've been abused by people like David can find help, can find a safe place to be."

I think she was at a loss. "Are you serious?"

"Very."

"And what is this supposed to be, Elizabeth? Retribution?"

"Penance, Ruth. This is your penance for sacrificing my sister's childhood for your comfort and ego."

"You don't understand, do you? It's about family, darling. The family must be preserved at all cost."

"It was never about family for you. It was the image— the illusion—of family that you wanted. And you sold Meredith and me for that." I stood up and looked into her face. "Goodbye, Ruth."

EDMAN WAS SITTING on a flowered loveseat in the living room. He stood up when I walked in. I nodded at him, and he went to the front door and gestured for Lester and the crew to come in.

They stood in the front hall, watching me. I pointed to the stairs. "Second door on your right at the top of the stairs—take it all. I want everything out of here tonight."

I don't know how much Edman had told them, but Lester

walked over to me and put a massive hand on my shoulder. "We'll take care of it."

Edman and I stayed in the living room while the guys did their thing, taking furniture and armloads of Ruth's clothes out to the trucks. After about ten trips, I wondered if they would have room for everything. Ruth stayed on the sun porch while all this was going on.

Finally, Lester came into the living room. "We're all finished here," he told me.

"Thank you. Do you have the address to the apartment?"

He nodded. "Yup. And Maynard gave me the keys. You want us to take the lady with us?"

"Yes. Please."

Ruth walked to the cab of the panel truck with her usual dignity. She could have been on her way to the opera or a fundraising dinner for all anyone would know.

She looked at me from the passenger seat. "We're not finished yet, Elizabeth."

"Yes, Ruth, we are." I turned and walked back into the house, with Edman at my side.

WE SAT IN the living room after Lester and the guys drove away, Edman next to me on the flowered loveseat. He put an arm around my shoulder, pulled me into his chest, and let me cry.

After a few minutes, he must have thought I'd done enough crying for the time being. He patted my shoulder and pulled away. I wiped my eyes and smiled. So very Edman— it's okay to cry, but only for an allotted time.

"I'm proud of you," he said.

"Because?"

"Because you did what you had to do. You took them all down, and you did it for your sister."

"I hope that's why I did it. I wonder how much I did for me."

He put a hand under my chin and made me look at him. "Does it even matter?"

"I guess not. I feel like I've been playing God—deciding other people's fate. I'm not sure I like it."

"We all do that every day in varying degrees. When you think about what Meredith endured, they all got off pretty easy."

"Whatever happens, please don't hate me." This is what my sister told me in the message she left the night she died. This is what she'd meant: She'd lit the match and our family, such as it was, went up in flames.

Edman looked at my swollen eye. "We need to get you to a hospital."

He called Fred to see where the EMTs had taken Tom. We drove to Regions Hospital, my second trip there in less than two weeks. Tom's partner, Sherry, was standing guard outside one of the curtained sections in the ER.

"Whoa! What happened to you?" she asked when she saw my face.

I smiled at her. "I lost. Can I see him?" I nodded my head at the curtain behind her.

She hesitated, then said, "Sure."

Tom was lying on a narrow gurney, dressed in a green print hospital gown, his eyes closed, but he smiled when I stroked his cheek. I bent over and kissed him.

"I'm sorry, nurse," he said, without opening his eyes, "but there's this girl I've been seeing, and believe me, you wouldn't want to tangle with her."

"Very funny."

He opened his eyes. "Are you okay?"

"I don't know. Maybe. I will be."

Dr. Weird Eyes, from my last trip to the hospital, pulled back the curtain and walked in. He looked at me and shook his head. "Did you hear what I told you before? Concussions are not to be taken lightly." He looked at my eye and prodded my cheek. At first, I thought he was checking for broken bones but then wondered if it was punishment for not listening to him the last time. It hurt like hell.

"I'm going to have Dr. Weisman take a look at you," he said. "And your friend here is on his way upstairs to get some stitches and an MRI."

"I'm not going in that long tube," Tom said. "I'm claustrophobic."

Dr. Weird Eyes must have heard it all before. "We'll give you something to help you relax, but I need to see what's going on inside your head."

"There are naked dancing girls," Tom said. "I'm not going in that tube."

Dr. Weird Eyes nodded. "We'll see," he said and left.

"If the doctor thinks you need an MRI, then you need an MRI," I said. "Besides, maybe he'd like to see all those naked dancing girls in your head."

He took my hand. "I want Sherry to drive you home after the doctor looks at your eye."

"Edman can take me."

"Will you just humor me for once? I'd feel better if Sherry took you home."

The orderlies came then to take Tom upstairs. Seconds later, Dr. Weisman showed up to examine me. I was lucky, he said, that there was no damage to my eye. I wanted to tell him that I was lucky to still be sane.

After he left, Fred came in. He crawled up on the table next to me and we sat there, neither of us talking. He put his head on my shoulder.

"It's over now, Fred."

"I know."

"And we're still here. You and me."

"I know."

"And we'll be okay."

"I wish she were here to see what you did for her. She'd be so proud of you."

"I think she knows."

He cleared his throat. "Edman and John told me what happened."

"And?"

He lifted his shoulders. "I'm glad David's dead. I wish I'd been the one to pull the trigger."

"I know the feeling." I told him about David's new will, the transfer of money to the agency, and Ruth's new home.

"Good" was all he said. He wiped his eyes and looked at me. "Martha's here. John called her. They're a mess, knowing about everything that happened to Meredith. You need to talk to them."

I felt like saying, *And this is where I came in*, taking care of the folks. Only a few weeks into this new role and I still didn't have it in me. Maybe I never would.

John and Martha sat in the waiting area, looking old and tired. When they saw me, they moved across the room, engulfing me in an embrace that I didn't think would end. Not that I wanted it to—it was almost as if we were all clinging to what was left of the lives we'd known—of the family we'd once been.

Martha pulled me against her chest. "I'm so sorry, baby," she said into my hair. "I'm so sorry."

We stood like that, John rubbing my back, Martha holding me like she had when I was a child. I felt raw and tired and beyond tears at that moment.

"I didn't know," she kept saying. "I should have seen it. I should have helped her."

"That bastard would have been dead years ago if I'd known what he was doing," John said.

"We should have known," Martha said. "We should have suspected—something."

I stepped back and looked at both of them. "People like David are very good at hiding what they do. And Ruth spent a lifetime creating illusions. There's no way you could have known."

"I feel like we let you down," John said. "I let you both down. I should have protected you."

I touched his cheek. "I think that my sister and I wouldn't have survived any of it if you hadn't been there. You are the closest thing to parents we ever had. And I know if Meredith were here, she'd tell you the same thing."

Martha was exhausted—I could see it on her face. I made John take her home and I sat alone in the waiting room, waiting for word about Tom.

Sherry walked in. "Tom wants me to drive you home. Let me know when you're ready to go. And I'll need to get your statement sometime soon—after you get some rest—but I'll need you to come to the office later today."

Twenty minutes later, Dr. Weird Eyes came in and said they were still waiting for the results of Tom's MRI to be read. Then he said, "Dr. Weisman thinks you're okay to go now, but, please, I don't want to see you back in here for at least six months."

I WENT TO find Sherry. Instead, I found Edman and Fred in the cafeteria, sitting at a corner table, drinking coffee.

"Have you seen Sherry?" I asked them.

"Not for a while," Fred said.

"I'm ready to go home, and she was supposed to take me."

"I can take you, Lizzie," Fred said.

Edman stood up. "I've got this. I'm still on the clock—more money for me."

"Are you staying?" I asked Fred.

"I think I'll hang around until Tom's ready to go."

"Tell Sherry I left. I don't want her waiting for me."

Edman pulled up in front of my apartment. It felt like a lifetime had passed since I'd left there the morning before. And maybe it had. Everything was different now. Ruth and David were gone, both in their own way, dead to me. And my father, who'd just been a blip on the radar of my life, was gone for good now too.

"The status quo, kid," Edman said. "You sure know how to shake it up."

"Yeah, I think you showed me how to do that." I leaned over and kissed him on the cheek. "Thank you."

"Wait till you get my bill before you thank me."

I WAS MORE tired than I could ever remember being. My emotions were raw, my face a mess, and all I wanted was to crawl into bed and not think about anything for a very long time.

I stepped into the living room and switched on the light. Lee Atwater was sitting on my couch.

"Long day?" she asked.

My stomach dropped. I looked out the window, hoping Edman hadn't left me, but his car had disappeared.

"How did you get in here, Lee?"

She smiled. "You know these old Victorians—they all have the same useless locks. So easy to pick. Tom lived in a place like this for a while when we were in college. Did you ever see it? He and Meredith were dating then. Seemed like she was always there."

"What are you doing here?"

"I told you before that we needed to talk."

The hairs on the back of my neck stood up. "You were right: it has been a long day. Maybe we can get together later. How about lunch?"

"No. I'm here now—let's talk. Why don't you sit down?"

She pulled a gun out from behind her on the couch. You'd think after all the guns that had been pointed at me in the last twenty-four hours, I would be well beyond any sense of fear. Not so. I was scared shitless, and the look on her face didn't help.

She waved the gun at a chair across from her, and I sat down, literally on the edge of my seat.

"What is it that we need to talk about?" I asked. This felt so different from my time with David. I knew then that Edman was on his way. Edman knew where I was, and at any second, he could show up. Now, I was alone in my apartment with another maniac, and everyone had gone home to bed.

"Let's start with Meredith. She was such a little liar, don't you think?"

She stopped as if waiting for a response. "No," I said. "Meredith was never a liar."

She narrowed her eyes. "Don't defend her. She was a lying, conniving tramp. She thought she was better than everyone else. She thought she was better than *me*, and just to prove it, she stole Tom away from me—twice. How could she do that to me? Tom and I were engaged to be married." Her voice was too loud.

How do you deal with a maniac? I had no idea. "You weren't engaged, Lee. Tom said you made that up."

"Now who's the liar?" she screamed. "Tom would never say that. You just don't want to admit that your sister was a tramp." She stood up and started pacing.

"Lee, did you go out to Meredith's that night?"

She stopped and looked at me. "I had to. Don't you see? I *had* to—she was trying to steal Tom away again. He'd just come back into my life. I couldn't let that happen. And now, *you*! I've seen him come and go from here at all hours—leaving here early in the morning. You're not any better than she was. You're a tramp just like your sister." She pointed the gun at me.

I was trying to figure out which way to roll once she pulled the trigger. If I rolled to my left, maybe I could make it to the dining room and through the kitchen and out the back door—maybe.

As nonchalantly as I could, I glanced toward the kitchen, trying to gauge how much ground I'd have to cover. A shadowy form moved into view. Tom put a finger to his lips.

I didn't know where he'd come from, but I felt a surge of hope, followed by despair. What if this was it? Tom and I dying together in each other's arms, like some sappy romance legend. That's not how I wanted this to go.

I looked at Lee. *Keep her talking,* I thought. "Lee," I said, my voice calm. "I'm sorry. I didn't understand your feelings for Tom. I like you. I think of you as my friend, and if you want Tom, you can have him. I'll walk away and wish you two all the happiness in the world."

She lowered the gun. "What are you saying?"

"I'm saying that you should be with the man you love. I didn't realize that you still had feelings for him. If I had, I never would have interfered. You two should be together—forever."

She lowered the gun a few more inches and looked at me skeptically. I wondered if I could throw her off balance with one calculated dive at her stomach and give Tom a chance to make his move.

I waited too long. She figured it out. The gun came back up, aimed at my heart. "Liar!" she screamed. "You're lying. You don't mean any of it. You want to keep Tom all to yourself!"

I sensed that she was ready to pull the trigger. I bolted to the left just as someone kicked in my front door.

Sherry yelled, "BCA! Drop your weapon! Drop. Your. Weapon!" Her gun was aimed at Lee.

Tom moved in from the kitchen and grabbed Lee's gun from her hand.

Sherry handcuffed Lee and told Tom she'd take care of the paperwork, and he could take the rest of the night off. She smiled and escorted Lee out the door and on to a jail cell somewhere.

"How did you know?" I asked.

"I didn't for sure, but Lee's been on my short list for a while." He looked tired, and his skin was almost white. He dropped down onto the couch. "The first time I interviewed her, something just felt off. Her responses seemed a little too controlled—too practiced. And all those times out of the blue when she kept running into me last spring. I hadn't seen her in years, and all of a sudden she's everywhere."

"Coincidence?"

"Too much." He motioned for me to come and sit next to him. "She showed up one time when I was having coffee with Meredith. The look on her face was the same one I'd seen in college—scary. When you started asking me about my history with Lee, it made me wonder more about her. We've had her under surveillance for a couple of days. Her car has been parked down the block the past couple of mornings. I went back through Meredith's cell phone records for the night she was killed. I couldn't figure out why Lee kept calling her. I think she knew Meredith was in a precarious place, and she was goading her. Trying to push her over. That's why I wanted Sherry to drive you home. Do you *ever* do as you're told?"

"I couldn't find Sherry."

"You should have waited. If we hadn't run into Fred when we did, and he hadn't told us that you'd already left, I don't know what would have happened to you."

"I'm okay. We're all okay."

He cleared his throat and looked at me. "So, what's this about stepping aside so Lee could have me? Didn't take you long to come up with that."

"Hey, I'd throw you to the wolves if it would save my ass."

He kissed my cheek. "I will never let anything happen to your ass."

TWENTY-NINE

November.

I STOOD IN the doorway of the bedroom watching Tom sleep. I walked across the room, leaned over, and kissed his stubbly face. "If you want to get a shower in before you leave for the cemetery, you'd better get up now."

He smiled and pulled me onto the bed with him. "Maybe we could stay in bed all day, and you and I can—"

"Can what?"

"Take your clothes off and I'll show you what we can do for the rest of the day."

I pulled away from him. "Nope. You're not going to distract me. Fred will be here soon."

"Are you sure you don't want me to be there? Getting your ninety-day sobriety pin is a very big deal."

"I know, but this is one of those things I have to do for me."

He sat up and kissed me. "I'm proud of you—you know that, don't you?"

I put my hand on his chest. "Please don't be proud of me."

"Why not?"

"I don't know. I guess it's just that I should have done this a long time ago, and if you say you're proud of me, you'll jinx it."

"Then you're crazy, you know that?"

"Yes, but in a fun sort of way, don't you think?"

"Sure. Whatever you say. What time do I have to be at the cemetery?"

"Noon."

He pulled me to him again. "So, how does it feel to have a virile stud living in your new house?"

"Well, the virile stud seems to be taking his own sweet time moving all his crap in here."

"Until my sexy roommate gets rid of some of her stuff, I have nowhere to put mine."

"I'm working on it. Just give me some time."

Tom's face got serious and he was quiet.

"What?" I finally asked.

"You know the first night we slept together?"

"Yes."

He slid a hand around the back of my neck and stroked my cheek with his thumb. "We talked forever."

"I remember."

"And we promised each other no lies, no secrets—everything in the open." His eyes were so intense, but I didn't want to look away. "In the boathouse, when David got shot, I wasn't unconscious the whole time."

"I know. You came to, right before I left to go to Ruth's."

"I came to before that."

My heart stopped. I thought it was over. I thought we were healing. I couldn't go back. "How long before that?"

"I saw everything, Liz—when John came into the boathouse, when he shot David, what Edman did."

I didn't say anything for a while. "Why didn't you tell me that before."

"I needed to figure out what I was going to do about it."

"And what did you decide?"

For the first time, he broke eye contact. He took my hand. "Well, John hasn't been indicted and Edman still has his license. So, what do you think?"

"Was there ever a question what you would do?"

"Of course there was. I took an oath to uphold the law. I didn't take it lightly. What John did was outright murder, and Edman made himself an accessory. I struggled with my decision for a long time."

"Why didn't you tell me?"

"You had enough to deal with at the time. And it was something I needed to come to terms with on my own."

"So, what made you keep quiet?"

He shrugged. "Not everything fits into our neat little rules of how the world is supposed to work. I don't agree with vigilante justice, but everyone in the boathouse that night loved Meredith. David deserved to pay for what he'd done, and John needed to feel that he'd finally protected her."

We were both quiet for a minute. Finally, I asked, "Are you okay with your decision?"

"It's what I needed to do for Meredith—and for you."

"Thank you."

A horn honked. "Fred's here—I gotta go. See you in a few hours."

Fred's Jag was parked behind my car in the carport.

"You ready for your big day?" he asked when I climbed into his car.

"I think so."

Fred looked at the cottage and over at the guesthouse that John had just finished painting. "Does it ever creep you out to live here—I mean, not because of Meredith, but because David died here?"

I thought about it. "No, I really don't think of that very often. But when I do, it kind of feels like we set her free here. I don't know how to explain it, but she loved this place so much that he needed to die here. This is where we vindicated her. This is where we slayed the dragon so we could all move on. Weird, huh?"

"No, not weird at all. How are John and Martha settling into retirement?"

"I don't think they understand the meaning of the word. They're always doing something—cleaning, fixing, painting. And Martha's doing her best to fatten up Tom."

Scott and Dana had an apartment near the University and were both in school. Dana said she wanted to be a social worker like Meredith had been. Now John and Martha were all moved into the guesthouse, and everything felt like home.

"You and Charlie are coming tomorrow for Thanksgiving dinner, right? It's my maiden voyage, and I need some moral support."

"You've cooked dinner for people before."

"Never sober."

FRED PULLED HIS car over to the side of the access road at the cemetery where the McCallisters had a large mausoleum and family plot. There must have been thirty people there waiting for us. I looked at Fred.

"All the people who loved her," he said.

"I thought it was just going to be family."

"Where does *family* stop?"

Good point.

We walked over to the group waiting for us. Tom, John and Martha, Dana and Scott, Dana's parents, the Beckwoods,

Fred's fiancé, Charlie, Rachel and Edman—whose flirting had taken them both to a whole new level—and Meredith's boss and friend Barb Forseman, several of her coworkers from the agency, and even a few clients.

The weather was unseasonably warm for late November in Minnesota, and it was a beautiful day. It had taken me months to pick out the perfect granite monument for my sister, with the perfect rose etched along the sides. I was surprised to see the monument covered by a tarp.

Barb Forseman came over and took my arm. "Liz, I still can't believe that you signed over the Summit Avenue house to the agency. We'll never be able to thank you for your generosity. Having such a safe and beautiful place will help so many people begin to heal and start the rebuilding process."

"It's what Meredith would have wanted."

We stepped away from the group. "I've been thinking a lot lately about you and your sister and all that happened, and I have to ask you…"

"What?"

"David never touched you, did he?"

"No. Never."

"Have you ever wondered why that was?"

"I've thought about it."

"I think he never touched you because Meredith sacrificed herself for you. I think that was the deal she made—that he could do what he wanted to her, and she would never tell, as long as he left you alone."

I managed, barely, to hold back the tears. "Yes, that's what I think too."

There were a lot of things that made sense now, like Meredith's summer fling with Father Mark Dutton. The shame my sister felt must have been more than a fifteen-year-old girl could handle alone. In her own way, she was trying to make people think that Dana's father was just some boy from school. The problem was that the secret pregnancy was so well hidden that her childish attempt to make it okay in other people's eyes was never even an issue.

Someday, when all the healing had taken place—or as much as I could hope for—I would let myself think about it all. Right now, I guarded my thoughts, trying only to let in the ones that didn't hurt too much.

Barb nodded her curly head toward the monument. "We made some alterations to your monument. I hope you don't mind."

Fred pulled away the tarp. Meredith's name and dates of birth and death were etched into the stone, along with the saying her friends had added: "You'll never know the lives you touched… And we will never forget you."

This time I didn't fight the tears as I ran my fingers over the words. It was a fitting epitaph for the sister I had lost, for the friend who had gone out of my life forever.

I looked around at everyone there. Everything I had was because of Meredith and what she'd done over the years to protect me. It was her gift to me, and I wasn't going to let her down.

"Whatever happens, please don't hate me."

I could never hate you, Meredith. You gave me my life.

* * * * *

ACKNOWLEDGMENTS

MUCH GRATITUDE TO my kind and amazing editor, Tara Gavin, for taking a chance on me and seeing what I saw in Liz McCallister's story; and to the great staff at Crooked Lane Books, who have made me feel welcomed as you took me into your home.

Thanks again to the usual suspects, who keep me moving forward in this writing endeavor:

Phyllis Lindberg for invaluable research and brainstorming;

My family and friends for their continuing love and encouragement;

Tom Hughes for his attention to detail and exacting thoroughness in reviewing my manuscript.

And finally, to all the readers who picked up this book. You are the necessary piece of this puzzle. I am grateful for all of you and I hope you enjoy *Where Secrets Live*.